The Shivering
Copyright © 2017 Joseph W. Bebo
Copyright © 2004, 2009 (as Ghost Games) Joseph W. Bebo
Published by Joseph W. Bebo
(An imprint of JWB Books Publishing)

Joseph W. Bebo
PO Box 762
Hudson, MA, 01749
Email: joewbebobooks@gmail.com
Editor: James Oliveri
Interior and Cover Design: Elyse Zielinski
Back picture of Author: Debbie DiFulvio

Library of Congress Cataloging in – Publication Data
Joseph W. Bebo
The Shivering /Joseph Bebo – First Edition

ISBN: 978-0-9982182-2-9
Thriller; Horror

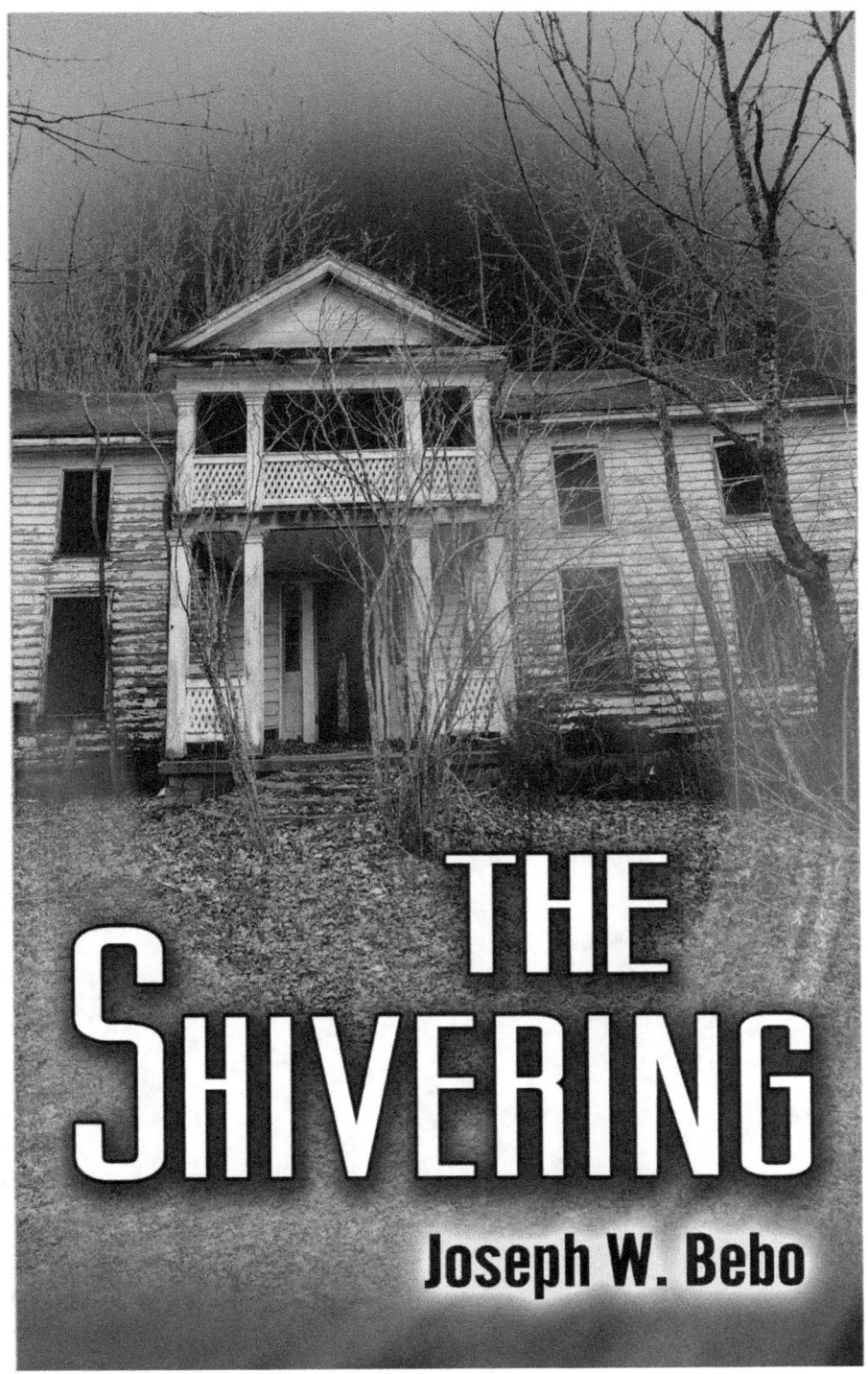

THE SHIVERING

Joseph W. Bebo

Prologue

Spotted rays of sunlight filter through the leaves to splash upon a shimmering patch of grass. Cars zoom by on the highway between trees and stones here long before the road appeared. One house stands alone, unheated by the sun, in eternal shadow. It has no occupant except the ghost of shattered dreams and bitter memories. It knows nothing except the ravages time. Sitting like a malignant thing she broods and waits for the night.

Chapter 1

Mike Russo parked his pickup in the lot of his new apartment building. He had been at work even though it was a Saturday. Mike worked in construction, carpentry mostly, but he was a jack-of-all-trades, despite his young twenty-six years. In this, he took after his dad, who had been a master carpenter like his father before him. Mike followed his dad around like a shadow when he was a kid. When he died an early death Mike's world tumbled down around him like a house of cards.

He would have stayed at work longer, but today was his turn to entertain the group, a few friends who were into the occult and had formed a club of sorts to pursue their interests. They attended lectures on reincarnation, sessions on past-life recall, and séances to communicate with the dead. It wasn't that Mike was that spiritual, but he was lonely and young, and one of the women making up the group was a very fine specimen indeed. If it meant believing in some superstitious mumbo-jumbo to get to know her, so be it.

Not that Mike was a total disbeliever. Ever since his father's death, he'd been interested in the supernatural. There was so much unsaid, so much undone. He longed to contact his father, to reach over to the other side. This group gave him an opportunity to try. Besides, there was something to this stuff. The lectures didn't make much sense, just unverifiable speculation as far as Mike was concerned, but the past-life recall was another matter. It seemed to make sense in a lot of ways. At a minimum it was probably therapeutic.

He pulled his toolbox out of the truck and started up the front walk to his apartment. He had just moved here from East Boston where he had lived with his mother after returning from Viet Nam. A small New England community about fifty miles west of Boston, it was no more than a few white buildings next to the highway. Quaint country houses and small farms, all interspersed with woods and fields, dotted the area. Mike lived in one of the only apartment buildings in town, in the backyard of what used to be an old homestead.

He moved up the walkway past the squat, rambling, white structure, now deserted and falling into ruin. It stood right in front of the two-story red brick building that contained Mike's one bedroom apartment. His bedroom window looked out on the old house's back door.

He had only lived here a few weeks, but already he had begun to wonder about the old place. Why was it still there? Why hadn't they torn it down when they built the apartment building? Why did it look so sinister, crouching there like some living thing? His dog, Hunter, sure didn't like the place. Now that Mike thought about it, he didn't either.

He rushed into his apartment and slammed the door behind him, checking the clock as he stashed his tools under the sink. He loved working outdoors, building things with his own two hands, especially in the summer. It made him feel like he was getting the most of each day, even if it didn't pay as well as the jobs his friends, Sam and Richard, had. At least it kept him in shape and well tanned. With his dark olive skin and Italian heritage, he could pass for a different race in the summertime.

Mike stripped down hurriedly and jumped into the shower, doing a mental inventory of what he had in the house. He'd known they were coming for a week, but he hadn't prepared a thing. Now at the last minute he was starting to panic. His friends had high expectations. The last time they got together at Sam's and Judy's house, they served expensive wine and cheeses. Their home was immaculate and the atmosphere perfect. There was no way he was going to be able to compete with that. He was lucky if he had any beer in the fridge.

Throwing on some clean jeans and a T-shirt, he rummaged through the cupboards and refrigerator, looking for the makings of an appetizer. He couldn't even find a measly snack. His guests were due to arrive in twenty-minutes. He shouldn't have gone to work this morning, but the job was running behind and if he didn't keep things going they'd miss their deadline. Mike hadn't missed a target date yet and he wasn't going to start now. As his dad always told him, that's just not the way to make a good name for himself.

He'd just have to improvise. The important thing was the activity and the atmosphere, not the food. Once they were here, he could go out and get something for them. No big deal. So why was his stomach in such a knot?

The phone rang, distracting him momentarily from his worries.

"Hello," he said, wondering who it might be. He only had the phone installed this week, and wondered if it was his friends saying they'd be late. No such luck. It was his mother.

"Michael, is that you? I just tried to call you and got the wrong number. The man on the other end of the line was so rude. He swore and hung up on me. Can you believe that?"

"Hi Ma, how you doing?" said Mike, looking at the wall clock. His friends would arrive in twenty minutes. His mother could take that long just to say hello.

"Never mind me, how are you doing?" she said, accusingly. "You've been there three weeks now and not even a call to tell me how you are."

"Ma, I just got the phone put in this week, and with the job and all, things are kind of busy. I'm all settled in, everything is going fine. I'm just real busy that's all. I was going to call you later tonight. Are you doing OK?"

"Oh, I'll survive. I survived your father's death and bringing you and your brother up alone, I guess I can survive being abandoned."

"You're so melodramatic, Ma. Are you sure you're not watching too many soap operas?"

"Don't get wise, Michael. The least you could have done was call and let me know you're all right. I get worried."

"Don't worry, everything's fine. I love it out here. The job's going great and I'm making friends. Soon as things settle down a bit, I'll take a trip into town to see you."

"I'll be here. I'm not going anywhere. Just call from time to time and let me know how you're doing, OK?"

"Sure Mom, hey, I've got to go. I have people coming over and I've got to clean up the place." It was only now that Mike noticed the mess in the living room and the dirty dishes in the sink.

After hanging up the phone, he spent the remaining ten minutes rushing around the apartment frantically trying to put things in order.

He never should have agreed to host one of their get-togethers. It wasn't that he underestimated the effort involved. Mike knew all too well that it was a pain in the butt. It was just that they hounded him so much and put such pressure on him - especially Sam and Judy - that he had no choice, he had to do it. It would probably be the last time they asked him to host, that is if they even let him stay in the group.

Linda, the lady Mike was interested in, was coming with his friends, Sam and Judy. The other couple, Richard and Sara, would be following in a separate car. These four did everything together. They had all gone to college in Boston, and hung together like a family. They even lived in the same neighborhood, in Jamaica Plains, a suburb of Boston.

Mike had met Judy, Sam's wife, at a reincarnation seminar a year ago. The vivacious brunette with the butterball body and nice legs attracted his interest. Thinking she was single, he arranged to meet her at a past-life recall lecture later that week. He was moderately disappointed when she showed up with her husband, Sam, and another couple. His disappointment turned to pleasure, however, when he was introduced to their friend Linda, a dark-eyed beauty who wore a lacy, low-cut blouse and tight black pants. She had asked him all sorts of serious questions about his personal life.

Mike immediately hit it off with the group. He got along well with Sam and Richard, even though he had nothing in common with them. They were college grads with high paying high-tech jobs, while Mike was an ex-marine who worked with his hands. But Mike was well-read and athletic, and knew more about the Boston Red Sox than Ted Williams himself. The women thought he was cute, with nice shoulders and a tight firm butt. He beamed good health and vitality and had an honest good-natured disposition that made him likable to all who met him. Linda was impressed enough to give him her number when he asked for it discreetly at the end of the evening. They had even gone out a few times, but nothing serious had yet occurred, much to Mike's regret.

A knock informed him that his guests had arrived. He opened the door and let them in through the kitchen, which he had just finished cleaning. Mike's hands were still wet from the dishes as he greeted everybody. Judy exchanged kisses, while the others waved him off good-naturedly. Unfortunately, he didn't get a chance to kiss Linda who rushed past him with the rest of the group as they pressed into his apartment.

There was the usual good-natured ribbing and bantering back and forth. Everyone liked Mike's new apartment, especially the location. With the trees just turning pale green and the flowers blooming everywhere, the broad swath of lawn hemmed in by the young budding woods looked like a miniature resort. The only discordant feature was the old white house in front of the building.

"What's that place?" asked Sara, looking out Mike's living room window onto the strange dwelling. Where Judy was small and fiery, Sara was tall and lanky, with a laidback disposition that matched that of her husband Richard.

"What a weird looking house," observed Sam, joining the two of them by the window. Sam was short and stocky with a high forehead and reddish brown hair. Like his wife Judy, he was a bundle of restless energy and always quick with an opinion. "Why didn't they tear it down? Does anyone live there?"

"No, no one lives in it. And I don't know why they left it there," answered Mike. "I'll have to ask the landlord. Sure is odd, though. Whoever built the rear of the place didn't know much about carpentry. The back there is all falling down. Looks like it's sinking. There's structural damage as well."

"Mike dear," said Judy with a sigh. "We didn't want a lecture on architecture, thank you, just a little information."

"Where's the food?" chimed in Richard with the usual smile in his eyes, as if he was in on a very good joke known only to him. "I'm hungry as a bear."

Mike hadn't even had time to say hello to Linda, and they were already on him. She wore a stunning summer outfit that showed off her bare midriff. Mike, momentarily distracted, was caught off guard.

"Well, I..." he started to say.

"There's nothing here!" announced Judy from the kitchen in a shocked voice, peering into his refrigerator like she owned it. He was cooked.

"I haven't had time to get anything," he admitted.

"What?" cried Sam. "You're kidding, right? You've known about this for a week. We asked you if you needed a hand."

"Yeah, I know," said Mike. "I thought we'd go out and get something."

Sam and Judy glared at him as if he had just shot their dog. Sara had a look that said, 'I told you so.' Richard stood by the window talking to Linda and looking out at the old house.

"We've just driven fifty miles and you want us to go out to eat?" said Sam indignantly. "I think that's very unfair, especially after all the work Judy and I did last time. The least you could have done is prepared something for the group."

"Look, he's thrown all his dirty laundry in the corner," said Judy from the bedroom. Mike always knew she was a little instigator, but he couldn't get mad at her for long because of the cute way she pouted her lips, and her nice figure.

"Come on, Judy," said Mike in embarrassment. "You're not supposed to go in the bedroom. I don't go in your bedroom."

"Hey, Mike," said Richard from the living room window, still looking out at the old house. "Are you sure no one lives in that place?"

"Yeah, why?"

"Well, I swear I just saw something move in there."

"Maybe it's kids," suggested Mike. "The place isn't locked up as far as I know. Could be shadows from cars passing by on the highway. I know at night the lights do funny things."

"Hmm, interesting," said Richard, turning and following Linda into the living room.

They all sat in a circle in the sparsely furnished room.

"Now that everyone's here," said Mike, trying to perform damage control. "I can go out and get some things. What does everyone want?"

"You're such a dud," observed Judy truculently. "Do we have to do everything for you?"

"I told you he'd screw up," said Sara. "Nothing personal Mike, you're a perfect sweetie. I love you dearly. But you're not the hostess with the mostest."

Mike was starting to feel like a heel in front of Linda. If he wanted to make a good impression, he sure wasn't going to do it this way.

"Hey, give the guy a break," said Richard. He was wearing jeans and a white shirt, his dark hair thick and curly. "I'm as hungry as the next guy, but Sara's right, what did you expect, finger sandwiches?"

Judy was fuming. Sara and Richard made jokes at Mike's expense. Mike was starting to get miffed. The mood was tense.

"Since we're all here for a reason, why don't we just get down to business," proposed Richard. Everyone agreed - almost.

"Well, thanks to Mike I haven't had a chance to get into the right frame of mind for this," Judy complained, not letting up for a moment. It didn't pay to disappoint this woman. "I doubt we're going to get much done at this rate."

Her agitation seemed to be infecting. Richard's usual good-natured smile disappeared.

"Give it a rest, Jude," he remarked. "Maybe if you'd just kept your yap shut, you'd be able to relax more."

"Hey!" said Sam, coming to his wife's defense. "If anyone's to blame, it's Mike. This is the worst session we've ever had."

"Sorry," Mike replied lamely. "It won't happen again."

"If you can't take this seriously," said Judy. "Maybe you shouldn't be involved."

"Now that's not fair," interjected Linda, like Joan of Arc coming to his defense. "Mike's doing his best. I thought the important thing was our spiritual growth, not our stomachs."

"Linda's right," agreed Richard. "Let's just forget about the food and get on with it. I'm anxious to try running."

Today Judy was going to lead the group in 'running', an exercise in past-life recall. Judy had done this kind of thing many times before with her teacher, Nicole, as had Sam. Sara had also done it once with Nicole, while Richard, who had never 'run' before, was still a virgin. None of them had tried it with Judy guiding, something she had just learned to do. It promised to be an interesting afternoon.

Everyone was seated around the living room. Richard and Sara sat on Mike's threadbare, hand-me-down couch. Linda sat on a chair taken from the dining room. Mike was on the floor next to Linda, while Sam relaxed in Mike's favorite recliner. Judy was on a large soft pillow at the foot of the couch.

"OK, Richard," said Judy, starting the activities. "Take off your shoes and lie down on the couch. Sara, get up and make room, will you."

"Are you sure that's all you want me to take off?" said Richard, getting back into his usual mode.

"No, that will do fine," said Judy, laughing.

"Now everyone, try to relax and clear your minds so that we can act as a conduit to amplify the spirit guides."

She went on in a low, mesmerizing voice.

"Richard, relax and breathe deeply. Breathe from your diaphragm, the bottom of your lungs. Relax your shoulders. Breathe in, deep, that's it. Now out. Good. Relax the shoulders. Breathe in again. Now, imagine yourself lighter and lighter with each exhale. Exhale. Good. Inhale. Imagine exhaling all your weight with each breath, until you are so light you start floating. That's it, breathe deep. Exhale all your weight. Good. Now, feel yourself floating. You're floating off the floor. See yourself floating as you breathe in and out, deeply, getting lighter and lighter, floating higher and higher. You're floating at the ceiling now. You can look down and see us sitting here. Feel yourself floating, becoming lighter and lighter, like a balloon. Now you're filling up with air like a balloon with each breath. The air makes you lighter and lighter. With each inhale you are getting bigger and bigger. And as you get bigger and lighter, you float even higher. Now you are going through the ceiling. You're going through the roof of the building to the outside. Now you are floating over the building. You are so light you're floating higher and higher. You can look down and see the building and the parking lot and all the cars. Higher and higher, lighter and lighter. You're weightless now, floating on the air. You can look out over the trees and see the surrounding countryside."

Judy's voice droned on in that monotone she'd been taught to use in these sessions, as she guided Richard on his past-life journey.

Mike and Linda had never run before, but they had observed it once or twice. Each time he saw it, Mike was amazed at the details and facts people came up with. Although he wrote the whole thing off to imagination or some form of hypnosis, there was something to it. The people who did it swore they weren't making it up, but watching it unfold as it happened. He also knew you had to be careful with this sort of thing and only do it with a trained guide, because things could get dicey if it went bad. A person could get stuck in whatever world, imagined or not, they were running in.

"Now, look down at your feet," said Judy. "What do you see?"

There was a long silence, as Richard, breathing deeply and evenly, with his eyes closed and lying on his back, slowly answered in a far away, high-pitched, queerly strained voice.

"I see bare feet, big bare feet, wrinkled and white with big toes and bulging ankles."

"Who are you?" asked Judy.

"Janelle," said Richard, in the strange voice.

"Where are you?"

"I'm here. I'm right here."

"What do you do?"

"Why, I take care of the house and tend the children. Yes, I tend the little animals."

"You have children, Janelle?" asked Judy, guiding Richard through his past life recall.

"Yes, seven of 'em. Little darlings all of 'em."

"And how old are you?"

"I'm seventy-five."

"What year is it?" continued Judy.

"Nineteen sixty-six."

Judy shook her head and fell silent for a moment. "That can't be. That's only ten years ago. You couldn't have had enough time to be reincarnated. You'd still be alive as Richard."

Judy, in her inexperience, had broken one of the main tenets of 'running', don't confuse the runner while they were traveling. She plunged on anyway.

"What are you doing, Janelle? What are you doing right now?"

"I'm running," answered Richard in the strained voice.

"No, I mean what is Janelle doing now?" said Judy, thinking Richard was referring to the exercise.

"I'm running through the woods in my bare feet. My shins are getting all cut and scraped. I can hear them behind me. There's blood everywhere, but they won't get me."

Judy, sensing the panic rising in Richard's voice, tried to stay in control and calm him down.

"Now Richard, breathe deeply. You're getting heavy. You're getting sleepy. Relax Richard. Keep breathing. Richard?"

Richard didn't seem to hear her and made no response to her words, but remained lost in a world of his own making, a world that was evidently getting scarier by the minute.

"I'm running, covered with blood. Got to get away. Can't let them get me. Got to run! Got to climb a tree! They won't get me. Blood, blood, blood!"

Richard kept repeating the phrase in a falsetto voice, which grew louder with each occurrence. The others in the group, including Mike, were starting to get alarmed. They had all heard what could happen when one of these sessions went bad.

"Richard. You are Richard Jenkins," Judy insisted. "Financial analyst. It's nineteen seventy-six. It's Judy and Sam and Sara. Remember? Richard, come back," she pleaded. She was growing almost hysterical herself now.

Richard started choking. Sara was standing next to the couch with her hands to her head, yelling Richard's name.

"Judy, for God's sake do something!" she screamed.

"Got to run! Got to climb!" croaked Richard, his face strained and getting red, his feet moving as if he was jogging, although he stayed motionless on his back.

Finally, Mike moved forward and knelt by his friend, whose face was dripping with perspiration and turning purple. Richard's eyes were open, but he was seeing something far removed from the room around him. His arms were flailing about.

"They won't get me!" he said in a choked voice.

"Janelle," said Mike, leaning forward and touching Richard's jerking shoulder. "It's OK. No one's chasing you anymore. They've all gone. You're alone now, back in your home. No one is after you. It's safe. You can come back now."

Richard began to calm down and began to breathe easier, responding for the first time to something other than the horror he was undergoing in his mind.

"Everything is OK," Mike assured him. "Everything is as it was. You are back now. Remember Richard? You are back now."

"Yes, I'm OK now," repeated Richard, in his own voice and much calmer. Mike looked at Judy and gave her a sign that she could take over. She just stared at him dumbly and blinked her eyes.

"How did you...? What did you do?" she asked.

"Nothing. You can take it from here. Just calm down."

Richard sat up and scratched his head.

"What happened?" Sara asked him, beside herself with worry. "Do you remember anything?"

"Yeah," replied Richard, with a pained expression. "It was horrible. I don't want to go through that again, ever. It was the worst thing that's ever happened to me. I was no longer here. It seemed so real. I was an old lady running through the woods. I was seeing it through someone else's eyes. I was someone else! I climbed a tree. Then I couldn't breathe."

He shivered involuntarily at the recollection. Sara and Judy continued to calm him down, while Mike made some soothing tea for everyone, and the party wound down. It was getting late and Mike's guests had a long drive ahead of them.

Linda helped Mike with the dishes, as the others drank tea and discussed the day's events. Judy would be sure to go over the entire incident with her teacher the first chance she got.

Mike enjoyed his few minutes alone with the tall brunette, sneaking peaks at her as they talked about things in general and Richard's bad trip in particular.

"That was good the way you handled things in there," she said, as they finished up the last of the cups. "How did you know what to say to bring him back? How did you do that?"

"I don't know," answered Mike honestly. "I saw Jude was getting panicky, I just tried to calm things down, go with the flow, you know. He thought he was this old chick named Janelle, so I just tried to talk to her. It seemed to work."

"It certainly did. I think we all owe you a big round of thanks."

"Ah, it was nothing, really. I just got lucky."

At least Mike had the presence of mind to ask her for another date the following weekend. He got lucky again. She said yes.

Chapter 2

The sun, which was hidden from Mike by a canopy of maples and birch trees, was finally sinking behind the western mountains, as he went out back to get his dog, Hunter. Hunter was a golden retriever with a heart as golden as his long soft fur. As much as Mike loved the dog, however, when he had guests Hunter had to stay outside. After all, it wasn't every day he had visitors and he appreciated the company, especially on these long, lonely, heartbreaking beautiful spring days.

Mike was depressed as soon as his friends left. He hated the weekends with no one to share them with. However, the sight of Hunter, with his violently wagging tail and silly dog grin cheered him up immediately.

He left the lights off and turned on the TV, a small 17" Sylvania his mother had given him when he left his family home in East Boston. It picked up two network and two UHF stations, one of which was showing wrestling tonight. Andre the Giant was fighting Bruno San Martino for the title. It was a far cry from what he imagined his highbrow friends were watching.

He really had little in common with them except their interest in the occult, but he enjoyed their company just the same and tried to keep an open mind. After all, he had a lot to learn from these people. He never had the chance to go to college. Both Sam and Richard, who went to school together, had good jobs, and knew a lot of people who needed carpentry work done from time to time, so the relationship was beneficial in that regard as well. They, in turn, were always interested in his war stories and what it was like to be in the Marines.

He used to resent the guys who got to go to college while he was drafted and had to go off to war. You could have knocked him over with a feather during his induction when everyone on his side of the room was arbitrarily assigned to the Marine Corp and he was shipped off to Paris Island without so much as a thank you ma'am. But Sam and Richard made him realize that college guys really weren't so bad and had a lot to offer.

Mike kept thinking about the events of the afternoon, in spite of the frantic efforts of Bruno and Andre to distract him. As soon as he was alone and it became dark outside, Mike got the jitters. He was unable to get the panic-stricken sound of Richard's voice out of his mind. It was like he was being possessed. Who did he say he was, Janelle? Who was that, some old farm woman? Why was she running through the woods in her bare feet, covered with blood? What was that about?

Hunter was jumping up on the windowsill and whining. It was starting to annoy Mike.

"Get down from there," he yelled. "You'll break the blinds. What's wrong with you, boy? Stop that!"

He went to the window and pulled the dog gently down by the collar. As he was closing the shades, he noticed a flash coming from a rear window of the old house, as if a light was reflecting off something sharp and metallic. It was only a momentary glimmer, however, for when he stopped and stared out more intently, only blackness peered back at him through the old house's empty windows.

Perhaps some kids on a dare, playing around in the old place. Mike thought no more of it and dropped the blinds with a loud rush. He spent the rest of the evening with his dog, watching B-movies and drinking the remains of a cheap bottle of wine he had bought after his guests had left. He fell asleep around midnight thinking about Linda.

He woke about an hour later to the sound of Hunter whining and scratching the windowsill. First the dog jumped up on the living room sill and cried there. Then he ran to the bedroom and jumped on the windowsill there. Mike dragged the whimpering animal back to the kitchen where his sleeping mat and bowl were, and gave him some treats to calm him down.

"What's the matter, boy? Got a case of the jitters? Me too. Here, chew on this. Maybe it'll calm you down."

While Hunter gnawed on doggy treats, Mike went to the window and peeked out the blinds. There was an almost full moon. A low fog had come in like a smoky tide. The old house sprawled across the otherwise well-manicured yard like a ghost ship in a vaporous sea, misshapen and malformed, the twisted experiment of a warped mind. It was just about the oddest thing Mike had ever seen, that white house floating in the fog while the moon lit everything with an otherworldly glow. He expected the elves and goblins to pop out from behind the bushes at any moment, but nothing stirred, not even the leaves.

He went back to the kitchen to get his now sleeping dog a fresh bowl of water, then plodded back to his room and fell instantly to sleep.

He woke again a few hours later after having a bad dream he vaguely remembered. It was just five. The fog still hugged the ground and shrouded the old house. The moon had long since disappeared. The sun was about to make its appearance in the eastern sky. Unable to fall back to sleep, Mike had a quick bowl of oatmeal, put on his jogging shorts and a T-shirt, and headed out for a run in the damp, chilly morning air, Hunter by his side.

As they left the parking lot and headed down the highway, the sun was just poking through the low clouds. Mike thought about how good it was to be alive. He turned down a small country lane and ran along an eighteenth-century stone wall, past a row of modern, well-tended houses, by an apple orchard and a long field of tall grass, then over a slow-running stream on a lonely wooden bridge.

He liked to keep himself in shape. A lot of guys he worked with relied on the job to keep them fit, but Mike figured it was better to be ready when it came time to exert oneself. Anyway, he had to lead a crew of guys and that meant being one step ahead of everybody, one step stronger, one step faster, one step smarter. At least that's what his dad always told him, and his father knew what he was talking about.

Thinking about his father still caused him a sense of loss even after all these years. That loss made him feel unlucky in life, always dealt the losing hand. He refused to dwell on it, however, and concentrated on the physical exertion instead.

In spite of the glorious day and the exhilarating run, something was nagging at his peace of mind, something he couldn't quite identify, but troubling all the same. He passed it off as home-sickness and pushed himself harder for being such a sorry sap. He thought of all the guys who didn't make it and silently scolded himself for being so sentimental.

It was still early, not yet eight o'clock, but already the temperature was in the low eighties. He was soaked with perspiration as he jogged through the woods back to his apartment, along old trails that snaked back and forth behind his apartment house for miles.

As he approached his building, which was hidden behind thick bushes and trees, the old house came into view. It looked picturesque enough, at least from this angle, with lilac bushes framing a stately front façade. But as he came closer and the rear of the house came into view, the strange, unshapely architecture of the place struck him.

Instead of going up the walkway to get into his apartment as he normally would after a jog, he cut across a small patch of lawn between the buildings to the rear of the old house. As he approached it, his dog, Hunter, raised his ears and darted off, circling the structure repeatedly at high speed. Around and around he went, with his tongue out and his eyes wide, as if the hounds of hell were chasing him.

Mike called and tried to stop him, afraid he would hurt himself, but the dog ignored him and continued to speed around the old building like a greyhound after a hare. Finally, he came to a sudden halt at the partly opened rear door of the shed. His body was rigid and stiff. He pointed his snout at the entrance and bared his teeth. His tail stiffened and his hackles rose. A low growl escaped his throat.

"What's the matter, boy?" asked Mike, as he grabbed the dog by the collar and dragged him away from the farmhouse door. "You're spooking me. What's your problem?"

Hunter continued to whimper and didn't want to leave. As Mike was pulling it away, it turned sharply and bit him on the hand. He yelled and let go of the collar. The dog immediately ran back to the house and stood there growling as before. Mike, shocked at being bitten, smacked it on the nose and scolded him as he dragged him away by the scruff of the neck. Taking the animal back behind the apartment building, he chained him to his tree. Then he went inside to clean and bandage his hand.

It wasn't a bad bite, just a nip really, but Hunter had never turned on him like that before. Mike hoped it wasn't a sign of something more serious. He'd have to keep an eye on him. After washing and bandaging the bite, Mike called Richard to see how he was doing after his harrowing experience of the previous day.

"Hi, Richard. How's it going?" he asked, after Richard answered the phone. "I'm surprised I caught you in, thought you'd be out playing golf or something."

"Too hot. Besides, I didn't get much sleep last night," he replied in a gruff, phlegm-choked voice. "Had the damnedest dreams, kept waking up. I had to change my T-shirt three times, I was sweating so much. It must have been the heat and that damned weird thing that happened while I was running. Boy, I'll never do that again."

"Well, I just called to see how you were doing. Sorry about yesterday. I guess things didn't turn out so well. I really blew it, didn't I? I'll have to think of something special to get back into Judy and Sara's good graces."

"Never mind them. Just make sure you buy the beer next time the boys go out."

"You got it, buddy," Mike said, relieved that his friend harbored no grudge from the day before. "How about tonight?"

"Naw, can't. We have plans. Let's try for later in the week."

Mike hung up the phone resolved on spending another night alone. The thought made him even more depressed than he had been earlier. He was having trouble identifying the source of his dismal mood. It had been a pleasant weekend. Granted, he had disappointed his friends, but it all turned out OK in the end. He had even been a hero of sorts. The job was going well, a little behind schedule, but nothing he couldn't handle. He usually felt good after a run with Hunter, but today he felt like his heart was an anvil. What's going on? Was he going soft or something? Maybe it was just the stress of moving away from home, having a place of his own with no one to share it with.

Much later that day, he decided to give Linda a call. He let the phone ring ten times unanswered before hanging up. The fact that she was out this evening only made him more dejected.

Around midnight, after a long evening alone, he shut off the tube to go to bed. Looking out the window to the front yard, he got the oddest feeling he was being watched from the blackness of the old house's empty windows. It seemed to have a consciousness, an awareness of him as he stood there looking at it in the moonlight. He dismissed the feeling and lowered the blinds.

He shut off the lights and went to the bedroom, where the open window let in the light of a pale full moon. He could see the house framed through the window like a malignant painting, bathed in an eerie glow. He wanted to close the window and pull down the shade to shut out the haunting image that seemed to pulsate in the half-light, but the thought of crossing the few feet of floor, for some reason, filled him with dread. It was as if a thousand guns were trained on the spot ready to fire. The absurdity of it filled him with anger. He called himself a few choice names and walked to the window like he wanted to put his fist through it. Staring out at the old house with disdain, he slammed the window shut, and pulled down the blind sharply, plunging the room into darkness. The shade snapped back to the top of the window sill with a loud crack and spun around rapidly like a whip. It seemed to move of its own volition, far longer than it should have. Spooked, Mike swore and pulled it down again, still mad at his unexplained fear.

The heavy feeling of being watched, even with the shades closed, still oppressed him. It felt like his very thoughts were being eavesdropped on. He had a childish impulse born of some innate fear of the dark, to run to his bed and throw the covers over his head. Instead, he stood in the middle of the room and laughed out loud, bold and boisterous. Suddenly, Hunter started howling in a strange fearful way that sent a chill up his spine. Jumping into bed, he pulled the quilt up to his neck and called his dog. Hunter came bounding into the room and jumped in the bed, where he stayed for the rest of the night.

Despite his desire to sleep, Mike was having difficulty nodding off. No matter how hard he tried to get the feeling of being watched out of his mind, it persisted, until he found himself sleeping with one eye open, like he had learned to do on patrol in the jungles of Viet Nam. He had thought he had forgotten how, but old habits die hard, just like marines.

He woke up drenched in sweat, the blankets and pillows strewn about the bed, after having a nightmare where he was fighting a black clad figure with no face. It was already light, after seven. He had forgotten to set the alarm and was late for work. Some of the guys would already be at the job before him, something that had never happened before.

He showered and rushed out of the house, forgetting his tools, which he had to go back for. He arrived at work at ten after eight, to the mild jibes of his crew for his unusual tardiness.

"Get lucky last night, boss?" one of them joked.

"Not as lucky as you'll be if I don't fire you," he joked back.

It didn't take long for the demands of the job to take his mind off the strange events of the weekend, and before long he had his shirt off and was soaking up the warm rays of the sun as he pounded nails into a roof beam. Yes, it was good to be alive.

Judy met with Nicole for her usual Monday evening appointment, and told her about the disastrous weekend.

"Sounds like the vibes weren't right," observed Nicole, a large black woman with a wide pretty face and colorfully-clothed, round body. "You can't do these things if there is any anger or hostility in the air."

"Oh, it was just horrible, Nicole," said Judy, sipping her tea as the sitar music hummed in the background and the smell of incense wafted through the air. "You're right. It wasn't the right vibes at all. You should check our locations from now on."

"I don't know if that's necessary, Judy. Just use your own common sense. If things don't feel right, don't be afraid to do something else, you know, something a little less intense. Tell me, you say Michael was able to talk Richard down? How did he do it?"

"I don't know," admitted Judy, thinking back on the words Michael had spoken. "He called Richard by his running name, the name he gave us."

"That's good," said Nicole. "That's the only name he would have responded to that deep in the trance."

"Then he told him, er, I mean her that no one was after her. That it was just like it was before we came and disturbed her."

"Hmm, interesting. He seems to have an intuitive knack for saying the right thing. I wonder if Madame Zarloff would like to meet him. She would be able to tell if he has any gift or not."

"Madame Zarloff?" said Judy. "Why, I've only just met her once myself. Sam's never met her and he's been studying with you for a full year now. It's not fair."

"I'll see if she'll meet Sam and Richard as well," replied Judy's spiritual advisor. "And of course, you'd be invited."

This made it a bit more agreeable to Judy, who said she'd think about it.

"Is everything all right?" asked Nicole.

"Sure," answered Judy. "Why?"

"Oh, I don't know, you just seem a little perturbed today."

"Other than having my weekend plans ruined and my training set back six months, I don't know what I'd have to be upset about. Aren't you being a bit hypercritical?"

Her teacher looked at her quietly and smiled. "Don't you think you're being a little evasive?" she said finally.

"No, Nicole, I'm fine, honest."

Judy was lying of course. She hadn't felt fine since Saturday evening. She had complained all the way home about Michael's terrible hospitality and whether or not he should be allowed to remain in the group. She got madder and madder the closer to Boston they got. By the time she and Sam got home, she was yelling at him about something she couldn't even remember now. She hadn't been able to concentrate on her exercises with Nicole, and then snipped at her when she suggested that Michael meet Madame Zarloff, the grand dame of the local occult set.

Something was troubling her, a vague uneasiness that started in the pit of her stomach and tightened at the back of her neck. Something was eating into her well-being like a worm in an overripe apple. The fact that something was troubling her and she didn't know what it was only made her angrier. But it would pass. Judy was sure of that. Everyone has their ups and downs, their time of the month, their moody blues. It would pass, Judy told herself, like a storm cloud on a summer day. It would pass.

Chapter 3

The week went by uneventfully. With each passing day his date with Linda grew closer and Mike's anticipation increased in proportion until he could barely stand the suspense. They had gone out a couple of times before, but this time he felt sure something special was going to happen. The important thing to remember was to keep his cool. Nothing will turn a woman off as sure as a desperate guy. Mike could only hope his desperation wouldn't show.

He had talked to Sam during the week. Judy was still ticked off, but had decided to forgive him. She wanted to have a follow-up session on Saturday. No running or anything, just some simple exercises to practice their past-life recall skills, like reading palms. It seemed innocuous enough, so Mike acquiesced. He could meet Linda there and they could go on their date afterward.

It was Judy's ambition to be a spiritual guide like her teacher, Nicole. The events of the last weekend didn't bode well for her success, but all her friends were determined to help. They would continue to be her guinea pigs, just as long as no one got hurt.

Saturday arrived crisp and clear. Mike drove his Ford pickup down Highway 111 to Route 2 and Boston, arriving at the Kelly's restored Victorian home in Jamaica Plains around 9:30 in the morning. Sam used his company bonus as a down payment and had bought the place for a steal a few years earlier. It needed extensive repairs and renovation, but Mike had done much of the work at cost. It had a big fenced-in yard with plenty of large trees and shrubs that practically hid the place from the street.

The others were already there. Sam and Richard were playing Frisbee in the back yard. Judy and Sara were sitting on the porch. Linda hadn't arrived yet.

"Hey, the hostess with the mostest has finally showed up to enjoy someone else's hospitality," announced Judy, not waiting for the formalities to start before taking potshots at him. If it wasn't for her big boobs and nice legs, Mike would have resented her a lot more than he did.

"Hi to you too!" replied Mike, slightly offended, but knowing he deserved it.

"Did you at least bring something?" asked Sara, getting up and walking toward Mike to extend her cheek for a peck.

Mike kissed her lightly and handed her the pastries covered with icing he had bought at the central store near home. The place had a meager selection at best, but at least he hadn't come empty handed. He knew he'd be able to eat the sweet cinnamon-laced stuff even if no one else could.

Judy took the box from Sara with a look of curiosity and disgust. "Look gang, Mike brought some frosting topped with a little cake. Roland should love this."

She called their dog, a stunted, half-sized, brown and white mongrel as she shook the box back and forth to attract his attention.

"Stuff it, Judy," said Mike. "I love those things."

"Yeah, the breakfast of champions," joked Richard, who joined the girls and Mike on the porch.

Sam, tall and handsome in his pressed slacks and polo shirt, shook his friend's hand, while Richard, dressed in jeans and T-shirt like Mike, snapped a few wisecracks at the newcomer's expense.

He was saved by the arrival of Linda, who immediately monopolized everyone's attention. She had on tight red slacks that clung to her lower half like a light cotton skin, and a white top that only came partway down her stomach. Mike drank her in like water from a spring. Getting excited, he remained immobilized on the porch while the others went to greet her. He was completely forgotten by the group as they clustered around Linda gossiping and laughing until he was finely able to stand and make his way to them.

"His majesty has finally deigned to rise and join us," Judy said, in her inimitable way.

She looked at Mike scornfully as he made his halting greetings. She hated the way he looked at Linda with those big brown eyes and his long dark lashes. She hated that he was so good looking. She hated that he seemed to be so good at everything, especially the very thing she wanted to excel in, without even trying. He didn't even take it seriously. He was just using it to get girls, the cad. She didn't care much for the outfit Linda was wearing either, even though it was very attractive and obviously comfortable. How did she expect the guys to concentrate and empty their minds when she dressed like that? But then again, the guys' minds were pretty much empty anyway, so maybe it didn't matter how she dressed.

They all moved back to the porch, shaded from the warm sun, to have brunch and tea. Judy served light pastries, cheese, and assorted fruit. Mike ate his sweet frosted cinnamon cake. They talked about past-life reading. Judy reiterated the technique.

"Remember, relax and breathe deeply from the diaphragm. Clear your mind. Just let the images appear."

They moved into the cool of the spacious dining room, where an eternal breeze blew the curtains in all directions. They took turns having their palms read by Judy, who sat in the center of the room. Unfortunately, things did not go well. All she could elicit was a hackneyed set of images from their mutual pasts. They all knew each other too well.

Judy tried reading Mike's palm, but he was nervous and his palm sweaty. The more she told him to relax and clear his mind, the more nervous he got. The practice session was turning out to be a dud. Richard started cracking jokes. It was all downhill from there.

The novices tried taking turns reading each other's palms, following Judy's instructions, but again, they all knew each other too well to get clean, unfiltered images. Finally, Judy suggested that Mike and Linda try it.

Mike took Linda's palm, which was dry and cool, and tried to clear his mind. It took all his efforts not to look at the smooth curve of her body. He concentrated on his breathing, envisioning the air being inhaled to the bottom of his lungs and exhaled from the top. He imagined it going down the back of his body and up the front, as he softly stroked the palm of her hand with his fingertips. She was so close that he wanted to kiss her. These thoughts disrupted his concentration. It was only after the greatest effort that he got his breathing under control again.

Gradually, faint images started to appear in his mind, getting clearer with each stroke of his fingers across her palm.

"I see mountains," Mike said quietly, "high, snow-covered mountains. There's a little girl with curly hair riding in a sled being pulled by a reindeer. She's smiling and hugging the old man sitting next to her. It must be her father or grandfather."

"It's Heidi," quipped Richard.

"Shhh, stop that," whispered Judy. "Go on, Mike."

"The girl has on a white fur hat and a long brown coat. Her cheeks are rosy and her eyes are sparkling. She seems very happy."

Linda opened her eyes and looked at Mike in amazement.

"How did you know I used to have a white fur hat? I used to go sledding with my granddad at Santa's Workshop in New Hampshire. I loved the mountains in the winter time."

"Try saving the commentary for later," Judy instructed. "It breaks the vibes."

After a short time, Mike started describing another scene.

"I see a road along a reservoir or lake. It's night. A car's traveling down the road. There are two people in the car arguing. There's another car coming down a side street. It seems to be swerving back and forth across the median. They're both coming to the intersection. They collided."

At this point Linda pulled her hand away from Mike's and yelled, "Stop it. Stop!"

"What's wrong?" asked Judy in concern. "What's the matter?"

"How could you have known about that?" Linda inquired, staring at Mike with wide, frightened eyes. "I haven't told anyone about that accident. My high school boyfriend was killed. It took them three hours to pry us out of the car. It was horrible. How did you know?" she yelled with tears in her eyes.

"I'm sorry," replied Mike, disconcerted and alarmed. "I didn't know, I mean, I just thought they were images from some past life, not real, not here and now."

That ended the session for the day. This wasn't quite how it was supposed to be. Instead of picking up some vague unverifiable past life images, Mike had picked up actual events from Linda's past. Judy wondered if Michael was clairvoyant.

It didn't take long for Linda to compose herself and for the group to venture back outdoors to take advantage of the sunny day. If Mike was worried about his date, he needn't have. If anything, Linda was even more affectionate than usual and left at five to get ready for their evening. Mike cleaned up and changed at Richard's house, which was close by, then picked Linda up at her apartment.

Mike had made reservations that evening at the Wayside Inn, an authentic two hundred-year-old eighteenth-century restaurant located outside Boston. A reproduction of an old gristmill stood across the road, grinding grain to meal with power from a steam-driven waterwheel. The whole scene bespoke of another time and was very romantic.

After dinner by candlelight in the crowded dining room, they strolled through the grounds of the old mill, where she kissed him long and tenderly below the slowly rotating waterwheel. Mike was in a state of bliss. He hadn't felt this good since his first case of puppy love.

The Inn was halfway between Linda's apartment and his. It was already late when they finished dinner and they were both feeling good from the bottle of wine they had shared. It didn't take a lot of persuading for Mike to convince her to spend the night at his place.

He pulled into his parking lot and helped Linda out of the truck. As they walked arm in arm up the front walk past the old house, they looked at it with curiosity. What was it doing there, so incongruous and out of place?

Once inside, Mike opened a bottle of wine, which he had been saving for a special occasion, and put Hunter out. He usually didn't leave the dog out at night, but he didn't want him disturbing their lovemaking. Hunter whined pitifully as he was chained to his tree, but Mike, excited by the prospects of the evening, ignored him.

Linda shared his bed that night. He couldn't remember seeing anything so utterly beautiful beneath him. Her smooth, tanned skin contrasted wonderfully with the white sheets. Her body was magnificent. Her mouth was so soft and voluptuous he practically fell into it. He made love to her as she kissed him passionately, orgasming so quickly he hardly had time to enjoy it.

Embarrassed, he rolled off her and apologized as he kissed her breasts. Her body shuddered with pleasure. They made love again, then fell asleep in each other's arms.

Later that night Mike was roused by Linda, who was shaking him and saying his name in alarm.

"Mike, Mike! Wake up! You're having a nightmare. Are you all right?"

"Yeah, sure. What's wrong?"

"You were making the weirdest noise. You scared me. I didn't know if you were having a seizure or what."

"What was I doing?" Mike asked, wide awake now.

"You were making this awful sound, like a siren. Ahhhh! Ummmmmm! Real loud. And you were pointing your fingers, like you were warding something away."

"Yeah, I remember now. I was in the kitchen of an old house, looked like a farmhouse or something, but it was deserted. There was an antiquated fridge and stove, and some other appliances. They were coming alive and starting to come after me. I was sending out a ray from my fingertips to ward them off. I must have been making a ray-gun noise. Hey, it was only a dream."

"Well, it must have been a doozy."

"I guess so. I've always had vivid dreams, but lately they've been real strange. Must have been something I ate. I probably do this all the time, just never had anybody here to observe me before, though I don't remember having one like that."

"Well, I'd appreciate it if you keep you dreams to yourself. I'd like to get some sleep."

"You can sleep, after I do this to you."

He made love to her again as if it were the first time. They fell asleep as they lay.

The next day, as Mike drove Linda back to her apartment in Boston, he half jokingly suggested she move in with him. To his surprise she took him up on his offer. Linda couldn't have explained why. She certainly hadn't known him that long, but the prospect of living with the hunky guy suddenly appealed to her. Maybe it was because her current roommate was such a bore. Maybe it was because she missed having somebody to snuggle close to at night. Maybe it was just the way Mike held her. Whatever the reason, she had been thinking about the idea all morning. Anyway, it would be about the same commute to work for her, except now she'd be driving in the opposite direction.

She collected a few articles of clothing and other things she couldn't do without, then they headed back out to Mike's place. It wouldn't be long before she moved in permanently.

All would have been perfect except that Mike's dog was missing. That morning, when he went out to get him, Hunter was no longer chained to the tree. Mike called and looked everywhere, visiting each of his pet's favorite spots in turn, but the dog was nowhere to be found. Later that afternoon, after they had returned to his place with a few of Linda's belongings, he continued his search with Linda's help, but still couldn't find the dog.

Mike called the police and the local pound, but no one had reported seeing Hunter anywhere. He canvassed the neighborhood that evening, as well as his apartment building, but no one knew anything.

The next day, dejected and beside himself with worry, Mike put a notice in the local paper and stuck up posters with the dog's picture all over town. However, in spite of his concern over his missing dog, he still managed to keep Linda happy on their first few days together.

Living with someone was new to Mike. He had plenty of girlfriends in high school and a few after coming home from the service, but this was the first time he had an apartment of his own. Before this, he'd be lucky if he and a girl had a place to be alone in at all. Living with his mother in the family's two-bedroom East Boston brownstone didn't give him much privacy. That's probably why he moved out as soon as he could afford a decent place of his own.

Mike found it difficult to meet women after he left high school. He hated singles' bars and nightclubs, and there weren't that many eligible females hanging around the construction site. That was one of the reasons he started going to the lectures and the past-life seminars, that and the unconscious desire to reconcile with his long dead father.

As the days wore on, Mike relished his budding new relationship. He couldn't wait to get up in the morning and come home at night. Work, which had always been his number one priority, suddenly took a back seat. Oh, he kept the job on schedule, with the same high quality he was known for, but he didn't obsess over it like he used to. Now he obsessed over Linda, her eyes, her skin, her hair. All would have been perfect if his dog hadn't been missing. He couldn't help worrying about him and wondered where he had gone.

Richard tried to concentrate on his computer screen, but his mind kept straying like a wayward pony. He'd tug it back and reign it in, only to have it go off again on some tangent or other that always led him back to the same scurrying thoughts, images of him running through the woods, not him exactly, but an old woman in a plain gray dress and bare feet.

Richard rubbed his tired eyes. He wasn't getting much sleep these days. He was irritable and on edge. Every little thing seemed to grate on his nerves, especially Sara, his wife. Her whining voice was beginning to make him sick, and he sure didn't like the way she talked about Michael. Michael said this and Michael did that, it was revolting sometimes the way she went on about him, the way all the girls flirted with him, especially Sara. He'd have to keep an eye on those two.

To make things worse, Mike now had a date with that piece of ass Linda, the lucky stiff. Now there's a broad I'd like to diddle, he thought crudely. Catching himself with a start, he tried to focus on his computer screen again, but the little black and white symbols that covered the display remained an indecipherable gibberish. It might as well have been Martian. His mind flipped unbidden back to thoughts of someone running in the woods.

Chapter 4

The week wore on like a slow parade, each day gliding by like a float of splendid colored flowers, and with each passing day, Mike and Linda got to know each other a little better. Of course, being somewhat new to this type of arrangement, they had their good days and their bad. Most of the time they were awake together, they were having sex, three, sometimes four or more times a day. It seemed they just couldn't get enough of each other, as if they had been denied something all their lives and were finally getting a chance to have it.

Unfortunately, they didn't talk much. Oh, Linda would ask him questions about himself and try to get the conversation going, but Mike was usually absorbed in some ball game or inane TV show, and barely responded. Linda was a little disappointed, but he was real sweet and good to her and never raised his voice. The sex was good, so why complain?

The fact that Linda and Mike were living together was the big news of the hour. Linda fielded no end of questions from Sara and Judy regarding Mike's private life. Mike got grilled just as mercilessly by the men about the secret charms of Linda Reynolds.

Mike's concern for his missing dog also grew with each day. Hunter had run away before, but he always came home for a good square meal after a couple of days chasing rabbits and squirrels. This time, however, a week had gone by with no sign of him. It was highly unusual and very alarming. No one had seen the dog. There was still no word from the police, who speculated that perhaps someone had stolen the animal. After all, the apartment building was close to the highway. Someone driving by might have seen the dog and taken him. Mike didn't think that was very likely, however. First, you really couldn't see the rear of the apartment building from the road, and second, Hunter wouldn't have just stood by and let some stranger cart him away. He would have yelped, bit, and barked. No way, Jose! But what other explanation was there for the dog's disappearance?

One night, a week after Hunter disappeared, Mike woke from a deep sleep to the sound of barking. Linda lay next to him, breathing with that soft snoring sound he was just beginning to get used to. There it was again, a muffled bark, as if a dog was under the ground somewhere, maybe in the basement.

Mike jumped out of bed and ran out of the apartment in his bare feet and pajama bottoms, not bothering to put on his slippers or robe. He ran to the basement of the building, down to the floor where the wash room was, and called his dog's name. There was no response in the still night.

He stood in the hallway in silence, going to each door and listening for any sound of barking. As far as he knew, he was the only one in the building who owned a dog, an exception to the otherwise strict rule. It helped that Mike did work for the landlord from time to time, and Hunter was an unusually well-behaved animal.

There wasn't a sound. Mike moved along the hallway listening as he went. Then he heard it again, faint and soft, a dog barking, strained and plaintive. He ran up the short flight of stairs to the first floor landing and out the back door of the building onto the small yard where Hunter's tree was, on the side nearest the highway. There were no cars driving by at this late hour, only the loud sound of crickets and frogs chirping in the moonless night.

He ran around to the front of the apartment. The sight of the old white farmhouse startled him, sitting there like a crouching reptile, menacing and hungry. It seemed to watch him from its black, strangely illuminated windows. Mike slowed to a walk and approached cautiously, listening for the sound of barking. All was quiet except the insects singing in the night.

He walked slowly to the front door of the ancient building and tried it. It was locked. He moved along the side of the house, but found all the windows shut up tight as well. Finally, he went to the rear of the structure, to the shed, and peered into the blackness of the partly opened door.

"Hunter! Hunter? Are you in there, boy?" he called softly through the door. Silence. Nothing. He stood there and called again, but still there was no response. He tried pushing open the door, but it was held shut by boards nailed across the top.

Suddenly, something small and feral darted out from the blackness of the doorway growling in a high, sharp snarl, its teeth snapping at Mile's ankles. He jumped up and away as if the ground were electrified. Avoiding the rabid little creature's attack, he back pedaled a few feet before turning to make a dash to his truck a short distance across the yard.

Bounding into the back of the pickup, he reached for the crowbar he kept near his tool box and turned to face the animal. To his surprise, there was nothing there. He could have sworn it was right behind him, nipping at his heels, but now there was only empty grass and shrub. Jumping down from the back of the truck, he marched back to the house with his new weapon held tightly in his hand, but the aggressive animal had disappeared as quickly as it appeared. It all took place so fast Mike wasn't even sure it had actually happened. The sounds of the night came back to him as if they had been in suspended animation. The wind, hardly perceptible earlier, had picked up considerably, swaying the leaves of the trees all around him back and forth with a loud rustling sound like a sea of whispers.

Mike went back to his apartment frustrated and confused, wondering if he'd just had a hallucination or if he really had been attacked by some kind of badger. It sure seemed real, but it all happened so fast. And the barking, had he really heard that? It was getting so he couldn't tell dreams from reality any longer.

He woke Linda while getting back in bed and explained what had happened and that he thought he'd heard Hunter barking.

"Are you sure it wasn't that thing that attacked you that was barking?" she asked, more interested in getting back to sleep than hearing his story.

"No, it was too small to make the kind of bark Hunter makes. I could have sworn it was him."

He didn't press it. After all, they both had to get up early the next morning. But Mike couldn't sleep and got up several times to check the house. As he lay there in bed, he thought he heard the persistent sound of something gnawing on wood just audible over the sound of the wind. However, when he'd get up to investigate it would stop or get drowned out by the night noises. So he could never quite locate its source or identify it.

When he finally did drift off to sleep he had dreams of Viet Nam, where he was searching house to house in the streets of Saigon for suspected Viet Cong infiltrators. He was moving slowly through a large ornate building, through rooms with richly carved and exotic furnishings, when suddenly, a large figure shrouded in black leaped out of one of the dark doorways surrounding him. As it came closer, the face became discernable in the darkness, a rat-like thing with snapping jaws. Mike stepped back and aimed the barrel of his rifle at his attacker only to find his automatic weapon had turned into a bo staff, one of those sticks with padding at both ends the Marines used for un-armed combat training. He screamed in rage and fear as the thing with the snapping jaws bore down upon him.

"Mike! Are you all right?" yelled Linda, as she shook him awake. It was just six AM. "You're scaring me half to death with your dreams."

"Sorry, Lin. It must have been hearing those barks last night. It got me all spooked. I'm worried about Hunter."

"Well, I'm starting to worry about you. You kept me up all night. Maybe you need to be alone for awhile."

"That's just what I don't need," replied Mike, taking her hand and apologizing again with a kiss. "I'll sleep on the couch next time I'm having problems sleeping. I'm sorry."

He was hard to resist lying there with no clothes on all cute and innocent. Just as she was about to get things going again with a kiss of her own, he opened his mouth and broke the spell.

"I could have sworn I heard a dog barking last night. I'm going to check out that old house first chance I get. Maybe he's trapped in there or something."

"I wouldn't go in that creepy old place if I were you," warned Linda, getting up and going to the closet. "Anyway, the police seem to think someone took your dog. You said yourself he was worth some money."

"Well, *I* don't think so. I think that old house is the most likely place for him to be. He was snooping around there the other day, acting strange."

"Oh, by the way, the landlord called yesterday, just after you left for work. He wants you to do a job for him. I asked him about that place. He said it was some sort of landmark. When they sold him the land, the city stipulated that he couldn't tear down the building, but had to build around it. Cost him a pretty penny. He didn't really know the history of the house, though. You'll have to go to the library or something for that."

"Well, I'm going to check that place out. I see lights flashing in there, and dogs barking late at night. Something's going on in there. For all we know, there's a family of gypsies living in the basement."

"I'm afraid you're the only gypsy living around here," she told him, patting his head as she went into the bathroom.

Later that week the group got together to attend a reincarnation lecture in Cambridge. They met at an ivy-covered lecture hall near Harvard Square that was packed with students and academic types, all eager to hear the latest theories on reincarnation, expounded by one of its leading proponents, a Dr. Harvey Rice of Stanford University's parapsychology department.

Dr. Rice explained how on average it took roughly 600 years for a soul to reincarnate after death, which means if you died at the dawn of civilization in 3000 BC, you'd be reborn approximately 4.4 times on average by 2000 AD. Furthermore, Dr. Rice explained, there are approximately 100 billion souls waiting for roughly 50 billion bodies, which meant there were twice as many souls than bodies. The results of all this, according to Dr. Rice, was a lot of old souls being born into primitive bodies, which in turn explained the turmoil and trouble in the world today, and why birth control is absolutely to be avoided.

Mike took the whole talk with a grain of salt. He wondered how the good doctor could calculate, with such certainty, the time it takes so many souls to be reincarnated into so many bodies. It seemed that Dr. Rice was much more interested in satisfying his sexual desires than his spiritual ones. Mike was less than impressed.

Judy took the opportunity to mention her spiritual advisor's suggestion of meeting Madame Zarloff.

"You say she's Nicole's teacher?" Mike asked, sitting between Richard and Linda in the back seat of Sam's car with Linda partially on his lap.

"Yes," answered Judy. "Her son died years ago from a drug overdose. She started seeing psychics and spiritualist in hopes of contacting him and soothing his way into the next world. Then she had a stroke herself and almost died. She says she actually did die on the operating table, saw them running around like school kids trying to save her. But she wasn't dead. She saw a bright light and a voice told her she could go now or come back. She knew that if she came back she would never die. Now she's convinced she can't die. She's ninety-one years old and still going strong."

"She's supposed to be an incredible spiritualist," added Sam, as they pulled into his driveway.

"You guys want to come in for a night cap?" he asked, getting out of the car. "We were going to open up a bottle of wine and talk about the lecture."

"No," said Mike, speaking for Linda and himself. "It's late and we have a long drive. Besides, I'm hoping there'll be news about Hunter."

"You still haven't found your dog yet?" Sam inquired. "That is strange. I can understand your concern."

Even if there was no word on his dog, Mike was just itching to get Linda home. She had been driving him crazy all night, practically grabbing his privates in the car on the way to Sam's house. He hoped Richard hadn't noticed.

That night, as they made passionate love, Mike couldn't shake the feeling of being watched, even though the first thing he did on entering his bedroom was close the shade of the lone window to block out the sinister silhouette of the house. They made love multiple times during the night, each time like the first. It was almost as if something was compelling them to do it.

The next afternoon Mike met the others in front of the massive oak doors of Madame Zarloff's Commonwealth Avenue apartment. Everyone was there except Linda. Judy's teacher, Nicole, with her slanting green eyes and ebony skin, also joined the group. Madame Zarloff was Nicole's teacher and had initiated her into the world of the occult. She liked to meet Nicole's pupils from time to time, to make sure she was teaching them correctly.

An elderly man dressed in a gray business suit met them at the door and abruptly informed them that only the men would be allowed in today. Madame Zarloff did not want to see the women.

Judy objected strenuously, but Nicole, used to the ways of her eccentric old teacher, explained it in terms even the petulant Judy could understand. "She needs to focus her energy on the men for this exercise. She doesn't want anything distracting them."

The three men entered and followed the butler up to the old grand dame's rooms while the girls waited impatiently on the street below.

The apartment was furnished from another era, with dark wood tables and cherry wood cabinets full of costly china and exotic bric-a-brac. A grand piano stood in the center of the sitting room, a room decorated as if out of a Victorian novel with fringed lampshades and oriental rugs. A tiny woman, bent with age, with small, wizened features, greeted them as they entered the room. She had silver-gray hair and wore a black silk dress that was clasped high at the neck with an ivory pendant. Silver necklaces hung around her neck. She had silver bracelets on her wrists. Her fingers were covered with silver rings.

She gave them tea and cake, then one by one, as the others waited, she took each of them into the adjoining room and talked to them alone.

Sam was first. Mike and Richard waited in silence, where they could overhear the conversation easily. She asked Sam a few questions and told him things about himself. It was nothing he couldn't have gotten out of a weekly horoscope, not very personal at all. After only ten minutes, she was done with him and escorted him out of the apartment with the words, "Be careful. You are a very young soul." Mike and Richard waited without saying a word. Richard was next.

Madame Zarloff spent a good deal longer with Richard, much to his discomfort. Instead of the polite but innocuous conversation she'd had with Sam, she started lecturing Richard about the way he treated his wife and lusted after other woman. She seemed to know everything about him, things only an intimate would know. Mike, sitting in the next room, grew embarrassed for his friend. After forty minutes of this, she led a humiliated Richard out of the apartment.

Mike had been waiting patiently for an hour. He found the whole thing fascinating, and was not at all bored. He occupied his time studying each of the items in the room as if it were a museum piece. He could almost see the history in each piece of furniture, in each painting, each vase and statue. A large fern sat in a corner of the room. A glass case full of first edition books stood against the far wall. Richard had fidgeted after only a few minutes, but Mike sat still in his chair the whole time, his hands folded calmly in front of him, waiting.

Finally, after escorting Richard downstairs, Madame Zarloff came for Mike.

"Thank you for waiting so patiently," she said, as they sat down at her table. "I had a few things I had to get off my chest with Sara's husband."

Mike said nothing, but sat there embarrassed.

"I'm never going to die," she told him, without preamble. "I died on the operating table and came back. Now I can't die."

Mike didn't know what to say.

"Give me your hand," she said abruptly. She stroked his palm with her long cold fingers.

"You are a very old soul," she informed him finally. Her voice was strong and clear. "You were a great religious man, a monk or a high priest of some sort. You have a great gift. You are here to taste life, after so much sacrifice and learning. You are a very old soul."

"You miss your father don't you?" she asked, changing the subject abruptly. "You loved him very much. There's still a lot you want to say to him."

"Yes," replied Mike, speaking for the first time, in a choked voice. "Is it possible to contact the dead?"

"That depends what you mean by contact. When a person dies, the energy that defies all odds to become a conscious mind lingers for awhile and retains its identity. Under the right conditions that identity may persist for a longer time and actually manifest itself. It is these entities that allow us to remember our past life experiences."

The explanation didn't make much sense to Mike, but her calling him a very old soul pleased him and made him feel slightly superior to the others when he met them again on the sidewalk.

"Well, what happened?" asked Judy, as soon as he reached the street.

"Nothing," said Mike. "She just read my palm and said I was a very old soul. She talked about my father."

"She did a reading?" exclaimed Judy in surprise. "She never does readings."

"Well, she did one for me. Said I was some kind of monk and that I was an old soul come back to enjoy life a little bit. This is one of my last reincarnations."

"Get out of here!" yelled Judy, punching Mike in the arm. "I don't believe it."

The group continued to gawk at Mike and ask him questions about his session with the Madame, until Mike, using his missing dog as an excuse, jumped into his truck and headed home.

After the three men left her apartment, Madame Zarloff retired to her bedroom. These evaluations exhausted her, especially the first two. She loved Judy dearly. She tried so hard she did. But her talent was limited. She just didn't have the temperament for it. Her husband, Sam, was even less spiritually gifted. All the soul he might have had, had been rigorously snuffed out of him during higher education. He belonged with machines and numbers, not with things of the spirit. Richard Kelly was another matter all together. She had seen his type before. He needed some attitude adjustment and fast or he was headed for trouble. She could see it in his seppuku eyes.

The last one, Michael, the one Nicole had told her about, was quite different. What a nice, well-mannered young man. She had observed him the whole time, and he seemed to handle all her little tests very well. He certainly had an interesting reading, a lot of wisdom and power in that one, a rare combination, but there was something troubling him, something more than his unfinished business with his father.

As a matter of fact, Madame Zarloff had sensed something as soon as they entered her apartment, something subtle but sinister. Something faint but troubling had attached itself to the three of them. Each one seemed to carry a little piece of blackness around with him. Such was the price of modern life. We pick up bad karma just going to the corner grocery store.

She continued her purification ceremony, cleansing the room and finalizing the sessions, clearing her mind of negative thoughts and influences. Whatever was dogging these youngsters was their own doing. They would have to undo it themselves, and may the Holy Mother Goddess protect them.

Chapter 5

The next day, Sunday, Mike made up his mind to check out the old house. He hadn't heard anything regarding his dog in over a week. He was beside himself with worry and didn't know what else to do.

Linda had gone shopping in Boston and was meeting some of her friends later in the afternoon. Living together was not what either of them had thought it would be, and took a lot more work than expected. They both led busy lives and often went days without talking. Mike slept on the couch more nights than not, so as not to disturb his new roommate as he sat up late into the night too upset about his dog to sleep. She somehow thought they'd go out more, to restaurants and clubs like they did when they were dating. He thought they would spend their nights cuddled in front of the TV watching his favorite shows. The previous night they made love, but hardly spoke.

Mike showered after a quick jog and grabbed a sandwich from the fridge. He then went out to the old house.

The day had started off sunny, like all the days this week, but had clouded up suddenly after lunch. It was gray and overcast, although still hot and humid. The weather report promised thunderstorms that evening. Mike hoped that Linda would be home before then.

He tried one of the windows at the broad front of the house. To his surprise, it was slightly ajar and he was able to push it open with little effort. He would have sworn it had been locked that night he heard the barking. It led to a long front room. He stuck his head in and called his dog's name.

"Hunter, Hunter? Are you in here, boy?" There was no response.

He sat on the windowsill and swung his legs into the house. He was in a long narrow room with a polished hardwood floor. A doorway stood at the other end of the room leading into a large foyer where the front door entered. In the middle of the opposite wall was an ornate fireplace decorated with the most unusual tiles Mike had ever seen. Etched in blue on a white background, they had scenes from different European locations - windmills, the Eiffel Tower, the Leaning Tower. He had never seen anything like it and wondered how something so well made could sit and gather dust like this in an old deserted building. Then he heard a creak in another part of the house, somewhere near the back.

"Hello, is anybody there?" he yelled, going to the far doorway and peeking around the corner. Entering an empty hallway, he noticed stairs going up the opposite wall and three more rooms coming into it. At the rear was a slanted doorway where the foundation had shifted, giving onto the back of the house, too dim to see.

Mike walked across the small hallway and peered into the opposite room. It was long and empty, just like the first, with a polished hardwood floor and fireplace faced with blue etched tiles. The windows let in a pale gray light.

He looked at the stairs to his left and noticed the rich texture and intricate woodwork. Someone had spared no expense. He called up to the second floor rooms. "Hunter, Hunter! Are you up there boy?" He didn't go up. There was no response.

He turned and looked at the dark doorway at the back of the foyer. It stood yawning at him like an open mouth, daring him to enter. He walked toward it, but as he moved forward it seemed to recede from him as if he were on a conveyer-belt moving in the opposite direction. He stopped and shook his head, confused and slightly disoriented.

Moving along the staircase, he observed its workmanship, which seemed to pulse and move before his eyes. He blinked and looked away. Noticing another doorway at the far corner of the foyer, he went toward it. It opened onto a narrow kitchen, with the table still set for some long uneaten meal. Old magazines were strewn across the empty floor, bare walls sat where appliances once stood. He was going to enter, when he heard a knock coming from the dark rear of the house.

Turning from the kitchen Mike was startled to find the slanted doorway standing dark and silent before him, as if it had jumped in front of him suddenly. He could have sworn it was several feet away, toward the other side of the hall. He stared at the uninviting rectangle for some time, reluctant to enter. It was sagging and tilted as if the whole rear portion of the structure was sinking into a pit. He peered through the doorway into the darkness. A dingy hallway snaked its way toward the back of the house. Shadow seemed to engulf it like a tunnel through iron black hills. He called his dog's name. There was no response.

Suddenly, a golden-yellow blur rushed out of a door at the end of the hallway and bounded toward Mike like a stampeding buffalo. He hardly had time to make out what it was before he was bowled over by his dog as he bolted for the open window, scampering on the hardwood floor like a cartoon character when he changed directions.

"Hunter!" Mike exclaimed, overjoyed and perplexed at the same time. "Where have you been? Boy, I'm glad to see you!"

Hunter ignored him, and bounded out of the window like a steeple-chaser. Mike followed as best he could, and had to chase the dog halfway through the woods before he was able to get him under control.

The animal seemed none the worse for wear after almost two weeks in the wild, or wherever else he may have been. A little thin and dirty, covered with briars and sores, but nothing a little shampoo and doggy-treats wouldn't cure. At least Mike hoped so. Had he been in the basement of the old house the whole time?

Hunter couldn't have exactly told him where he had been, even if he had the brain and thoracic structure to talk. He would have been unable to explain how he came to be unchained from his tree and in the pitch-black basement of that terrible place. He vaguely recollected, as much as dogs can recall such things, running through the woods, chasing something that smelled wild, but he couldn't have told you much more than that. Then he heard his master calling his name as if out of some thick cloud of ink, and he had run to that voice as if his life depended on it.

Mike was so happy to have Hunter back that he called all his friends. Linda was happy for him, but less than pleased that she'd now being sharing the one-bedroom apartment with a large canine. Their time together had been pleasant enough, if not idyllic, but that was when they'd had the place to themselves. Linda never had a dog before, and to make matters worse, Mike refused to leave Hunter outside during the night. He didn't even like chaining him to his tree unattended in the daytime anymore. He told her it just wasn't good to tie them up like that, it ruined the dog's spirit. Though it had never bothered Mike before.

That evening Mike and Linda had their first argument.

"I don't see why you can't keep him outside, at least when it's nice," Linda objected, as they lay in bed that night. They had just had sex. She loved his broad shoulders and chest, his narrow hips and washboard stomach, the way the sun colored his olive skin to a dark golden tan. He certainly was attractive enough, and the sweetest guy you'd ever want to meet. Why did he have to be such a dud?

44

"I told you. He's been missing for two weeks. He's traumatized and malnourished. The vet said to keep him quiet for a few days. I'm certainly not going to leave him outside again, not after what happened. It'll be fine. He's used to staying in. He's very well behaved."

"Well, this apartment is too small for a dog that size and two people. We'll have to figure something out."

"Yeah, like what?" replied Mike, getting angry. He seldom lost his temper, especially with women, but the bitterness rising in his gorge was choking out all restraint.

"Like buying a house or getting a bigger place. Or maybe I can just make it easy for everyone and move out."

"Hold it, Honey," said Mike, truly alarmed at the prospect of her leaving. "Don't say that. We'll figure something out. You know I plan to build my own place, but I can't afford it yet. Maybe if we get that bonus for finishing early. I need to find the right piece of land at the right price. It'll take some time. Meanwhile, we can save money by staying here. Give it a chance, OK?" Things were moving kind of fast for him. They had only lived together a few weeks and they were already talking about buying a house together.

Linda didn't know what she wanted. She had always been so sure of herself, seen her opportunities and made the best of them, but now she was as confused as a teenaged drifter. What was happening to her? She felt a desperate urge to find a man and start a family before she ended up like her spinster aunt, but revolted at the loss of her independence and freedom. She hated Mike's possessiveness. He hated someone trying to change him.

"I guess you have to live with someone to really know them," observed Linda.

"What's that supposed to mean," said Mike, hurt and annoyed.

"Never mind, I'm tired and want to go to bed."

The dog began to howl and bark.

"Yeah," she groaned sarcastically. "Some well behaved dog. He's having a conniption. Why don't you get up and quiet him down before the neighbors complain." The guy downstairs was already pounding the ceiling.

As Mike came up to Hunter where he sat in the darkened kitchen, the dog released its bowels in a watery brown stream. Mike retched and turned away.

"Hunter!" The smell was overpowering, fetid and rank. The dog seemed to know it had done something terribly wrong, and cowered whimpering in the corner on its blanket.

Mike used the last of the paper towels to clean up the mess, but it was still smeared on the linoleum floor when they ran out. Linda walked in to see what was going on.

"What's wrong? You're keeping me up. I have to go to work in the…" She stopped dead in her tracks.

"Oh my God! Now what has that dog done."

"Calm down," replied Mike, standing there in his pajama bottoms. "I've got the situation under control. I'll mop it. Poor dog must be all messed up. His schedule is screwed up. Probably hasn't had a real meal in days. God knows what he's been eating."

"That poor dog has just made this place smell like a pigsty on a hot day. I can't stay here with that!" she told him, pointing vaguely to the kitchen floor, but also to the dog, who lay with its head between its paws in the corner.

"Don't do anything rash. It's way too late to drive, and where would you go?"

"There're a lot of places I could go. Richard and Sara have an extra room. I'm sure Richard wouldn't mind."

"I'm sure," said Mike, sizzling. "Look, let me finish cleaning this up. I'll spray some air freshener and open some windows. It will be fine. Just go to bed. I'll be there in a minute."

She gave him a look that said not to bother, and turned on her heel and left. Mike finished cleaning up the mess, using a dirty mop and some Comet he kept under the sink. He sprayed Lysol in the air to cover the stench, which permeated the apartment. He actually contemplated tying the dog outside, but thought better of it. His anger at his pet was far outweighed by his relief at finding him just when he had given up hope.

It was already late. Mike lay down on the couch. He was just starting to doze off when he was disturbed by a scuffling sound. He looked up to see the dog scratching at the living room window.

"What's wrong, boy?" he asked, going up to him. "What's bothering you tonight, eh?"

"What now?" moaned Linda sleepily from the bedroom. "Can't you keep that dog quiet? I've got to get up for work in a few hours."

"Me too," he answered back from the other room. "He must be having a hard time."

"Put him out. Please put him out," she pleaded in exhausted tones.

"OK," he replied.

As he pulled the dog away from the sill, he thought he saw something move in one of the windows at the rear of the old house. He stopped and looked again more carefully. There was that strange faint glint again, coming from the window, as if something was watching him.

Dragging Hunter to the kitchen, he whispered, "Is there someone in there, eh boy? Was there someone in there with you? Did they take you?"

Mike had never wished an animal could talk more than now. He would have given anything to know his whereabouts for the last twelve days.

He didn't have the heart to take him outside. Instead, he threw a pillow and a blanket on the dining room floor and slept there with the dog. He soon grew used to the smell and eventually dozed off for a few hours of fitful sleep. He woke with Linda stepping over him as she left for work.

Mike and Linda were not the only ones having problems. Sarah and Richard were having trouble as well, arguing day and night. Richard accused her of having sex with his friends, yet stayed out all night with no explanation, missing work as well. Sam and Judy were preoccupied with vague physical complaints that persisted to plague them. Neither was able or willing to help the other. Their days seemed to be a dreary burden, as if they were being dragged through them against their will. None of them were the fun-loving, upbeat people they were a few weeks ago. Something had changed.

Chapter 6

Mike had a long week of grueling work ahead of him. They had fallen behind on the job, just at the finish. Now they would have to work overtime and twice as hard to meet their bonus deadline at the end of the week.

In spite of this, the next day he decided to find out more about the strange old house in front of his apartment building. He tried calling the town hall and local library from the package store near the job, but no one answered. Both were in the small center of town not far from his apartment. He decided to skip lunch and drive there himself.

It was only a short distance from the site to the small center of town, a cluster of white wooden, two-story buildings situated around a small grassy square in the middle of which stood a flagpole. Across the street was a white wooden church. It didn't take much to imagine the place as it had been a hundred years before. It probably hadn't changed much since then, except for the fact that there were cars lined up in front of the buildings instead of horses on a hitching post.

Mike pulled his truck into a space in front of the first white building and went up to the entrance, which read 'Town Clerk, Licenses and Fees', and tried the glass-paneled door. It was locked, the interior dark. There didn't appear to be anyone in. He walked up the sidewalk to the second two-story building, similar in appearance to the first, except larger. It lodged the County Assessor's office, as well as the building inspector's. He knew both men in passing. Their doors were also locked. Everyone must be out to lunch, he reasoned, as he crossed the street to the third building, a three-story schoolhouse that had been converted to a library when the Middle School had moved to a new location.

This building was also closed. He read the sign. 'Hours: 9:00 am to 3:00 pm, Tuesday through Thursday. 10 to Noon on Saturday. Better than banker's hours. He headed back across the street to his truck. He had missed lunch for nothing.

Just as he was about to drive off, a station wagon pulled up. He recognized the driver, who was the building inspector. Mike got out of his pickup and approached the small balding man as he was unlocking the door of his office.

"Hi," said Mike.

"Can I help you?" asked the man suspiciously, not recognizing Mike with his cap and sunglasses on.

"It's me, Mike Russo. Remember? I did Neil Gibbons' barn out on the old Mill Road."

"Oh, yeah, sorry, I didn't recognize you. What can I do for you, Mister Russo?"

"If you have a few minutes, I'd like to ask you some questions."

"I just stopped by the office to pick up a few things," explained the busy man. "I've got to look at some new houses out in Harvard."

"I won't take up much of your time," Mike assured him. "I just wanted to get some information about that old house in front of my apartment building out on one-eleven. You know, the white rambling place sitting right in front of the Carriage House Apartments. I asked Tom, my landlord about it, and he said it was some kind of landmark."

"Oh, yeah, the old Stillman place."

"The old Stillman place? What is it, what's so historic about it?"

"Well, I don't know much about the history of the house. You'd have to check that out at the library. Jessica, the librarian, should be able to help you. She knows a lot about that stuff."

"What stuff?"

"Oh, ah, local history and folklore."

The city official seemed a bit short with Michael after his mention of the house. He hurried about his cluttered office, grabbing blueprints and large sheets of paper, which he stuffed into his legal-sized briefcase.

"I'm sorry I can't help you further. I really don't know anything about the place."

"Well, you must know something," said Mike, following the man out to his car. "You're the building inspector. You made them leave it there."

"The city designated it as an historical landmark. I just enforced the ordinance."

He seemed to be evading Mike's questions as he got into the car.

"I really can't help you. Try the library. I think they're open on Saturday."

"Yeah, from ten to noon."

"There you go."

"Look, I skipped my lunch just to talk to you. Can't you tell me anything, like how long it's been vacant, who lived there? Who are the Stillmans?"

"Sorry, I really have to go," replied the little man, as he vanished down the highway in a cloud of exhaust. Mike went back to work, hungry for both lunch and information.

Because of the time he spent on the phone that morning and hunting down answers that afternoon, he had fallen behind on his work and had to stay late into the night to finish up. It had long since grown dark and he was alone in the new house, working on the finishing for the staircase, a fine craftsman's job that took patience and skill, and which only he could do. He was using some of the ideas he had seen on the stairs in the old house. The painters and electricians, who had long since left, could not continue until Mike finished. He had to get it done before they arrived in the morning.

It was after nine before he realized he hadn't eaten anything except a couple donuts and a cold slice of pizza all day. Worse than that, he had forgotten to call Linda to let her know he'd be home late. The way things were going, it wouldn't be before eleven at the earliest. It hadn't been convenient to hop in the truck for the half-mile drive to the package store and the phone. Now a cold beer might taste real good and give him the stamina to finish. He decided to take a break, even though it would mean he'd get home even later. If he didn't call Linda soon, he might as well not go home at all.

He drove the short distance to the store and made the call.

"Nice of you to let me know you're not coming home. I was starting to get worried," she said as soon as she recognized his voice.

"Sorry. It's been real busy today. Tons of small things only I can do. It's the last minute rush, you know, deadlines coming up."

"What do you want me to do about the dog?" she asked, not interested in the job or the deadline. "You know he won't eat for anyone but you. He's really a pain in the butt. I don't trust him. He scares me."

"Don't be silly, Lin. Hunter wouldn't hurt a flea. He's harmless."

"Well, I don't know what dog you're talking about, but this one growls and bares his teeth at me when you're not around, and I want him out of the house." Her voice was starting to rise in pitch.

"We'll discuss it later. I've really got to go. Give him some doggy treats and I'll feed him when I get home."

"I don't want to discuss it later. There won't be a later. I hardly see you anymore. And when I do…"

"Not now Linda. We'll talk about it when I get home. I've got to finish up or I'll be here all night. Bye."

He hung up without waiting for her reply, something he was sorry about as soon as he did it. He tried calling her back, but she wouldn't answer the phone. With any luck, she'd be asleep by the time he got home. He walked across the parking lot and bought a six-pack of Heineken at the market. Taking it back to the site with him along with a couple more slices of pizza, he picked up where he left off.

It was four hours and several beers later when Mike looked up at his handy work with pride, bathed in the light of his bright halogen lamp. It looked exceedingly like the staircase he had seen in the Stillman house, except with less expensive material. Suddenly, his reverie was interrupted when something moved just out of his vision, a flash in the shadows of the empty house. His lamp clothed all in blackness that was not covered by its light.

Mike cocked his head and listened. Was that a gnawing sound he heard just above the night noises? A shadow flashed in front of an empty window just out of his peripheral vision. He turned sharply, hammer in hand, and looked about, using his flashlight to spray the corners with brightness. Expecting to see some badger or raccoon leering at him, all he saw was empty flooring and pasteboard walls. Suddenly, his light went out and he was plunged into darkness. At that moment something tugged at his thick work boots, as if tiny teeth were nipping at his shoe laces.

He stumbled back and kicked out wildly, almost losing his balance in the process, and made his way out into the cool night. Spinning around several times, he looked for the source of the sensation, but all was quiet. Nothing stirred but the tree tops waving gently in the light breeze. He decided to call it a night and got in his truck for the short drive home. Again, he wondered if what he felt was real or just his beer-induced imagination. Twenty minutes later he stumbled into bed. Contrary to his hopes, Linda was not sleeping.

"It's after two. Couldn't it have waited until morning?"

"I told you, honey," answered Mike, praying desperately for a few hours of sleep. "Everyone's waiting on me. If I don't finish this up, we'll miss our deadline, and I'm counting on that bonus." He didn't want to mention the most recent bizarre episode. He was in enough trouble for one night. He still didn't know if he had imagined it or not.

"Well, it's not worth making yourself ill over. You need your sleep."

"Don't worry, sweetie, it'll be over soon. We're almost there."

Mercifully, she was too tired to argue, and soon fell to sleep. To avoid disturbing her further, he decided to sleep on the couch, where he tossed and turned all night unable to drop off. His mind kept speculating about recent events and the mysterious old house. What was it doing here? Why was it deserted? What seemed to animate the place with its gloomy presence so that even his dog sensed it? Things were getting strange. He half expected it was his own mind playing tricks on him. Maybe it was some kind of post-traumatic stress syndrome or something. He'd certainly heard enough stories about guys coming back from Viet Nam who seemed perfectly normal, but who wigged-out for no apparent reason after a few years. The stress of living with somebody, even someone he found extremely attractive, was more difficult than he had bargained for. Then he heard the gnawing.

Chapter 7

Mike's bonus deadline came and went without the job being finished, despite the superhuman effort he put in during those last few days. Even working late and all weekend, they didn't make the bonus date.

He had been counting on the extra money, enough for a down payment on a good piece of land he had been looking at in Bolton Springs. Now who knew how long it would be before he made enough money to buy it, even if it stayed available at the current price. Every day he spent finishing up the current job was another day he couldn't bid on a new one. He prided himself on sticking to his commitments and doing what he had to do to get the job done, but a few last minute electrical snafus set them back a couple of days, and by the time they got going again the bonus deadline had passed. He wasn't the only one disappointed on the job that day.

He had been too busy to visit the library that Saturday morning but promised himself he'd do it the following weekend. He'd have a little more leisure now that the pressure was off. They would still be ready in plenty of time for the closing date and could finish up at their own pace now. It might actually be enjoyable.

Mike and Linda had made plans to join the group at Richard and Sara's house on Sunday to practice some more past-life recall. Mike was less than enthused about it because of what had happened to Richard, but Linda had never 'run' before and Judy was anxious to practice on Michael himself.

The Jenkins lived in a single-story, two bedroom ranch house only a few blocks away from the Kellys. Like Sam and Judy, Sara and Richard were so far childless. Being in their mid-twenties they had plenty of time for that, but their biological clocks were ticking.

Mike and Linda arrived right on time. Sam and Judy were already there.

"So here comes the couple of the hour," announced Richard, enjoying his role as host as much as Michael had hated it. "The virgin sacrifices."

"Hey, that's not funny!" said Mike in mock concern.

The mood was light. Something seemed to lift from everyone. Richard was in rare form with his constant jokes and puns. Even Mike's mood brightened.

"Glad to hear you found Hunter," Sam said to Mike. "How long was he gone?"

"Almost two weeks. Thanks," replied Mike.

"You say he was in the house the whole time?" Sam asked.

"I don't know. Where else could he have been? I looked all over. Then I checked out the old house and there he was, all spooked out."

"I don't blame him, the poor baby," cooed Judy, all of a sudden the animal's best friend. "It must have been so scary being trapped in there all that time."

"I don't know if he was trapped or what. He just sort of came out of nowhere when I called his name."

"And you went inside?" Sara inquired, intrigued.

"Yeah, sure, of course. I thought I heard barking one night and actually tried to get in, but it was late and dark, so I forgot about it. The next day I went through a window and there he was."

"What's it like in there?" asked Sam.

"Quite interesting," answered Mike, warming to his subject. "The architecture is very intriguing. The back seems to have been added with no plan or design, but the house itself is very well made, the finest wood and finishing, beautiful hardwood floors, thick oak ceiling beams, built to last a couple of hundred years easily. You should see the brick work and tiling on the fireplaces. They're absolutely incredible."

"And the whole place is deserted?" asked Judy, taking her place on the floor.

"Yeah," replied Mike. "I only saw the front rooms and kitchen, but even that was impressive."

"We should all go and check it out," suggested Richard. "Sounds like a paranormal experience if I ever heard one."

"I don't know," cautioned Sara. "It sounds kind of spooky."

"I'm not stepping a foot in that place," announced Linda. "It's haunted."

"What do you mean, it's haunted?" asked Mike, with a perplexed look. "You never mentioned anything to me about it."

"First of all, we hardly talk anymore. And second of all, you'd just tell me to calm down and take a deep breath."

"Exactly what did you see?" asked Judy, leaning close to Linda.

"Well, nothing exactly. Mostly it's just the dog spooking me. You know how they just stare at the wall or ceiling sometimes, then growl at the air, as if something is hovering just above their heads. Hunter does that every time he and I are alone together, day or night. It freaks me out."

"I've never seen him do that," observed Mike, in his pet's defense.

"I'm sure you've never seen him do a lot of things," she continued. "Like shit on the rug and growl at the furniture. After all, you're the one who said he was well-trained."

"He was," said Mike. "He's just a little freaked-out after his ordeal, whatever the hell happened. Though I have to admit he has been acting kind of weird. I'm sure you would too if you were kidnapped and kept in the basement for two weeks."

"You think that's what happened?" asked Richard, pouring a glass of wine. He wasn't running tonight, not tonight or any night. He learned his lesson that day at Mike's house. It was Mike and Linda's turn now.

"I don't know. It's the only thing that makes sense," reasoned Mike. "That's why it's probably not a good idea to go snooping around the place. Plus there are no trespassing signs. I'm sure it's private property."

"It's a public landmark," said Sam. "And that means open to the public, which means us."

"That's all well and good," continued Mike. "But what if there's some lunatic hiding in the basement with a gun or a knife?"

"In that case," said Richard. "Have a very nice time there tonight. Linda, you may want to stay here with us."

"I'd be safer with the lunatic," countered Linda, who couldn't drink until she had finished the exercise.

Without further ado, Judy gathered the group into a circle around Linda, who was lying on the thick living room rug with her head resting on a soft pillow. Judy went into her spiel, telling Linda to breathe deeply and imagine getting lighter and lighter as she rose off the ground and floated to the ceiling.

"Imagine yourself getting bigger and bigger, like a balloon," Judy intoned. "Now you're floating out of the room and into the air."

When Linda reached the right level of trance, Judy said, "Look at your feet. What do you see?"

"White boots," Linda answered. "White cowboy boots."

"Where are you?"

"New Mexico, near the border."

"Who are you? What year is it?"

"My name is Carl. I'm a prospector looking for gold with my uncle and brothers. The year is 1857."

"What are you doing now?"

"I'm in a cantina standing at the bar having a drink with my brothers."

"What's happening?" prodded Judy, keeping the action moving.

"Someone has just come in," said Linda. "A Mexican with a belt of bullets across his chest. He's unshaven and dirty and has shifty eyes, which are bloodshot and heavy-lidded. He looked at me as soon as he entered the room as if he wanted to kill me."

"Why? Why is he singling you out?" asked Judy, echoing the thoughts of everyone in the room.

"I don't know. Maybe it's my white boots or my fancy shirt or my nice new hat. Perhaps he's offended by my spotless gray jacket. I cut quite a figure. The women find me quite attractive, I assure you."

"What's happening now?" continued Judy.

"The Mexican is starting a fight. He has two companions just as menacing and well-armed as he is. None of us are armed. My brothers are trying to come to my defense, but the bandit is just ignoring them while his men walk them off. Now he's drawing his gun."

Linda's voice was starting to rise and quiver. Judy, after the fiasco of a few weeks ago and armed with her teacher's instructions, was ready.

"That's OK, Carl. They can't harm you. You're floating over the barroom now, high above it. See? Look around. You can see the mountains in the distance. You are safe. No one can hurt you, understand."

"Yes," replied Linda, calm now and breathing evenly.

"If you want," Judy suggested. "You can look down on the bar and watch the whole thing like a movie. Do you want to do that?"

"Yes," answered Linda.

"What do you see? What's happening in the barroom far below you that you can see, but that can't harm you?"

"The Mexican is shooting the handsome man in the fancy gray suit. He just pulled out his gun and shot the guy. The Mexican is emptying his gun into him for no reason. He didn't do anything."

Linda began to cry. "Poor guy, he didn't do anything."

"Who is it? Who is shooting you? Do we know him?" asked Judy, prodding for some past life association with the present.

Sometimes a guide will probe like this, so that a person can resolve whatever unfinished business he or she may have with someone else carried over from a previous life. But it was usually only done by a very experienced guide, and only when the conditions were right, certainly not after such a traumatic revelation as a murder. But Judy, being oblivious to the danger, plunged on anyway.

"It's Michael," said Linda. "Michael's the bandit. Michael killed me!"

Linda was sobbing now, big heartbreaking, gut-wrenching sobs.

"That's all right," said Judy, in a soothing tone, guiding Linda home. "You're floating away from there now. You're floating up like a balloon, up to the stratosphere and back east toward us. You're floating back to Boston. You're over Massachusetts now. You're floating back to us. Now you're over Jamaica Plain, there's Sara and Richard's house. You're floating down through the roof now. You're going through the ceiling. See us? You are above us now. You're starting to deflate."

In this way, Judy guided Linda back from her astral projected travels.

"Well, that was fun," said Richard, after everyone had recovered from the session. "I think we'd better stick to paying Nicole from now on if we want to run. This stuff is just too dangerous."

"Everything is fine," insisted Judy. "How do you feel, honey? Everything OK?"

"Yeah, I'm fine," answered Linda. "It was just sort of freaky seeing everything like that, like in a dream, but yet you're awake and able to describe it."

"Yeah," agreed Richard. "That's exactly what it's like."

"You want to try it?" asked Judy hopefully, looking over at Mike who sat on the floor next to Linda. "This whole meeting was to initiate you."

"Well, one out of two isn't bad," replied Mike, not the least bit interested in trying it after seeing what happened to Richard and Linda. Besides, he was too busy doing damage control. Linda was sure now that he had killed her in a previous life.

"You killed me," she said, shaking her head from side to side and looking at him incredulously.

"It's just your imagination, Linda," he answered. "It doesn't mean anything. It's not real, and even if it was, it's another time and place. It wasn't me, but somebody else, a different person, some other consciousness. It doesn't mean anything."

"That's not true," objected Judy. "You and Linda have some unfinished business that needs to be resolved."

"Linda and I were getting along just find until you started making all this trouble with your mumbo-jumbo."

"Hey," interjected Sam on his wife's behalf. "I thought you believed in this stuff. Sara's right, you're just in it for the chicks."

"Of course he is," agreed Sara in disgust.

"No, I'm not," said Mike. "I believe it, but I take the whole thing with a grain of salt. Who can say exactly what we're seeing when we go under. It's like a hypnotic trance. It's your unconscious minds and memories painting images for you."

"It's more than that," insisted Judy. "Doctor Rice says they're real past-life experiences, traces of previous existences still lingering in our genes and DNA, our very atoms. He tells us exactly how to interpret these things."

"Yeah, and he'd tell you he'd like to screw you too, but that doesn't mean he knows what he's talking about," answered Mike, starting to get angry. He had resolved not to take any of Judy's crap tonight, not after the week he just had.

"Well, isn't that nice," said Sam. "Please keep it civil, Mike, if you don't mind. We're not out on the construction site."

"For your information, we don't swear on the job. It's a five-dollar fine. But your wife has been on my back ever since you guys came out a few weeks ago. I've tried my best to make up for that, but you just keep throwing it back in my face every chance you get."

"No one's throwing anything at you, Michael," Judy assured him. "You're just in denial. What Linda saw was real and you just don't want to admit it. You two have some unfinished business."

The session broke up early, since Mike would not run and Linda wouldn't stop commenting on his having killed her.

"You killed me for no reason," she repeated. "Shot me in my new white boots."

Whatever love-life Mike may have anticipated had just been shot down just like Linda had been in her previous life. He'd be sleeping on the couch again tonight.

Before they left, Judy pressured Mike and Linda into having the next meeting at their place.

"We're giving you a chance to redeem yourself, Michael," she said.

"That will be fine," Linda answered for him. "And don't expect any help from me, Michael. You're on you own, cowboy."

Later that night, after a long ride home, where Linda persisted to berate Michael for his previous life's misdeeds, the argument continued in the apartment.

"Judy said we had unfinished business to take care of from a previous life," she told him, as they got into bed. "You have a hell of a lot of bad Karma to make up for."

"Oh, give it a rest, Linda," responded Mike, tired and irritable from the night's activities.

"Oh, I'm sure you'd like to forget all about it," she continued truculently. "But I'm afraid it's not going to be that easy."

"Linda, it was only a dream," Mike assured her for the fiftieth time. "It wasn't real, just an unconscious image projected on your conscious mind. You can't take this stuff so seriously."

"But I do take it seriously, Michael," she said. "That's the problem. I take it seriously and you don't. As a matter of fact, you don't seem to take anything seriously."

"That's not fair and you know it. I take plenty of things seriously, my health, my job, you!"

"If you took me so seriously, our relationship would be in much better shape. And if you take your job so seriously, why did you miss your big deadline, eh, mister perfect?"

You could cut the tension in the room with garden shears. Their agitation was growing with each word, filling the air with tension.

"You know I busted my ass on that job," said Mike in a soft voice. "You know as well as anyone. I never worked so hard in my life. That bonus meant everything to me. It was just one of those things, out of our control."

"Yeah, you busted your ass alright, but what about those palookas you hired to help you. Couldn't you have gotten a better group?"

"Cool it, Linda. I've worked with those men for months. They're as good a bunch of guys as you'd find anywhere."

"Oh, Michael, you only see what you want to see. Just like your dog. You think the thing's well behaved and it's not. Just like our relationship. You think it's all hunky-dory and it's a pile of crap. You're living in a fool's paradise. But when it's something real, something that counts, something spiritual, you discard it as useless superstition. That just about sums it up, doesn't it?"

"What do you mean, our relationship's a piece of crap," Mike asked, zeroing in on the words that stung him the most.

"I mean just what I said. This is the worst relationship I've ever been in. We hardly see each other, and when we do all you do is sit there and watch that stupid TV set of yours. You don't talk, or at least you don't have anything interesting to say. You sit and dolt on that stupid dog of yours all night. You like to watch the dumbest programs and shows. You're an idiot, Michael. I love you but you are a dithering idiot."

Linda's rant had been getting louder with each sentence, her anger growing with the volume. She felt the rage rising in her like a giant wave, unstoppable, overpowering.

Suddenly, a voice whispered, *"Why don't you…"*

It sounded like it came from a foot above their heads, directly between them as they lay in bed. Mike thought Linda had thrown her voice, like a ventriloquist. She'd gotten so worked up, so angry, that she just clenched her teeth and unconsciously threw her voice. Even though he had a rational explanation for it, the sound, a hoarse whisper right above his head, frightened him and made the hairs on his arms stand up. The knowledge that someone could throw their voice like that under stress was disconcerting. What other things were they capable of if pushed far enough? His concern was about to grow even more.

"What did you say?" they both asked at the same time.

"I thought that was you," Mike informed her.

"It wasn't me," she insisted.

"Are you sure you didn't throw your voice? You know, unconsciously?" He suspected that under the circumstances she didn't even know for sure whether she had actually spoken or not.

"No, honest, Mike," she insisted. "It wasn't me. I would know, trust me."

Mike shivered. He could see his breath.

"It's freezing in here," he observed. Then he laughed out loud, a boisterous, rowdy, confident laugh.

"Imagine a white light over your head," he counseled her. "Laugh and imagine a bright light. We are more powerful than any ghostly entity or empyreal spirit. Let them know you know it."

All animosity and anger had left them. Linda tried to laugh, but it came out shaky and brittle.

"I saw an old woman with uncombed white hair," she said, "just for an instant, in my mind."

"That's OK," answered Mike, now laughing loudly and trying his best to imagine a light over his head.

As they huddled together in the bed, their argument of moments before was completely forgotten.

Suddenly, the stereo came on loudly, making them jump. The dog started barking in alarm. Mike ran into the other room, wondering what could have made the radio come on. When he got there and flipped on the light, he noted the stations were changing as if someone was turning the knob back and forth. Afraid to touch it, he bent over and pulled out the plug. It went silent, much to his relief. As he was straightening up he glanced into the mirror above the stereo. It abruptly went askew as if someone had grabbed it. In that instant, he saw a dark form reflected behind him.

"Jesus!" he yelled, jumping back in surprise. "What the hell's going on here?"

A moment later he was huddling in bed next to Linda.

"What happened?" she asked.

"Nothing," he replied. "Just try to go to sleep."

He had brought Hunter in with him and had him lay next to the bed. Linda didn't complain. They didn't get much rest that night.

The next morning over a leisurely breakfast, they discussed the events of the previous night.

"This place is haunted," Linda observed.

"No it's not. That's ridiculous," replied Mike. "Are you sure you didn't, you know, stress out and throw your voice? It sounded like you were clenching your teeth. Maybe you did it subconsciously. You know, you've seen enough Shari Lewis on TV to pick up a few hints."

"Don't be funny, Michael. I heard it just like you. Sounded like an old woman whispering right above us. I heard it clear as day, and it sure as hell wasn't me. I know when I'm talking. It said 'Why don't you', but I couldn't hear the rest. It kind of faded out."

"Yeah, that's exactly what I heard," said Mike. "That's the strangest thing I've ever experienced."

"I saw an image of an old woman at the exact time I heard the voice," explained Linda. "Her face just popped into my head. She had flaring gray hair that stuck straight out like a halo, and a wide wrinkled forehead with a large nose and chin. I saw it plain as day, but it wasn't anyone I recognized, and I didn't see it again after the voice stopped."

"That's the damnedest thing I've ever heard of," Mike said. "Wait until the group hears about this."

"I wonder if it has anything to do with the old house," wondered Linda out loud.

"It was probably the upstairs neighbor, telling us to shut-up. 'Why don't you shut-up.' That's what it was saying. That's the only thing that makes sense."

"It didn't sound like your upstairs neighbor. How could you hear them if they whispered? No, it sounded like it was right in the room with us, right next to us. Ugh, it gives me the shivers. It was so intimate, but threatening all the same. And how do you explain the stereo coming on like that?"

"I don't know. Maybe it was an electrical short or something. The mirror moved too. Maybe there was an earthquake." Trust Mike to seek a rational explanation for the events of the night before. Even though he dabbled in the occult he didn't believe in ghosts.

"No, it would have been on the news, we would have felt something," she insisted. "No, this place is haunted."

"Well, whatever it was, it sure was strange," Mike admitted.

"Hey, not to change the subject," said Linda, rising from the table and clearing the dishes. "Remember the others are coming over this Saturday. We can tell them about it and see what they think. In the meantime, don't forget to get ready. I'll make a list of things to do and what to buy, but you're responsible for seeing everything gets done, OK? This is a chance to redeem yourself. If you do a good job, maybe you'll finally get Judy off your back."

"That would be nice. Don't worry, I can follow orders very well."

"Good, you have a lot to make up for from your previous life. You can start now," she said, reaching over his broad shoulders from behind and kissing him on the neck.

Chapter 8

The first thing Mike did after leaving the apartment was visit the construction site, where his crew was finishing up the last minute details. He'd work on the interior in the afternoon. Once he saw that everything was on track there, he headed to the local library in the center of town.

The door to the library was open and the lights on. The place appeared to be deserted, except for the librarian, who was standing behind the front desk.

"Hello," she said as Mike approached. "Can I help you?"

She was young, perhaps a couple years younger than Michael, with long tangled blonde hair and fine delicate features. She wore a white blouse and khaki slacks, which showed off her slim figure to good advantage. Her nose was too long and sharp to be attractive, but her eyes and mouth more than made up for it, especially when she smiled. Mike was instantly captivated by that smile.

"Yes," he replied, staring at the young woman before him. "I'm interested in information about some of your local town history. Specifically, anything you have about the Stillman house. You know, the old white farm house up one-eleven in front of the new apartment building."

"Ah yes, the Stillman place," she answered knowledgeably. "There's not much documented that I know of, although the name is on some of the historic papers and letters we have archived and on Filch. Are you a scholar, mister..."

"Russo, Mike Russo. And no, I'm in the construction business. I live in the Carriage House apartment building, the one they built around the old house. It's just such an interesting place, and a historic site from what I hear. I was just wondering about it and thought this would be a good place to start."

"Well, you've come to the right place. I've wondered about that house myself. I've only lived in the area here for a few years. That house has been deserted like that as long as I've been here. I drove by it one day and stopped to take some pictures. I'm a photographer. At least I try, when I'm not filing books, that is. It just struck me as such an odd place. I thought it would be a good subject to shoot. It was a nice day, but there was something about the house that wasn't quite right. I don't know, I couldn't get the light right, everything seemed draped in shadow. I couldn't for the life of me figure out where it was coming from, all the shadow I mean, since there were no trees or clouds. I tried for a while, but nothing was working, so I picked up my stuff and left. I got the weirdest feeling from that place."

"I was curious, like you," she continued. "I started asking questions about the place, but everyone I talked to either didn't know anything or didn't want to talk. I got the cold shoulder more than once for asking about it. I've done some of my own research though, and was able to find a bit of information about the Stillman family."

"Do you have some time, Mr. Russo?" she inquired, smiling pleasantly from behind the desk. "You might find it interesting. It's pretty slow here this time of day, especially with the Fourth coming up. Everybody's busy getting ready for the holiday. I can tell you what I know. Would you like a cup of coffee?"

Mike accepted out of politeness, and followed the comely librarian into a small alcove just off the lobby. They sat down in comfortable leather chairs set around a small table, surrounded by shelves of books.

"Max Stillman was from Boston," she began. "In the import/export business from what I can gather. Made a fortune in the early 1800s exporting southern cotton to England and manufactured goods back to Boston. He also dabbled in the sugar trade, a real entrepreneur. By the time he retired from the business just before the Civil War, he had amassed a considerable fortune. He sold his home in Charlestown and moved out here to the country.

He built the house you're talking about, not far from the center of town here. It was just these three buildings then. This was a schoolhouse. The church was on the corner here as well.

The house was much smaller then, just the main two-story structure itself. None of the rooms in the back had been built yet. Stillman moved there with his two grown sons and his daughter, Rose, the baby of the family. His wife had died having her in early 1850. As was usual in those days, Max raised his daughter as a live-in cook and maid.

When the war came, Stillman's sons enlisted in the northern cause and went off to fight. Neither of them came back. The eldest died at Antietam, and the younger, his pride and joy, at Gettysburg. Max Stillman died soon after of a broken heart they say, in early 1868. Rose was eighteen. This left her in sole possession of the house and the considerable estate.

That's where most of the documentation ends, but I was able to find some additional information in some letters written about that time.

As I'm sure you can imagine a young single woman with a bank account like Rose had plenty of suitors in those days. She must have gloried in the freedom of being out from under her father's thumb and the shadow of her brothers. Of course, people would talk about her and gossip. Soon she had a reputation for being a loose woman, but her wealth stifled most of the rumors.

She never married. People said she slept around. It was a big scandal, but Rose didn't care. She was rich and independent. She must have practiced some sort of birth control, because she never got pregnant, at least not at first. Whatever she did, it apparently worked well enough until she met the father of her first and only known child. She was quite old by that time, over fifty. The father was purported to be an unscrupulous con man from Boston. This was back in 1901. Despite her almost fifty some odd years, Rose had a child, a baby girl named Jeanette.

At that time, as I'm sure you know, having a baby out of wedlock was strictly taboo. Rose became an outcast. By all accounts, Jeanette was a precocious child, very bright and inquisitive. Rose brought her up alone in the large house. She had been shunned ever since the child's birth. Even her immense wealth couldn't shield her against the moral tide that rose against her in the puritanical society where she lived. She and the child were treated like lepers.

Max, Rose's father, spared no expense building the house. He imported the finest materials from all over the world, hardwood from Canada for the floors, Teak from South America for the interior, the brick and tiles from Europe, the best of everything. He hired the most skilled craftsmen and carpenters from as far away as Boston and New York. The place was famous even then for its workmanship."

"Yes," interjected Mike. "I can attest to that. I've been inside. It's very well built, beautiful thick oak ceiling beams and hardwood floors. The tile work on the fireplace is absolutely incredible."

"So you've been in the house, Mr. Russo?" asked the librarian.

"Yes, and please just call me Mike. I was in the place looking for my dog. And your name is?"

"I'm Jessica Wilson. Nice to meet you, Mike." She shook his hand.

"Nice to meet you, Jessica. I must say, you know a lot about the house's history."

"I made it a point to learn all I could about that place. I was thinking of writing an article for the newspaper about it, but no one seemed interested."

"Well, I'm very interested. Please go on."

"I talked to someone who knew an old lady who lived here at the time. She told my friend that Rose's illegitimate daughter grew up in the house alone with her mother. She said Jeanette didn't have many friends her own age, except for a few local children too young or poor to know better. When her mother died in 1921, Jeanette, who must have been around twenty, inherited the house and land."

"What was she like," asked Mike, vaguely recognizing the name from somewhere. Was that the name Richard had used when he ran? No, he recalled, that had been Janelle. But it was close enough to make him wonder.

"Here's where it gets interesting," continued the librarian. "Jeanette lived alone like her mother. But where Rose was a recluse because she was shunned by her neighbors, Jeanette was one by choice. For one reason or another she avoided people and kept to herself. It was Jeanette who first started building the additions to the house. She hired carpenters from out of town, none of the locals. They must have hated her for that, even more than the fact that she was a bastard child of a Boston whore, as some said."

Mike smiled at the librarian's colorful colloquialism.

"When was that?" he asked, keeping his end of the conversation going.

"Most of the work was done between the first and Second World War. She had enough money to do whatever she wanted. I guess the house became a kind of a hobby for her."

"Why is it considered a landmark?" asked Mike.

"I'm not sure, perhaps because it's one of the first homesteads in town or because of its workmanship. The history kind of ends there, with the Second World War. I guess Jeanette also had an illegitimate child late in life, like her mother, but I don't know what became of them after that. It's strange how the story just peters out with no more information. You'd think someone around here would know the rest. Like I said, when I came here in seventy-one the place had already been deserted for years. Then they built the apartment building you live in."

"There are probably a few old timers around that know something," suggested Mike. "Maybe we can talk to one of them."

"I don't know. Everyone's pretty closed-lipped about it. I'm hoping to talk to that old lady I mentioned, my friend's acquaintance. Maybe she knows something. What does your landlord say?"

"Just that it's a landmark and couldn't be torn down."

It was almost eleven. Mike had wasted the entire morning talking to the pretty librarian. He didn't believe he had ever seen such golden-yellow hair, the way the sun hit it as it filtered through the high windows and slanted into the mote-filled room.

"Well, thank you, Mrs. Wilson. You've been extremely helpful."

"That's Miss Wilson. It's been my pleasure. Perhaps we can talk again. I'd appreciate it if you fill me in on any information you get. I'll do the same if I hear something else. They say the place is haunted, you know."

"Oh, is that so?"

"At least the local kids think it is, and sometimes they're the best judges. You know, the innocent eyes of children, unencumbered with all that adult clutter we carry around in our heads."

"Perhaps they're right. The old place sure is spooky enough. I know my dog doesn't like it much."

"What do you mean?"

He wasn't sure he wanted to tell her about his recent paranormal experiences and framed his answer carefully.

"He kind of freaks out whenever we go by the place. Runs around the house at full clip like the devil's chasing him, then stops dead by the back door, shaking and pointing. Real strange. Then one night he disappeared. Didn't show up for a couple weeks. On a lark, I decided to check the place out. I didn't get very far, only the front rooms, when my dog comes barreling out of the rear of the house like a bear was chasing him. I guess he'd been in there all along. I'm beginning to think he was abducted by gypsies and they're living in the house."

"Hmm, could be. That's very interesting. I'd like to join you next time you go in there."

"I don't think that'll be any time soon, thank you. The place gives me the creeps. You seem pretty interested in all this stuff."

Mike walked across the lobby with her to the entrance of the library. A few folks were starting to come in, perusing the shelves or sitting at the tables.

"Oh, I've always been interested in the occult, witchcraft and those kinds of things. I hope you don't think me crazy or anything."

"Not at all. As a matter of fact, I'm also interested in the occult. A group of friends and I actually get together and practice."

"Practice what?" she asked, suddenly more interested in the good-looking stranger.

"Oh, we do past-life recall, stuff like that."

"Sounds very interesting. Can anyone join?"

"I don't know. I'm kind of new at it myself. I'll have to ask the group, but I don't see why not. We're getting together this weekend at my place. I'll find out then and let you know. In the meantime, thanks again for all your help, Jessica. See you around."

"Bye," she said smiling, as Mike left the building.

The rest of the week went by leisurely. Mike and his team had plenty of time to finish up the work, and he was eager to bid on a new job, hopefully one that would take him through the rest of the summer and into the fall.

By the middle of the week, he had already obtained most of the things on Linda's list and was anticipating the group's visit with eagerness. This time would be different. They were all going to have a good time. He had a lot to tell them. Luckily, there had been no more paranormal occurrences.

In spite of the cordial breakfast they'd had that morning, Mike and Linda had dropped back into their familiar argument.

"We never go out anymore," she complained.

"We're having the others over this weekend," he countered. "I'll take you out on the Fourth. Maybe we can go into town and see the fireworks."

"I shouldn't have to make a fuss before we do something. You should think of it on your own. You should be more spontaneous."

Mike chalked it all up to that time of month and trusted things would get better. He told her about his conversation with Jessica the librarian. Linda became concerned when she learned the girl was young and blonde.

"She's really not that pretty," lied Mike. "She'll probably end up an old maid or something. She's really the spinster type."

"Well then, you two should get along just great," Linda replied.

Chapter 9

The day of the get-together arrived. The weatherman promised a mostly sunny day in the mid-seventies. This time Mike was prepared. He had a wide selection of fruit and cheeses, coffee and pastries, roast beef and chowder. Despite her threat not to help, Linda had bought a few items to help decorate the apartment. It actually looked like a home, with drapes and a tablecloth, comfortable pillows and working lamps. They had even splurged and bought a new 24-inch color TV, Michael's first.

He was trying to put Hunter out back, but he did not want to go. Mike had to pull him out of the kitchen by the collar. The dog resisted, dragging its paws. Suddenly, it turned on him and bit him on the hand, a good nip, penetrating the skin cleanly.

"Ow!" yelled Mike, grabbing his hand and swatting the dog on the snout as he did so. "The damned dog bit me again," he told Linda, who had just entered the room.

"I told you," said Linda. "That dog's vicious."

"There must be something bothering him," replied Mike, looking at his dog with concern and holding his bleeding hand. "He's never acted like this before. I'll take him to the vet first thing Monday and have him checked out."

"You'd better go to the hospital and get that hand looked at," she advised him, looking at his wound in alarm. "That looks like a pretty bad bite. You might need stitches."

"It's nothing," Mike assured her, holding his hand under the faucet and wrapping it with a towel.

"The dog could have rabies," she answered.

"Hunter doesn't have rabies."

"How do you know? He was missing for two weeks. You'd better get it looked at just in case."

Linda handed him a gauze bandage from the medicine cabinet and some long adhesive tape."

Mike brought Hunter outside and carefully tied him to his tree. The dog now seemed submissive and scared. Mike became worried. How did he know Hunter didn't have rabies? Anything could have happened to him during those fourteen days that he was missing. He'd had his rabies shots, but...

The others showed up at that moment, all of them driving together in Sam's Volvo. Mike walked across the yard to greet them, taking the bottle of wine and the pastries they offered. They stared at the old house with interest as they walked by it to the front entrance of the apartment.

"What happened to your hand?" asked Richard, as they entered the artificial coolness of Mike's building.

"Oh, nothing. Hunter just nipped me a little."

"Old Hunter bit someone?" said Richard. "I didn't even know he had teeth."

"So, you out of work now?" asked Sam, as they entered Mike's apartment. Linda was in the kitchen waiting to greet them.

"What do you do now, collect unemployment?" he continued.

"Yeah, that and bid on new jobs."

"How long does that take?" Sam inquired, looking concerned.

Sam and Richard worked in the burgeoning high-tech field. They made good salaries, double what Mike made in any given year not to mention the huge bonuses, and were never out of work, although the oil crisis would soon put a damper on things.

"It shouldn't take long," said Mike, optimistically. "A week or two at most, then hopefully I'll be working for the rest of the summer."

"I don't know how he can do that contracting stuff," observed Judy, looking at Linda, who was showing everyone into the living room. "It all sounds very insecure to me."

"No more insecure than any other job," replied Mike. "When the economy is good, everything is good. People will always build new houses and fix up old ones. It's pretty steady."

"And that's why we call you mister science," said Richard. "What have you got for brunch? I'm starved. And don't tell me we're going to the greasy spoon twenty miles down the road to eat."

Everyone was pleasantly surprised at the hospitality, especially at the changes Linda had made to the apartment.

"Nothing like a woman's touch to make a place look comfortable," observed Richard.

It didn't take long for the discussion to get around to the old house. Mike retold the history of the house to the spellbound group. Then Linda recounted the experience they'd had the night they heard the voice whispering above them.

"Unbelievable!" said Sam.

"You're kidding?" said Judy.

"No way!" exclaimed Sara.

"Far out!" added Richard.

"It's the God's honest truth," insisted Mike, who recounted the whole thing in his own words, verifying Linda's story with his own embellishments.

"Unbelievable," repeated Sam again.

"I think it has something to do with the house," speculated Linda.

"Let's go in there," suggested Judy. "Let's check it out."

"I don't think so," objected Mike. "We don't know if the building's safe, or what's in there."

"You said yourself how well it's built," replied Sam. "That they don't build houses like that any more. It sounds pretty safe to me, what's the problem?"

"For all we know there may be some crazy person living in the basement."

"Or a ghost," volunteered Linda from across the living room. They were sitting on the couch and chairs, and pillows thrown about the floor. "Let's just forget it and do what we came here to do. It's Michael's turn to run, isn't it?"

"How'd you learn the history of the house?" asked Sam, ignoring Linda.

"His new girlfriend told him," she answered.

"She's not my girlfriend," replied Mike. "She's the librarian at the local library."

"The library, eh. You've got to watch out for those librarians."

"Thanks, Richard, I'll remember that."

"Don't change the subject, guys. I want a peek at that house," insisted Judy.

"What can happen if we all go together," asked Sara. "It'll be fun."

"It'll be fun all right, the whole place could fall down around our ears," objected Mike reasonably. "And besides, there are no-trespassing signs all over the place."

"Listen to Mister Macho over here, afraid of a few signs," said Judy. "I thought you were supposed to be tough."

"I never said I was tough," replied Mike. "It's not safe or legal to go in there. Let's just drop it, OK."

"What do you think we've come all the way out here for, anyway?" Judy persisted. "All you've been doing is talking about that place. Now all we want to do is check it out for ourselves. That's better than you doing it alone, right?"

"Yeah, I guess so, but…"

"OK, it's settled then," Judy interrupted. Being outvoted by his friends, Mike reluctantly went along.

After brunch, he led the group across the yard to the front left side of the old house, and went up to the window he had used to gain entry previously. It slid open easily. He climbed in.

They were hidden from the road by a broad rhododendron bush and the jutting corner of the building. The others followed him into the long front living room. Even Linda went, more from not wanting to be left alone than any curiosity.

The dwelling had been deserted for ten years or more according to the best information, but the insides were surprisingly free of the passage of time. The floors were polished to a fine shine, the windows free of any grime or grit. The fireplace was as pristine as the day it was laid, its tiles gleaming in the lazy rays of the sun that slanted into the room. The walls and ceiling were free of cobwebs or dirt. Mike led the others across the long room to the far door.

He peeked out the doorway into the darkened hall, the front entrance to the house. To his left, at the far end of the foyer, was the slanted entrance to the rear of the building, which disappeared into darkness. Directly across the hallway was the door leading to the other front room. Just to the left of that was the steep staircase with its finely-wrought railing. Mike stepped into the entrance way to examine the banister in more detail, surprised how well he had imitated it after only seeing it that one short time.

"Wow, some place," exclaimed Richard right behind him. "When can we move in?"

"Look at this!" said Sara, from the fireplace. "Look at these tiles."

The group spread out immediately to marvel at the front rooms of the house, a few crossing to the opposite doorway.

"Hey, this room's got a fireplace too," cried Linda, losing her trepidation in the rush of discovery. "These tiles are even more beautiful."

Mike followed Judy, who made her way up the stairs to the second story. The further he got into the house the more trepidation he felt. By the time he was at the top of the steps, he felt he was standing on a great precipice about to fall off. He stopped and grabbed the banister.

"Wow," said Judy from one of the rooms. Mike forced himself to follow, gritting his teeth, and joined her in what appeared to be a master bedroom. It had a high ceiling and a fireplace of its own. An old porcelain stove stood in the corner. It all looked as untouched as if it had been built yesterday.

Judy was standing near an open closet speaking low as if talking to herself. As Mike entered, she turned and arched her back, throwing her arms up in the air. Then she flung them down, stretching them toward him, her fingers clutching the air just inches away from his face. Mike jumped back and yelled in alarm.

"Look what I have for you, sweetie," she hissed in a harsh voice, sticking out her tongue. Only the whites of her eyes showed. Mike backed away, his senses alert. Her tight black skirt was hiked up over her hips, her light sweater hitched up to her bra. Her hair was disheveled. She looked at him as if she wanted to maul him, like a predator stares at its prey. Mike stared back not sure what to do. For a moment he forgot everything he had ever known. Terror seized him.

"You want some of this?" she said in another's voice.

Starting toward him, she grabbed his arm. Without thinking, he slapped her, just hard enough to snap her out of her trance.

"Judy!" he yelled sharply.

She shuddered and seemed to shake herself awake.

"What happened?" she stammered, holding her reddened cheek. Then she shook her head and looked at him. "Thank you," she said quietly.

The others came running up the stairs.

"What's going on here?" Sam asked, looking at Mike suspiciously.

"Nothing," Judy replied quickly. "Michael just saved me from cutting myself on this glass here." She gulped visibly and looked at him knowingly. "Thank you, Michael."

She then walked out of the room as if nothing had happened. Mike followed and stood in the hallway as the others examined the room. He felt drained, as if every move was an effort. Nothing made any sense. He wasn't even sure if what he saw was real, or if he had hallucinated. Mike had never taken LSD, but was sure this must be what it felt like. Had he just had a psychotic episode? Or had Judy actually been possessed? Following the others back downstairs, he held the banister tightly.

"You OK?" asked Linda, looking at him as he came down the stairs.

"Yeah, sure," answered Mike, shaking off his fear. Whatever was happening, it was starting to make him mad.

"Take a look at this," said Sara, walking toward the back of the house, as the others followed. "It's the kitchen."

They went through the doorway into an elongated room that reached along the rear of the house. An old, round-topped table stood along the near wall. A broken sink and rusted counter sat opposite it. Above the table was a long window that looked out the side of the house to the wide parking lot. Newspapers and magazines were strewn across the floor.

"Look's like someone left in a hurry, right in the middle of breakfast," observed Richard, as they all crowded into the kitchen.

"Yeah," agreed Sara. "The table is set and everything, creepy."

Mike looked at Judy as she walked by, but she acted as if nothing had happened. He had a bad feeling. He had seen enough and was ready to leave. Unfortunately, the rest of the group had other ideas.

"Come on, guys. Let's get out of here," he said.

"Yeah," agreed Linda. "I want to go."

"What are you talking about?" Sam asked. "This place is fantastic. We should have brought a camera. This house just screams paranormal."

"That's what I'm worried about," persisted Mike. "We've seen enough. We should go."

"Remember what Professor Rice says," Judy reminded them. "We are stronger than any ghosts or spirits."

"Check this out," said Richard from the foyer. "Is this wild or what?" As the others joined him, he pointed at the entranceway to the rear hall as if it were an unexplored cave. "It's all slanting and tilted. The whole thing's warped like some funhouse."

"Yeah," agreed Sam, right behind him. Mike held back, reluctant to follow.

"They must not have built it properly," he observed. "It doesn't look safe. We shouldn't go in there."

"Why is it so dark?" asked Linda, peering into the gloom.

"Most of the windows must be blocked off," answered Richard, who had now entered a few feet into the hallway. "It's cool in here, like someone has an air-conditioner going. Must be ten degrees cooler than outside."

Linda followed the group as if pulled by a string, stiff and stumbling. Mike reluctantly went as well, feeling like he was being swallowed rather than walking into a hallway. The shadows engulfed them.

The hallway felt like a living thing, like a tunnel into a malignant black gullet. The light seemed to recede, as if ashamed to shine. Unlike the rooms they had just been in, this part of the house was filthy and festooned with cobwebs.

"Cripe," complained Richard, sweeping spider webs from his hair as they entered the first room on the left, into what appeared to be a large bedroom. Three bare cots without mattresses stood in the middle of the room, their exposed springs black and rusted. Little light filtered in through the boarded-up windows. Large vines rose up the far wall, where dirt had busted through the flooring. Dust floated like smoke in the beams of light that made it into the gloomy interior.

The stillness of the place was oppressive, as if the sound was being sucked away. Mike couldn't wait to leave it as soon as he entered, but lingered instead, as at the scene of a fatal accident. It appeared to be a children's room by the small size of the cots. Dust and dirt covered everything, from the bare corroded floor, up the faded, torn wallpaper, to the cracked and crumbling plaster on the ceiling.

"Ugh!" said Judy, voicing everyone's opinion. The contrast between the front and back of the house was striking, but even more, there was something disturbing about this place, a presence everyone felt but no one wished to voice.

Mike slipped out of the room and looked down toward the end the crooked hallway, where Linda was standing. She was staring through a doorway into the basement. She had a frozen expression that instantly alarmed him.

"Everything all right?" he asked, walking up to her. There was just enough light filtering in through a grimy rear window to illuminate the scene. But it couldn't dispel the darkness emanating out of the black hole of the cellar, which Linda was looking into.

She didn't answer, but continued to stare into the dark stairwell, which descended into a dank, stone-walled pit, cold and forbidding

"This is where Hunter came out of," Mike told them, following Linda's gaze and immediately getting a chill. The darkness of the tunnel-like entrance drained his will and left him weak-kneed and dizzy. The others soon came up behind him. Linda hadn't spoken a word.

"What's this?" inquired Richard.

"Hmm, look's like the basement," answered Sam. He pushed in front of the others and peered down. "Anyone got a flashlight? We should definitely check this out."

"No way," replied Mike. He tried to warn them. Something was wrong. "I wouldn't go down there if I were you."

"Don't be such a wimp," said Richard, pushing past him. "You construction guys are such pussies."

"Hey, watch your mouth, buster," scolded his wife.

Richard took a small flashlight out of his pocket, and started down the stairs into the basement. Sam followed close behind. Mike hung back with the women.

Suddenly, just out of his field of vision, something flashed from the room at the front of the hall. It happened so quickly, and Mike's attention was so focused on the cellar, that he wasn't sure what he saw. It was just a blur of shadow against the darkness, but it made him start. He spun around sharply and looked, but there was nothing there. He was going to tell the others, but before he could say anything, an even more bizarre chain of events occurred.

Richard, who had descended toward the bottom of the stairs with Sam right behind him, flashed the small penlight around the flagstone basement, crowded with dust and debris. Piles of shingles and dirt, and rusted pipes were scattered everywhere. Then he saw something that he would never forget - a small child, emaciated and naked, with white skin and black hair. Its large, wide, black eyes stared up at him hungrily. It began to crawl up the steep basement stairs toward him. Its hair was pasted to its head as if it had a fever. Its teeth were pointed and sharp. As Richard looked on in horror, it opened its mouth to let out a soundless scream, its jaws getting wider and wider until it took up its whole face.

Richard screamed and threw up his arms, flinging the penlight into the darkness. In his haste to reach the top of the stairs, he knocked over Sam, who had been right behind him.

Sam had seen nothing, but he heard the bone-chilling scream. Or at least that's how his brain interpreted the nightmarish sound. He had noted Richard's alarm, but couldn't see what the problem was. Suddenly, he was assaulted by the most hideous noise he had ever heard. He froze in fear. Even after Richard had knocked him down and stepped over him, the sound kept going, like a thousand sirens. He crawled and scrambled up the steps, and put his hands to his ears trying to block out the terrible wail. It sounded as if all the damned of hell were howling behind him.

Linda was staring at the black, formless, smoke-like thing she had been looking at the whole time, too petrified to move. It started moving up the stairs toward her, floating on the air like a vapor of shadow, its face getting more defined and hideous as it came.

Each of them was submerged in their own private horror. Judy heard the crying of a dozen newborn children, wailing at the top of their lungs. Sara stared into the open doorway of the cellar, which looked like the mouth of a large, wormlike creature that was swallowing them in its black, gaping throat.

Screaming in unison, all five ran toward the front of the house. Mike stood there alarmed and perplexed. He hadn't seen or heard a thing except the earlier fleeting movement out of the corner of his eye.

"Jesus!" he cried. "What's wrong?"

No one answered. Instead, they ran screaming down the hallway for the front of the house, Sam in the lead. In his panic, he made a wrong turn and stumbled into the first bedroom. Seconds later his high-pitched yells were rending the air, drowning out the others. Mike ran to his aid and found him lying on one of the small cots, his hands and feet entangled in the iron springs and coils, bouncing up and down as if he were humping the thing.

"Help!" he cried in panic. "Something's got me."

"It's the bed you idiot!" said Mike, pulling him from the cot and noting he had a bloody nose.

Helping Sam from the room, they rushed the rest of the way out of the house. As Mike guided Linda out the front window he noticed her stony expression and dull eyes. She had not spoken a word, but let herself be pulled along mindlessly. Mike decided he liked the screaming better.

"That was horrible!" observed Judy as they made their way back to Mike's apartment. "Did you hear that crying?"

"Did you see that hideous mouth?" asked Sara.

"I saw something in the basement," Richard told them, still in shock, unwilling to put his vision into words.

"Did you hear that howling?" Sam asked them, confused as to what had just occurred.

As each recounted what they had experienced, it became apparent they had each seen or heard something different. No one could collaborate the other's story.

"That's odd," said Mike. "You each saw or heard something different."

"A group hallucination?" wondered Sam out loud.

"More like group hysteria," replied Mike. Despite what he said, he was beginning to think something more than just their imagination was at work here. He had seen something move out of the corner of his eye, but the things these people were talking about just didn't make any sense at all.

They were all glad to be out of the house. It was like waking up from a long nightmare. As time went on, each of them began to doubt the reality of what had occurred, especially since each had experienced something different.

"I saw something floating in the air, like a thick black smoke," Linda explained. "It was like it was holding me there. I couldn't move or speak. Then it started to come at me and I saw her face. It was coming up to me, like it wanted to get inside me. Oh, it was horrible!"

She buried her face in her hands and wept.

"I told you there was something down there," said Richard, trying to vindicate himself after his panicky retreat. "You'd better call the cops. There's someone down there."

"I don't know about that," answered Mike. "It's probably not a great idea to let the police know we were trespassing."

"Well, you better do something. Have them check it out. Tell them you're seeing things at night."

"I have. They think I'm seeing things at night," joked Mike, trying to lighten up the mood.

All thoughts of any further activities that day were put aside. Everyone had had enough excitement for one afternoon. Even the roast beef and chowder went untouched. The group had lost its appetite as well as its nerve.

"I'd call the cops if I were you," warned Richard, as they got ready to leave. It was early, hours before they had planned to depart. "Have them check that place out."

"Yeah, and have that hand looked at," volunteered Sara.

"Let's get together on the Fourth at our house," suggested Judy. "We'll have a cookout and do some exercises out on the yard. It'll be fun, much better atmosphere. The vibes are distorted here because of that house. Something bad went on in there and it's polluting the whole area. What's everyone doing Monday?"

"We'll see," said Mike, without committing, wondering if maybe he'd had quite enough of the occult.

"Sounds good to me," chimed in Richard, always the party animal.

Sam had recovered from his ordeal, which was already beginning to fade in his memory.

"How about you, babe?" he asked his wife.

"I'll have to talk to Brian and Ann," said Judy. "We were supposed to go there in the evening to watch the fireworks. You can see them from their roof. I'll let you know Sunday evening at the latest, Sara."

Mike walked them all to Sam's car. Linda stayed in the apartment and started washing the dishes. The sky was turning dark in the east, but was still pale blue and rosy in the west, half hidden behind the trees.

"I'll call you tomorrow and let you know about the Fourth," he said again, as he shut the door and waved good-bye. No one said anything about the house or their excursion, each now wondering if what happened had been real or not.

Mike's hopes of impressing his friends had failed miserably. They would probably never visit him again. He walked back to his apartment, across the yard between the walkway and farmhouse, to bring in his dog. Everything was now dark in shadow.

Looking at the squatting structure to his left as he walked by, he could have sworn he saw something move in one of the rear windows. He walked to the window and looked in, covering his eyes with is hands like a visor as he did so. Nothing. Blackness was all that returned his gaze.

Something small and furry suddenly thumped into the window from the inside, almost shattering it. Mike jumped back in alarm. Regaining his composure, he banged on the sill with his palm and peered in, but all was now quiet. Whatever it was had been scared off.

Shaken, he pulled himself away and went to get his dog, wondering about the strange events of the day. Had they really seen something or was it all their imagination, the product of their own frayed nerves and contagious fear? Mike had the distinct feeling that distinguishing fantasy from reality would soon become very important.

Chapter 10

That evening Mike and Linda had a terrible argument. Linda refused to spend a single night more in the apartment. Mike told her she was being unreasonable, that what happened today was just the result of her overwrought nerves. It was probably the worst thing he could have said. She started to cry and told him he didn't take her seriously. She was nothing but a live-in sex doll to him. They didn't do things together. They never had any fun. He spent more quality time with his dog than he did with her.

"Would you do as I asked and keep the animal outside?" she complained. "Would you believe me when I said the dog was vicious and should be put away, even after it had bitten you twice? When I tell you I saw something terrifying and that we should not be staying anywhere near that house, do you believe me? No! You don't believe a thing I say."

Michael had no choice but to drive her into Boston to stay with her old roommate until she could make arrangements to move the rest of her things. He returned home well after midnight, broken-hearted and depressed. He slept on the couch with his dog. His lonely days and nights were about to begin again.

He spent a shiftless Sunday moping around the apartment, and called Judy in the evening to tell her he couldn't make it for the Fourth.

"Maybe next weekend," he said.

"It's just as well," she answered. "We can't break our plans either."

He didn't have the heart to tell her he and Linda had broken up. After all, it was Sam and Judy who had introduced them in the first place. He was sure Judy would take Linda's side and lecture him on what an insensitive cad he was.

Monday the Fourth was even more depressing than the weekend had been, if that was possible. Mike spent the day alone. He took a run with Hunter in the woods, but nothing seemed to dispel his gloom. The beautiful country just broke his heart, and the exercise made his gut hurt, giving him none of its usual pleasure.

For a change, he cut into the woods off the highway and ran along a wooded path he hadn't been on before. It seemed to circle far behind his apartment. At one point Hunter darted off into a thicket and didn't return for some time. Mike, already spooked by the recent loss of the dog, called after him in concern.

"Hunter! Here, boy!"

There was no sign of him. Mike could see a trail faintly branching off from the main one he had been jogging along, mostly covered by ferns and bushes. He pushed them aside and ran along the path calling his dog's name.

He followed the trail deeper into the woods, where the trees grew closer together and the ferns higher. The sun was having trouble penetrating the tightly intertwining branches above his head. Just when it seemed the path would give out, he came upon a small clearing, in the middle of which stood a tiny cemetery plot, two gravestones ornately decorated with angels and curlicues. A corroded wrought-iron fence surrounded the stones. The bigger stone had faded lettering that read, 'Maximillian Stillman – 1791 to 1868. On the smaller stone was the inscription, 'Rose, beloved daughter of Max Stillman – 1850 to 1921'.

Mike stood and stared at the plot for some time. His dog was there, circling the iron-gate with his nose glued to the ground.

"So, what have we here, eh boy?" Mike said, relieved find his dog.

Hunter continued to circle the fence with nose to the ground.

"Come on boy, let's go home," said Mike, growing tired and impatient to leave.

The animal ignored him and continued to move around the fence.

"Let's go, Hunter. Here boy!" he called.

Still the animal ignored him. Mike reached out to grab his collar, but the dog hunched down and bared its teeth, growling at him. Mike had never seen him do anything like that before, but stood his ground.

Hunter reacted with swift anger, lunging at his legs, his teeth snapping the air. Mike lifted his leg up sharply as the dog came at him, and brought his foot down on his head, pinning it to the ground. He kept it there until the animal seemed to calm down, then let him up. Hunter immediately ran down the path back toward the main trail. Mike chased him, but couldn't catch up, yelling the whole way for the dog to heel. Following the path back to his apartment building, he was relieved to find him sitting by the side door as if nothing had occurred. It was all just a game. Michael wasn't so sure.

"Hunter!" he yelled. "What's wrong with you? What's the matter, boy? Maybe Linda's right. I just might have to take you to the vet's."

Even though it was threatening to rain, he tied Hunter to its tree and left him there. He no longer trusted the animal. It was the loneliest, most depressing Fourth of July he could remember. He tried calling his friends, but no one was home this festive night but him. He called Linda several times, even after her roommate informed him she had gone out for the evening and wouldn't return until late. She did not return his calls.

The next day he took the dog to the kennels up the road and left him there for the vet to look at. He told the doctor how the dog had run away and bitten him since his return. The vet said he'd keep him under observation for a few days, confirming that Hunter's rabies and distemper shots were up to date.

Later, Mike checked the union hall, but there were still no jobs to bid on. He didn't know what to do with no construction site to go to. The work his landlord had wanted him to do was just a small pick-up job, and Mike had given it to someone else since he had been busy finishing up his previous one.

He visited one of his crew at their log cabin home on a wooded lot in Stowe, and looked at some property that was too expensive for him now that his bonus money had evaporated. That night he called Linda again, but still couldn't get in touch with her. A little later his phone rang. It was Sam, probably the last person he wanted to talk to.

"Hey Mike, how you doing? How was your Fourth?"

"Not bad, Sam," he lied. "How about yours?"

"Great, we went down to the Esplanade. They had concerts and a big firework display. I guess they're going to do it every Fourth of July from now on. You should have come. We missed you."

"Thanks, but I wanted to keep it low-key this year. I hate crowds."

"I know what you mean," said Sam, getting to the real reason for his call. "Hey, I heard you and Linda broke up."

"How do you know about that?" asked Mike.

"Are you kidding? You think Linda would keep a thing like that from Judy for long? Linda told her the first day after moving out. Boy you must be bummed."

"Yeah, you could say that. Have you talked to her?"

"Sure, she was with us at the fireworks. She said she didn't want to talk about it.

"Great," said Mike, feeling worse than ever. Sam seemed to offer so little hope. Linda didn't even want to talk about him.

"Hey, we're all getting together Saturday at the house. Linda's going to be there. Why don't you come? Maybe you two can start over again, you know kiss and make up."

"I don't know if that's such a good idea, Sam. But thanks anyway. I'll think about it and let you know later in the week, OK?"

He hung up thinking there might be some hope after all. He knew all along he'd go. He just didn't want to seem too eager.

The next day Mike got a call from the vet. His dog Hunter had bitten two of his assistants and the vet himself, a total of seven times in all. The animal was obviously unmanageable. For the safety of everyone involved the vet strongly recommended putting him down. Mike refused, saying he'd take care of it.

"I'll be over to pick him up later this morning," he said.

He hung up the phone feeling his heart sink to the floor. What was happening to his dog?

When Mike arrived at the vet's to pick up the dog, Hunter seemed quiet and sedate. None of the handlers wanted anything to do with the animal. He was muzzled and locked in a cage. Mike took him out without a problem. It was as if the dog knew it had just been reprieved and was on its best behavior. Mike thought everyone, including himself, had been overreacting. You just had to be careful around the animal, treat him gently, not spook him. He'd be OK with a little time and tender-loving care. He certainly wasn't going to have the dog put down over a little bite. At least the doctor didn't seem to think it was rabies or distemper, and admitted he could be spooked by what had happened to him. Maybe someone had abused him.

When he got home Mike filled Hunter's bowl with water, then went down to the union hall to check for work.

Hunter lay on the kitchen floor waiting for his master to return, his head resting on his blanket next to his water bowl, his eyes closed, resting. Suddenly, he looked up at the door as if someone was entering, but there had been no sound. He howled. An old woman stood before him. He rose and circled the floor growling, but the figure made no sound and stood as still as stone. Even though he had relieved himself before Mike brought him in, his bladder let go in a yellow stream. He whimpered. His hackles rose in fear. Hunter heard a whisper and tried to bolt toward the door, but it was shut and locked.

"Doggy want a bone?" she croaked. "Doggy want a bone?"

Sam walked into the darkened bedroom. Judy was lying in bed with a wet cloth over her eyes.

"Honey, can you look at this," he asked. "This sore on my nose is starting to look funky."

"Please," she said irritably. "My head is killing me. Keep it down, will you. I can't look at your nose. The light hurts my eyes."

"Sorry, hon. Maybe we should both make an appointment with Doc Richards."

"I don't have time for doctor appointments," she told him from the bed. "Just let me rest, will you. We've got the gang coming over Saturday and I'm already exhausted. Why do we have to be the only ones to entertain all the time?"

"Because we're the only ones who have any class."

"Please let me rest," she pleaded, waving him away.

Sam walked back into the bathroom to study his face.

A few blocks away Richard and Sara were having one of their increasingly frequent arguments.

"Where were you last night? This is the third time you've been home late this week," complained Sara. "Where did you go? It was after eleven."

"I told you," replied Richard. "We're working on a new project. I had to stay late at the office. Get used to it."

"I called your office," she countered. "They said you had left before five!"

"What, are you checking up on me now?" Richard asked heatedly. "If there's any checking up to be done around here, I should be the one doing it."

"What do you mean by that?" asked Sara, not liking his implication.

"I mean, who have you been screwing around with? Is it someone I know, one of our friends? Or is it some stranger?"

"Richard!" she yelled in shock. "How can you say that?"

"Bitch!" Richard yelled into her face. "You bitch!" He turned and walked quickly out of the house, slamming the door behind him.

Sara didn't know what to do or think. Richard had never acted this way before. It must be the stress of the job, she thought as she went back to the TV show she had been watching. She was having trouble sleeping lately. At least she had her favorite shows to keep her company.

Richard got in his Saab 900 Turbo and squealed out of the driveway. He'd had all he could do not to slug that two-timing broad right in the face. She had a lot of nerve coming down on him like that. If he ever caught her screwing around with any of his friends, he'd kill her.

Instantly, images of her making love to someone else came unbidden to his mind. He tried to drive the thoughts from his brain, but almost drove off the road instead. He stopped and clenched the wheel. Then he had an idea that actually made him feel better. Following a sudden impulse, he drove toward the west end of town.

Richard had never acted this way before. He was normally easy-going and jovial, but lately something had been bothering him, an anger that was eating into his soul, overwhelming him. It was accompanied by a persistent sexual hunger that made him feel like a bull in heat.

"Hi," said Richard, as Linda opened the door.

"What are you doing here, Richard?" she said in surprise.

"Are you alone?" he said, breathing hard.

"Yeah, my roommate's out on a date. Why?"

"Can I come in?" he asked hopefully. "I have a little blow. Thought you might like to share some with me."

"Richard, I had no idea you were into that stuff. Does Sara know where you are?"

"She could care less. She's out screwing around somewhere. I just wanted to get you high."

"Why, Richard, you naughty boy." She opened the door wider and let him in.

Mike returned to his apartment. Parking his truck, he walked past the old farm house, which sprawled across his front lawn like a dying white whale. It seemed to leer at him through its slanting windowsills and crooked doors, as if mocking him. He dismissed the vague sense of foreboding he had felt all day and entered his apartment.

The scene that met his eyes was horrible beyond description. The place was filled with blood and vomit. His dog, Hunter, was on its back with its feet sticking straight up in the air, an oversized soup bone protruding from its gaping jaws, its eyes wide in pain and sudden terror.

Mike yelled and threw himself back against the wall, then clasped his hands in front of his face and ran out of the apartment. Tears welled up in his eyes. He swore vehemently and punched the wall. Then gaining his senses, he ran back inside to see if he could help his dog, but there was nothing he could do, Hunter was gone. Wrapping him in a blanket, he rushed back down highway to the vet's, driving as fast as he could even though there was obviously nothing the doctor could do.

At the kennel, they took the dog from him and confirmed that he was dead, consoling Mike the best they could. It was for the better they said, considering the dog's recent behavior. He should have been put down earlier. Mike drove back to his apartment in shock

Chapter 11

The next day, against his better judgment, Mike called Linda. He needed to talk to somebody and share his grief. Linda was the first person he thought of. She answered the phone on the second ring as if she were expecting a call, but sounded disappointed when she recognized his voice.

"Hunter just died," he blurted without preamble. "They wanted to put him down. He just started biting people. He tried to bite me again the other day and I took him to the vet's. He bit everyone there so they wanted to put him to sleep. I guess you were right. He just kind of went crazy after getting lost. Poor guy. But I just couldn't do it. I took him home. He seemed fine, so I left for a short time, just a half-hour to go down to the union hall. When I got back I found him dead on the floor. He choked on a soup bone. Can you believe that, a soup bone!"

Mike's outburst lasted a full five minutes without a pause.

"I'm sorry," said Linda, without emotion.

There was an awkward pause as Mike searched for something to say and Linda waited.

"How you doing?" he asked finally.

"OK, how about you?"

"Not good, but I'll be all right. How was your Fourth?"

"OK. Went to the fireworks with Sam and Judy."

"Yeah, Sam told me. I miss you."

Another long pause.

"Look, Mike, I really can't talk right now. I'm expecting another call. I'm sorry about your dog. Maybe I'll see you around."

She didn't mention the upcoming get-together at the Kellys. Mike hung up even more depressed than before. Walking to the living room window, he looked out at the dark, rainy, overcast day. The squat white farmhouse looked back at him through black, non-reflecting windows, a grotesque rambling thing that seemed to be brooding in the midday gloom.

Losing all sense of time, he stood staring at the pile of wood and shingle lost in thought. His trance was broken by the telephone, which was tweeting like a canary from the kitchen. Glancing at the clock on the way to the phone, he noticed it was twenty-two past two. An hour had gone by! He had been standing in front of the damned window for an hour without realizing it. Isn't that what they call a blackout?

Mike was more than a little disoriented when he answered the phone.

"Hello, Mr. Russo? This is Jessica Wilson from the library. I have some more information for you regarding the house."

"Oh, hello Jessica. Nice to hear from you. How was your holiday?"

"Very nice, thank you. I went out to the western part of the state on a retreat with some friends this past weekend. It was very spiritually invigorating."

"That sounds nice. I could use some spiritual invigorating right about now."

"Oh, is something wrong? You don't sound so good."

The sympathetic human contact made it hard for Mike to hold back his tears, which swam just below the surface of his mind.

"My dog died yesterday," he explained. "He choked on a soup bone."

"Oh! I'm so sorry. That's horrible. You must feel terrible. What kind of dog was it?"

The sympathy and hurt in her voice was more than he could bare, and he started sobbing like a child.

"A Golden Retriever," he blubbered into the phone. "I'm sorry. I don't mean to carry on like this. It's just a bad time. My girlfriend left me, moved out. I'm not working. Things are kind of piling up."

He could barely control his voice, his words interrupted by huge, heartrending sobs.

"You poor man. I feel terrible. Is there anything I can do?"

"No, I'll be all right," he said, blowing his nose. "I'm so embarrassed."

"Don't be," said Jessica. "It's good to get it out. There's nothing trivial about a pet dying like that."

"What were you going to tell me about the house?" asked Mike. "Maybe it will take my mind off things."

"Well, I don't have any information yet myself, other than what I've already told you, but I know someone that has, and she's agreed to talk to us, both of us."

"Great! See, you've cheered me up already. When? Who is it?"

"Her name is Hanna, Hanna Gilmore. She's a real old timer, lived here all her life. She's eighty-seven years old and sharp as a tack. She knows all about the place and isn't afraid to talk about it."

"What do you mean, isn't afraid? What's there to be afraid of?"

"I don't know, but nobody else seems to want to talk about it except the local kids, and they say the place is haunted, something about an old lady who kills little children and eats them."

Mike was beginning to get his composure back and was feeling a little better.

"I don't know about ghosts," he said. "But I'm thinking of having the police check it out. So, when does this lady...?"

"Hanna."

"When does Hanna want to meet us?"

"How does next Sunday afternoon sound?"

"Sounds good. I'm going to a little get-together on Saturday. A little past-life recall thing. Would you like to come? I mentioned you asked to join us and no one seemed to mind."

Mike had completely forgotten to mention it, except perhaps to Sam. He probably wouldn't go if he had to face Linda and all her allies alone.

"Are you sure it's OK?"

"Sure, positive," he lied. "The gang would love to meet you. I told them all about you."

"Great!" said the librarian.

"Then I'll see you Saturday and we can make plans for Sunday, OK?"

He got directions to her place, and her phone number and hung up, feeling immensely better about himself, although the cold fingers of death still tugged at his heart when he thought of Hunter gone for good. No more walking along the woods with Hunter zigzagging back and forth across the trail. No more running along the road with his dog at his heels. No more antics. No more trials. No more loyalty so strong only the grave could break it. His best and only companion had gone horribly into the void, choked on a soup bone he never should have had.

The week dragged by with interminable slowness as Mike tried to deal with his sorrow. The lack of bids was beginning to concern him, even though it had only been a couple of weeks since the job had ended. He'd have to start economizing, not that he was any kind of spendthrift to begin with.

He was beginning to suspect the old house might have something to do with the trouble he had with the dog. After all, it was after going in there that it had started acting strangely. Now that he thought of it, it was after going into the house that all his trouble with Linda had begun.

As Saturday approached, he got more nervous about introducing Jessica to the group. He was sure that Linda wouldn't like it, but that was all the more reason to bring Jessica along. Anyway, she had been the only one willing to help him find out about the old house. It was the least he could do.

He had talked to both Sam and Richard during the week, and told them he was bringing someone along to the get together. Neither objected, but Sam told him he should have passed it by Judy first. It was her group. She had formed it and introduced him to everyone. Mike owed her that much. Mike told Sam he wouldn't complain when he saw the attractive librarian, so in the end he finally agreed to help clear it with his wife.

Mike picked Jessica up at eleven and drove the forty or so miles into the city. The drive down Route 2 was scenic and enjoyable. The Boston skyline sparkled like a table of expensive crystal in the late morning sun. The others were waiting for them when they arrived. Linda looked as radiant and sexy as ever in a white see-through sundress.

Mike introduced Jessica to the group with awkward words and gestures. She worked them like a politician, winning the men over as soon as she stepped out of the car in her black Bermuda shorts and yellow halter-top; the women after she smiled and spoke a few gracious words. She knew just what to say to put Sara at ease and make Judy an ally. Linda, however, did not bother to hide her dislike for the newcomer, and showed it by flirting unmercifully with Richard.

"What a lovely place you have," Jessica observed on being introduced to Judy. "I've heard so much about you. The vibes are absolutely perfect here. This house has a nice green aura, a healing color."

"Oh?" said Judy. "You can see auras?"

"Why, yes. Yours is purple and blue, but there's dark redness near your head."

Judy looked at her in surprise.

Apparently Jessica knew quite a bit about the occult. As the group moved to a shaded corner of the backyard Jessica told them that she was a witch.

"I'm a practitioner of the white arts," she explained, "the old religion of the female God."

The group was standing around a lunch table set up with a variety of cheeses, fruits, and pastries.

Judy took the revelation in stride. The rest of the group looked at Jessica with a mixture of curiosity and suspicion.

"I haven't been feeling well since last weekend, after coming back from Michael's house," Judy confessed, rubbing her forehead between her eyes. "I've got the worst headache I've ever had. Not a migraine, but right between my eyes. It's been killing me. Sometimes I can hardly see it hurts so much."

"How's the hunt for work going, Mike?" asked Sam, changing the subject as they milled around the table.

"Slow," replied Michael, not going into detail.

Mike noticed Sara standing off to the side, not being her usual talkative self.

"What's wrong with Sara?" he asked Sam, when they were alone for a minute. "She looks like she's been crying."

"I guess Richard and her are having problems," said Sam. "He was kind of rude to her earlier and made her cry. I've never seen him so mean, must be pressure on the job or something. They're fine now."

Sam had a big bandage on his nose. Mike said nothing.

Jessica and Judy stood together talking, while Richard joined Mike and Sam. Sara busied herself arranging and then rearranging the table.

"Michael said you told him the history of the house?" Judy asked Jessica.

"Yes, he told me you all went in there last week," replied Jessica, addressing the whole group. "What was it like?"

"Spooky," answered Judy. "I heard the most awful sounds."

"We were all seeing things," said Sam, interrupting and annoyed at the direction the conversation was taking. He for one did not want to recall the incident at all.

"Is that why you ran out of there like a scared rabbit?"

"Aw, stuff it Jude," he replied. "I wasn't the only one who ran out of there. You were all right behind me."

"Yeah, but none of us got tangled in a cot," she laughed cruelly.

"Mike didn't run," offered Sara, coming out of her funk to join the others. Richard rewarded her with a dirty look.

"I saw a face," said Linda. "I saw an old woman's face. It came out of a black fog that seemed to float in the air just above the cellar door. It was the most terrible thing I've ever seen. And a few days before that, Mike and I heard a voice."

"Oh?" said Jessica, looking at Mike questioningly. "Sounds like a frightening place."

"Michael, it's your turn to run," announced Judy, getting the session back on track. She had been waiting weeks for this moment. Mike seemed to be the most naturally gifted of the group. Both her teacher Nicole and Nicole's teacher, Madame Zarloff, had said as much. He seemed to have an intuitive way of handling the unknown, a hidden confidence that only came out in extreme situations. She was dying to get him into the trance and see what he'd say. Of course, she would have liked to do a lot more with him, but remembered how untrainable and contrary he was. Mike didn't object this time, but took his seat in the reclining lawn chair that Judy proffered him as they all got comfortable.

A fresh breeze wafted through the large oak trees that sheltered this corner of the yard. The grass was cool and green between their toes. The sky peeking through the leaves high above was clear-blue and cloudless.

Judy put some soft celestial music on the boom-box and started her relaxation mantra. Mike followed her voice and was soon in a self-induced trance, imagining he was rising into the air as he got lighter and lighter. He was looking down on the others from above the trees. The Boston skyline glimmered close by in the east. He could see the hazy green and bluish mountains in the west. Houses and apartment buildings stretched into the distance below him. Somewhere along the way imagination turned real and he was no longer floating in the air. Following Judy's disembodied voice, Michael looked at his feet.

"What do you see?" she asked.

"Black shiny shoes with silver buckles and white stockings," he answered in a cultured voice, not quite his own.

"Look up, what do you see?" she continued, guiding him into the past.

"A dress, no robes. I wear gold and purple vestments of the richest brocade and silk. I have on a tall, ornate hat. There is a long, golden staff in my hand and a large gold and ruby ring on the second finger of my left hand.

"Who are you? What year is this?"

"I am Nicole, Bishop of Paris, visiting the Holy See in Rome. The year is 1375. I sit with my secretary in the papal curia dictating my memoirs. I have seen much in my forty-two years.

The great bells of Master Dondi's wondrous clockwork toll for the hour of nine. The room is lit only by a single candle, over which my faithful secretary hunches as he scribbles my words. I need him, for my vision has failed, so that the letters blur and become indistinct in the maddening, flickering light.

The universe is like a great clock and God is the master clockmaker. Its design is perfect in every way, every part fitting precisely with the next and carrying out its task perfectly, a flawless creation, a miraculous machine that works according to strict laws. Once set in motion, it will run to eternity of its own accord, moving through its appointed rounds, toward its appointed destiny. For if anyone should make a mechanical clock, would he not make it perfectly, so that all the wheels move as harmoniously as possible?"

Mike was talking in a calm voice, low and steady, long ceasing to need Judy's prompting. She sat there with the rest, mouth open and staring spellbound at the rich detail and eloquence of his speech.

"Have you got that, Giuseppe? Oh, please, you can call me Nicole. You do not have to call me Your Excellence like some country prelate. Don't be so formal, my trusted friend. Let me continue my dictation then.

The world has seen some very hard times these last forty years. Famine, war, plague, earthquakes, we have seen it all. The pagan Turks knock at the gates of Constantinople. Soon it will be Vienna, I fear. And that interminable war with the English will last a hundred years if we are not careful. Not even the pope can stop the fighting, I'm afraid. Ay, he is the cause of much of it. Even the plague has been seen again not long ago in London and other places, rearing its dreaded head after so many years in abeyance. Things now are just getting back to normal, as they were before the dark days of the great death."

Suddenly, in an imperious voice, Mike said, "Who is that who enters there? Who let you into these sacred precincts, old woman?"

Mike was no longer in the backyard of the Kelly residence, nor in the twentieth century although his body still lay in the chair. His mind had taken him back six hundred years and he now saw that time and place as if it were real. In a full-blown waking dream state with no consciousness of the world around him, Judy's voice was lost to him.

Mike continued talking to the intruder.

"What do you mean, why did I violate your home? What are you talking about, old woman? We violated no one's home. What? How dare you speak to me like that. Do you not know who you are talking to? Stop your incantations. I am Bishop of…"

Suddenly, the scene changed and he found himself in a darkly curtained room. He was no longer the powerful Bishop Nicole, but a small child of six. The room was vaguely familiar, with bare linoleum floors and small high windows. He was sitting in a tiny cot in the middle of the floor. A single bureau stood against a gray-papered wall. He was naked and filthy, crying and covered with his own feces, which he was smearing across the wall in broad wide strokes. The room smelt of human defecation. He screamed at the top of his lungs.

"Let me out! Let me out!"

The others in the group stood around Mike in a panic, as he thrashed around on the lawn chair, crying in a shrill, high-pitched voice for someone to let him out of the room. One minute he was an imperious high-churchman ordering someone out of his chambers, the next he was screaming like a six-year-old child. Judy seemed completely at a loss, unable to bring him out of it. Her eyes filled with panic.

"Oh no!" said Richard. "Not again!"

Mike's cries were growing shriller. Sam was afraid the neighbors would hear and call the police, thinking someone was getting murdered. He tried to quiet Mike down by shaking him, but that only made things worse. He was lucky to escape with only a bruised shoulder.

Seeing Michael's distress and Judy's inability to snap him out of it, Jessica knelt on the grass next to Mike and calmly started talking to him. As she did, she imagined a bright white light over both of their heads, imagined it until she saw it burning as brightly as the real sun in the sky.

"Oh, Mother, we are your children. We do Thy will." She said this to no one in particular, continuing to look at Mike.

"You are being pulled back. You are connected to us by an unbreakable, invisible elastic band, and it is stretched as far as it can go. Now it is snapping back to us and you are being pulled with it. Feel it as it accelerates faster and faster until you are flying through space and time to us. The years fly past, decades, centuries, faster and faster through time and space you go. Now you are over the ocean. The rubber band is contracting and you are being snapped across the ocean in a flash. Now you are over Boston. You are almost over us now, going slower and slower. See Sam and Judy's big brown house below with the wide yard in back?"

Mike, who was astral-projecting, could see them below him through the trees, all standing around his lawn chair. The grass and leaves were so green and shiny, it almost blinded him. He put his hands in front of his eyes and when he removed them, he was lying in the chair half sitting up with Jessica's face only inches away from his. The sensation of falling made him jump and almost tumble off the recliner. For a moment he just stared at her. He had an overpowering urge to kiss her, but before he could she moved away.

"He's OK. He's back now," she announced.

The others expressed their relief and tried to find out what had happened. To everyone's disappointment, Mike couldn't remember a thing.

"This happens sometime, with real intense trips," said Judy knowledgeably, although she had never seen anything like this herself before. Jessica still knelt close to Mike and looked at him searchingly. They told him what he had said, but no one knew of a French fourteenth-century bishop named Nicole.

"Sounds like a chick's name," observed Richard.

"That's my teacher's name," said Judy. "Maybe you picked up on that?"

"Who was the old woman?" asked Sam, interrupting. "What happened at the end there? Where were you, in prison or something?"

"I don't know. I don't remember an old woman," said Mike, growing frustrated at his lack of recall. After all, the whole reason for the exercise was to remember past lives. "All I remember is that I wasn't the same person at the end that I was at the beginning. I don't know who I was, but I wasn't the same person, I'm almost certain of that."

Judy recounted everything he'd said in detail with help from the others, so that it would not be lost to Mike's long-term memory. Over time his analytical left brain would hopefully be able to remember, even if his short-term recall couldn't.

"It will come back to you over time," Judy assured him. "That usually happens in these cases."

"Is that a good thing?" asked Jessica in concern.

"I don't know," answered Judy, shaking her head. "I really don't know."

After Mike and Jessica left, the rest of the group retired to the house. Judy wasn't feeling well and went upstairs to lie down. Sam sat in the kitchen with the others, drinking coffee and talking about the day's events and Michael's new friend.

"What do you think of Jessica?" Richard asked the others.

"Seems nice enough," answered Sam. "She certainly did a good job talking Mike down from his bad trip. Maybe there really is something to this witchcraft business."

"I think she's a fake," commented Linda resentfully. She was jealous Mike had found a new girlfriend so soon. She had forgotten how good he looked in jeans.

"Oh?" said Sam. "Why do you say that?"

"I don't know," replied Linda flustered. "She just is that's all."

"What did you think of Mike's little trip?" asked Richard. "Wild, heh?"

"Yeah," agreed Sara. "I wonder where he picked up all that detail. He's not a history buff, is he?"

"I don't know," said Sam, trying to ignore the burning itch on his nose. "But he sounded like he knew what he was talking about. I wish Judy felt better so we could get her opinion."

"Are you and Mike going to get back together?" Sara asked Linda. She had been dying to ask this question all day. As a matter of fact, it had been the cause of her and Richard's earlier argument. "Maybe you should give him a call before he gets too involved with this Jessica character."

"Why don't you mind your own business," interrupted Richard sharply.

"I could care less," Linda replied, looking at Sara's husband and smiling. "He's looks nice on the outside, but inside he's a spoiled little boy who needs a mother. I need a real man."

She gazed at Richard seductively with her dark eyes. He stuck his tongue out at her in a sexual gesture that reminded her of the previous night. Soon her bare foot was nestled in his crotch. Sam couldn't help notice and stared hard at his friend but didn't say anything. Sara pretended not to see. After a while she stood up.

"Well, we've got to get going. Tell Judy we're sorry she's not feeling well. Come on Richie."

Richard just sat there and grinned. He couldn't have moved if the house was on fire. Linda, who had come with the Jenkins, laughed and got up quickly from the table, running into the other room to put on her shoes. The three of them left a short while later.

Any other time, Sam would have spent considerable energy speculating on how the drive home would turn out for the three of them. Anything could happen in such an emotionally charged atmosphere. As it was, however, he had enough of his own problems to worry about, like his nose and the insistent itching. He went up to the bathroom to study his face in the mirror. He removed the bandage to reveal a good-sized reddish sore just next to his left nostril. It continued to consume his consciousness like a bullet wound. He peered at it and prodded it, trying one salve then another far into the night.

Jessica hadn't mentioned it, but each of their auras, which she could see as plainly as the features on their faces, had a dark patch attached to it, a shimmering negative piece of energy that seemed to hide in the dappled shadows of the trees as if conscious of her gaze. Even Michael wasn't free of it. It troubled her mildly, but she also knew enough to take these things with a skeptical attitude. She'd have to wait and see. She was already becoming too familiar with Michael, whose aura was fading as their familiarity grew. They drove home together in silence. He certainly was an interesting specimen. There is more to him than meets the eye.

Chapter 12

The next morning Mike got ready to pick Jessica up for their visit to Hanna Gilmore's, the old woman who had firsthand knowledge of the history of the house. He took a long shower and tried to wash the cobwebs out of his brain, but even the over-strong coffee didn't seem to help. He had gone without sleep before, it was no big deal, but he felt particularly drained and robbed of energy on this morning. Why did everything feel so hopeless?

He had dropped Jessica off the night before with hardly a good-bye, not even walking her to the door. Then he drove the short distance home without incident. The problem occurred getting from the parking lot to his apartment.

He stopped along the way to look at the house in the half-moon, and again lost himself in some murky subterranean thought. He came to forty minutes later still standing in the same spot. Through a series of mental gyrations he was able to persuade himself that only a few minutes had elapsed, and sustained that belief by not looking at the clock. But a blackout was something to be concerned about no matter how long it lasted. That concern made it impossible for him to sleep. He was still lying awake when the alarm rang at 6:30.

In his confused state he went out to his dog's tree, calling Hunter's name as he went, forgetting he was gone. The shock of the dog's death hit him all over again, that and the realization that he appeared to be slowly losing his mind.

He arrived at Jessica's an hour too early, but she was glad to see him. She cooked an old-fashioned breakfast of bacon and eggs.

Jessica lived in a small auxiliary house on the grounds of a large estate owned by some TV producer who was hardly ever there. When he was home, he raised horses and played farmer. The small house had once been the living quarters for the caretaker and his family. Now it was a lovely, although small apartment with a diminutive living area and a large kitchen. There was a bedroom and adjoining bath upstairs. They sat in the tiny living room while Jessica told him about the old woman they were about to meet.

"She's a friend of a friend of mine. We've exchanged letters, but I've never met her, though I've heard so many wonderful things about her. I can't wait to meet her."

"Is your Hanna a witch like you?" asked Mike, picking up on what she had said the day before, something he had all but forgotten but found himself asking about all the same.

"I don't know, Michael. We'll just have to see, won't we?"

Hanna Gilmore no longer lived in her family home just a few miles from Mike's apartment. Now she resided in the Rosebud Retirement Home situated in the next town over. It was a nice, pleasant country drive and Mike was enjoying the scenery, especially Jessica, who looked radiant in a simple flowered Sunday dress.

"You heard a voice?" asked Jessica, remembering something Mike had said the previous day.

"Oh, Yeah. Linda and I were arguing and heard a voice, a whisper. It said, 'why don't you'. Probably telling us to shut up. It sounded like it was right in the room with us. Scared the heck out of me. I thought Linda was throwing her voice or something. It was just after I had gone in that house and found Hunter. We were arguing because Linda thought I killed her in a previous life. That's what she saw when she was running. That's one of the reasons she moved out. She thinks I killed her and the house is haunted."

"How odd," observed Jessica, looking at Mike with a quizzical expression.

"She said I was a Mexican Bandit. We were arguing about it when we heard the voice."

"That certainly is a strange story," said Jessica, after hearing his tale. "I've heard stressful situations like you describe can bring out ghosts. They seem to thrive on the negative energy."

They arrived at the old folks' home, a large brown, three-story, wood-framed building, on a quiet street near the center of town. A number of old people were sitting on rockers and swing-sofas scattered along a large shaded porch, which covered the entire front of the building.

They inquired about Hanna Gilmore and were told she was around back in the garden. Following an attendant along the dirt drive to the rear of the house, they came to a screened-in porch overlooking a wild tangle of vines and plants, all in full bloom. The overgrown garden covered the entire, rather spacious back yard, which was framed by a white picket fence. Two ancient oak trees stood in the far corner, towering over everything. Hanna was seated alone on the porch. Mike and Jessica let themselves in through the screen door and introduced themselves.

Hanna was a stocky woman in her late eighties with white hair and a ruddy complexion. She stood instantly and hugged Jessica in greeting, smiling at her with a slightly crooked smile.

"Oh, you must be Jessica," she said, looking at the young woman with a steady gaze. "Laura has told me so much about you, sister. You got the gift, she says."

"Laura is a very good teacher. This is Michael," said Jessica, introducing him. "He's the one interested in the old Stillman house. He lives behind it in that new apartment building."

"Oh?" replied Hanna, looking at Mike for the first time. "You live near the house? Why so curious?"

Mike told her of his experiences and about his dog. She showed special interest in the story about the voice and asked him several pertinent questions.

"Well, if you've already been snooping around there," said Hanna, "then perhaps you know all you need to know."

She stopped and looked at him carefully, then continued.

"I'm not afraid of the truth. There's nothing to be scared of in the truth. If you walk with Her nothing can hurt you. Those things, they just happened. Those responsible will get their just deserts, I'm sure. But why should I tell you about it? What are you going to do with this information, brother? Are you going to use it for good?"

She looked at him hard with squinting, watery blue eyes. They matched the blue and white dress she wore, which was festooned with tiny yellow flowers. Mike held her gaze and cleared his mind of thoughts, letting her look into his soul.

"I love it back here," she announced, suddenly changing the subject. "Most of the old folks stay out front. They like to sit and watch the cars go by and gossip, but I like it back here by the garden, with nature. Nature is God you know, like I'm saying to you, friends." She looked at Mike sharply. He nodded in agreement and smiled back, his brown eyes clear and guileless.

"It's beautiful back here," observed Jessica in agreement. "The Azaleas are brilliant."

"I knew Jeanette Stillman when she was still a little girl," the old woman began, changing the subject abruptly. "We lived down the road from them back then. Wasn't much more than a wagon trail in those days, unpaved and rutted. We used to ride our old swayback through the woods in back to get to their homestead. She lived with her mother, Rose."

"Yes, that was Max Stillman's daughter," interjected Jessica, helpfully. "Both his sons were killed in the Civil War."

"Yes, I remember her telling me something about her uncles dying in the war. My parents didn't like me going over there. They said Rose Stillman had a bad reputation and that her daughter was illegitimate and would end up just like her. I was told in no uncertain terms to stay away from Jeanette. But she was so pretty, and they had such nice things that, well, you know kids, I just couldn't stay away from the place."

Hanna folded her hands, bent and gnarled from years of arthritis, over her lap. Her broad face was placid. The crooked smile still played on her mouth.

"Jeanette lived like a princess. And was she ever a beautiful little girl, with black hair and long curls. She had the longest eyelashes you ever did see. We went to school for awhile together in the building they use as a library now."

"Yes," said Jessica. "I work there."

"Isn't that a coincidence, sister?" replied Hanna, with a twinkle in her eye. Both of them knew there was no such thing as coincidence. Everything happened for a purpose. It was for humans to figure out what that purpose was.

"Let's see, this must have been around about 1901," she continued. "I was just ten. I was born in 1889, same year as Jeanette."

"Her mother died several years later. I think it was around 1920 or 21. We had lost touch long before that. It's one thing to play with the daughter of a blacklisted Christian when you're a tomboy running around barefoot playing in the dirt. But it just doesn't do when you're a young woman looking for a husband. I was long married by the time her mom died, to Harry, my first husband. He was a blacksmith. Too bad no one told him about the horseless-carriage."

She started laughing and coughing in fits, which took awhile to subside. She sipped some tea.

"We must a both been about thirty when her mother died. It was awful, poor Jeanette all alone at the cemetery. No one came to the funeral, wouldn't you know, just her mother's lawyer, who read the will and returned to Boston the same day. She got the house, the land, everything. I remember envying her at the time, having all that money and property and independence. It was unheard of for a girl to be on her own like that back then.

It was around the time her mother died, when she was living alone in that house, that she started acting strangely. This is only secondhand hearsay, you know. As I've said, I lost touch with her. I was raising young ones of my own and didn't have much time for socializing. It isn't like today when you can just drive to the store. Every time you ate or left the house was a major undertaking. Everything took hours. But one heard the rumors and stories, and there were plenty being told about Jeanette Stillman. They said she tramped around like a whore, but I didn't believe any of it. I thought they were just jealous lies by small-minded people. I knew my friend Jeanette was special.

I remember it was around that time that she started adding on to the house. She hired craftsmen from Boston and Concord, but did all the planning and laying out of the rooms herself. They said she was crazy. But she had a lot of money so they did what she told them. Again, I heard the stories but didn't think much of it, being busy with my own life and all. I never saw Jeanette in town or anything. Never saw her in church, when I used to go to church that is. Never saw her at the picnics or socials, those few we went to. She had no kids that were my young'uns age. They said she was a recluse and I believed them.

We'd go by her house from time to time. But from the road you couldn't see much. Don't you know, that place hasn't changed a bit in sixty years. Still the same last time I saw it about a year ago. The rest of the house, her rooms, well, they were covered with lilac bushes and trees and mostly hidden by the front part, so you really couldn't see them, and that's a good thing too, I'm telling you now, friends. My dear husband, Harry, he knew something was not right with the place, but I told him he was off his rocker. He was just jealous because out-of-towners got all the work. People said it was built all crazy like, but you couldn't tell from the road."

"That's true," agreed Mike. "That's exactly what it's like. And the front looks like someone comes and cleans everyday."

Hanna smiled her crooked smile and studied him with her watery eyes, still 20-20 after eighty-seven years.

"My Harry would have liked you," she told him. "He was a good man, my Harry, thank you Mother. Even-tempered and level-headed, and strong, he was. I know you two would have gotten along. I wish he was still alive so you could talk with him."

"Me too," said Mike.

"You miss your dad," she told him out of the blue. The sudden change of direction and mention of his father almost made him choke on his saliva. He mumbled some sort of meaningless response. Hanna went on as if nothing had happened.

"Now, listen to what I'm going to tell you, friends. Jeanette had her little girl right around the time of the Second World War. Her daughter's name was Maxine, after her grandfather. The father was some GI on his way to the war. It was a big scandal. It was all people talked about for months. My Harry was just as indignant as the rest of them, that she would go and fornicate with a man she hardly knew and have a child out of wedlock, without so much as a sliver of shame. But there was nothing he or anyone else could do about it by that time.

She brought the little girl up herself. They never left the house from what I can tell, and pretty much kept to themselves. So did we. Don't know about how she brought up the little girl. I know I had enough trouble with my three. All boys and all a bundle of nerves and energy, like to drive you crazy those three. But I love them dearly. All grown up now, married with their own kids. I'm a great grandmother now, don't you know? If that don't tell you ya lived too long, I don't know what will."

"Now don't say that, Hanna," objected Jessica. "You've got a lot of good years left in you yet."

"Some good in me, maybe. More years left, I doubt it, sister." She smiled crookedly at Jessica. "I heard nothing of Jeanette or her child from the end of the war through the fifties. Then, when was it? All these years and events get jumbled in my head. I swear sometimes I don't know if I'm talking about Jeanette or her mother or her daughter, I get so confused, I do. Now where was I? Oh yes, it was in the sixties, around sixty-five or sixty-six, something happened out there at the house, something terrible.

I never knew it, but Jeanette's daughter, who still lived alone with her mother, had her own children, seven of them, all from different men. Can you imagine that? The daughter was worse than the mother and grandmother put together. She had seven little boys, all between one and eight years old, if you can believe it, friends. She must'a been kicking them out faster than a rabbit. I worked as hard as I could with Harry for six years and could only manage three, and the last one just about killed me, I tell you."

She stopped and sighed, as if just the memory of it exhausted her. Her eyes, dim with the past, got more watery. "God I miss them."

"Don't they visit you?" asked Jessica, sensing Hanna liked talking about her sons.

"Sure, aint a week goes by when one or another of them don't pop their heads in, the grandkids more than not. They stay a few minutes until they get bored or something gross happens, then they skedaddle. Who can blame them? Who wants to talk to an old woman?"

"We do," answered Jessica.

"I'd be glad to stop by now and then, especially if there are things I know you need," volunteered Mike.

"Aren't you sweet," said Hanna, "a regular meals on wheels."

She cackled and wheezed with mirth as she got up and sauntered to a side table for Kleenex and fresh lemonade, just put there by a young volunteer. Hanna walked with a limp, bent over with arthritis, as she made her way back to her rocker and continued her story.

"Imagine my surprise hearing Jeanette's daughter, Maxine, had kids. She passed away a short time later. Some thought she was poisoned, but I never found out exactly how she died. Her mother took over the care of the kids.

Now hear what I'm about to say, friends. I knew something was up, and that it be no good. My Harry had been long dead by then. Died in a car crash in '54 out along old Route 2 there. Poor Harry, Mother rest his soul. What a waste. A couple kids going back to school out in Amherst from an all-night party smashed him head on. Never knew what hit him, poor man. Not a scratch on him neither. Just a little bump on the head, that's all. But he was gone all right, no doubt about that. Oh, Lord, he was so handsome all laid out in his suit, I tell you. I wanted to hug him, I did. Anyway, I knew something was going on there. I could feel it when I'd pass the place. By then I knew something about things most people don't know about, that I did. I learned by listening to the Mother's voice. Now I tell you, if you love Nature, you will never be alone, friends.

Soon after Jeanette took over the upbringing of the children they were all murdered. People thought that it must have been too much for her and she went crazy, but I knew better. I know what the truth was, and I'm not afraid to tell it."

She rocked back and forth and looked at the garden. It was starting to get warm. The lazy drone of the insects was getting louder. She took a sip of lemonade. Mike fixed a glass for himself and Jessica.

"They tried to keep it quiet," she continued. "But it was all over town. How can you keep such a horrible thing from getting out? Those seven children were butchered in their sleep, their throats cut. Then I heard they had a posse out looking for Jeanette, bloodhounds and everything.

I knew why those children were killed, I do, but it is too terrible to tell about, dear Mother. No, there's no call to go and do a thing like that, I tell you.

A few days later, I heard from one of my boys, who was working at the sheriff's department at the time, that they'd caught Jeanette Stillman, my old friend, in the woods back behind her house. The bloodhounds had chased her up a tree. And don't you know, before they could get her down, she hanged herself with her own apron. Hung herself right there on that tree. Can you hear me, children?"

She sat and smiled crookedly at them as they digested the rest of her story with stunned expressions.

"I don't know what they did with the bodies," she continued after awhile. "But I doubt they was laid in hallowed ground. More probably they're buried in an unmarked grave somewhere. I never did find out exactly what happened or why. But I can guess, there was something not right with my old friend or her house. I could sense it. It's surprising the evil things modern civilization can hide from us, with so much to distract us. After all, the brain is nothing but a bunch of molecules somehow making up our grey matter."

"Hanna used to be a school teacher," offered Jessica, still doing her best to digest Hanna's story.

"That's right, sister. Use to teach right in that same building I went to school in. It's the library now. How about that, friends? Things change yet remain the same, such is Her great plan. When my Harry died and the kids moved out, I needed something to do and they needed a part-time teacher. So I took a few courses at night down at the community college and there you go. Before you knew it I was a school teacher. Now don't that beat all. I guess you didn't have to know that much back then," she said with a laugh.

"I was teaching about the time all this happened. Maxine's kids never went to school. They were all schooled at home, if they were taught at all. Guess that's how they could just sweep the whole thing under the rug like that. None of them was baptized, don't you know. No legal record of them or their mother. Easy come, easy go. That's the way they did it. I knew they'd be sorry."

"Hanna taught more than school," said Jessica mysteriously.

"Life is our teacher, child. I know what happened, though everyone's got their own theory. Something happened to Jeanette after her poor mother died, ever since she started building those crazy rooms. Listen to what I say, children. Those rooms possessed her somehow. She indulged in something dark. God knows what she did those years she was alone, but there was something sinister growing there. It got worse each passing year until it exploded and Jeanette killed them seven children with a butcher knife. I mean there were times, mind you, when I was on the verge of doing something like that myself with my three hellions, but this was different, this was ritualistic."

"Do you know what Jeanette looked like?" asked Mike, after a pause.

"No. I only remember Jeanette as that pretty little rich girl with the long black curls. I never saw her when she was old."

"I wonder if it's her ghost haunting the place," said Mike, thinking out loud. Jessica and Hanna just looked at him.

"I don't know," replied Hanna slowly. "Evil comes in many forms. You must always be aware of your own power when confronting it. Anger and hatred can cause many bad things, but goodness and truth can overcome them. You must keep these things in your heart. Then no harm can come to you, friends."

"You sound like the Bible," said Mike. "The truth will set you free and all that."

"This is where the bible came from," she explained, touching her breast, "the living truth in our hearts."

She smiled serenely at them, her broad face beaming radiantly like the flowers in the back yard, beyond the screened confines of the porch. She looked at Jessica, her smile gone, her expression serious.

"Now listen to what I say, daughter. Watch yourself," she warned. "Laura has taught you well, but there is much she doesn't know. She can fly all right when the weather's good and there's no storms, but she's never been at the controls when the lightning's crashing and the thunder's peeling and the ground's shaking, and it seems like the very sky is going to fall. Always remember your special power, your strength, your purpose. Never forget She is with you always and forever. The Holy Mother sustains and nourishes us like a living stream. She is our shield and our sword. No thing will harm you if you walk with Her."

"Thank you, Hanna," said Jessica, tears coming to her eyes. "I can't tell you how much your words mean to me and how wonderful it is to finally meet you."

Hanna seemed to ignore Jessica and sat as if listening to something, although all that could be heard was the buzzing of the insects and the breeze through the tree tops. She stood abruptly and clasped Mike's hands. Mike was standing by the screen door ready to leave. Looking up at him earnestly she said, "Listen to what I say, brother. Evil's only protection is your disbelief in it. Believe in yourself, child, and what you see, and you will be all right. One only becomes strong through being tested in times of trial. Your trials are upon you, brother. The Good Mother be with you."

Chapter 13

Mike was exhausted when he drove Jessica home later that afternoon, as if he were the eighty-year-old. Jessica gave him a concerned look when he declined her invitation to come in for dinner. He said he had a lot to do. What he really meant was that he had a lot to think about, although he was sorry as soon as he left her house, as the gloom and depression descended on him. He dragged himself home and grabbed a can of pork and beans out of the cupboard.

Hanna's story kept playing in his head like a bad grade-B movie, interspersed with fantasies about Jessica. Soon these last images took over.

Another week went by and still there were few jobs to bid on and none of his bids accepted. He was beginning to get discouraged. He had just enough money in his bank account to pay the rent and live on for another couple months. After that he'd be looking for a room to rent by the week in some cheap, rundown motel. After that, the street would do nicely, thank you.

He haunted the local union halls and construction sites, renewing old acquaintances and making new ones, but no one seemed to have work for him. It wasn't that things were bad. There was plenty of construction going on. Mike asked himself why every other half-baked contractor in the county was working and he wasn't. All the guys that were on his old crew had found jobs with other concerns, although they all assured him they'd drop those in a flash if something turned up with him. He was starting to wonder if he'd been blacklisted or something. Maybe it was because of the missed deadline. But it was only an added bonus, an incentive for finishing construction sooner than planned. It was self-imposed and affected no one except himself. Guys miss deadlines all the time, by a lot more than a few measly days. This had been his first time.

Desperate for leads, he gave Richard a call, hoping he would know somebody who might need carpentry work in the city.

"Hi, Richard," Mike said when his friend answered the phone. "Haven't talked to you in awhile. How's it going?"

"Been busy," Richard replied with little humor in his voice.

"Yeah, me too. I know how things can get. Have you heard from the others?"

"You mean Judy and Sam? You can say their names can't you, or are you just a fair weather friend?"

"Sure. Is something wrong? Is everything OK?" Mike asked, concerned over his friends unusually surely tone of voice.

"Oh, they're just doing fine. Judy's in the hospital undergoing brain scans and Sam's got some sort of skin cancer or something. His face looks terrible. I can hardly look at him without gagging, his nose is so bad."

"That's horrible!" Mike said. "When did all this happen?"

"Just this week."

"How about you, Rich, how are you doing?"

There was a pause at the other end of the line. "Nothing I can't handle," answered Richard finally. "Can you hold on?"

Without waiting for an answer, Richard left the phone. Michael could hear him yelling in the background, loud and furious.

"Can't you see I'm on the phone? What's the matter with you, you stupid bitch? I'm on the phone! I'M ON THE FUCKING PHONE!" he yelled. "YOU STUPID BITCH!"

There was a loud crash and the line went dead. Mike considered calling 911 for a moment, then thought better of it. It was none of his business. He'd said as much in a drunken rant once or twice. It didn't mean anything. If they were having problems, Richard and Sara would work them out. They were intelligent, rational adults. Still, Mike was disturbed by the trouble that seemed to be assailing his friends.

Jessica called him a few days later. Her voice was small and she sounded as if she'd been crying.

"Hanna died," she told him, as soon as he answered the phone.

Mike felt an instant lead weight on his chest. He had only met her once, but felt he had known her all his life. It felt like his mother, who still lived in East Boston, had just died.

"Oh, I'm so sorry," he replied. "Is there anything I can do?"

"As a matter of fact there is. It would be wonderful if you could be a pallbearer. Her three boys will be there, and two of their sons, but they need a sixth person. She was old. All her friends and relatives except her sons are gone. Could you do it, Mike? I'm sure Hanna would have appreciated it."

"Sure," he answered, feeling a great sense of loss. "I'd be more than happy to. What happened? I mean, how did she die?"

"She just died quietly in her sleep, Monday night."

"Well, if you gotta go that's the way to do it. She was something else!"

Jessica gave him the time and information he would need to get to the funeral home.

"Oh, by the way," she said. "I've been checking around at the library, doing some reading, you know, following up on your little past-life experience last weekend. I think I found out who you might have been."

"Who?" asked Mike.

Bits and pieces of that afternoon had come back to him slowly, in spurts and snippets, so that he was able to fit together what he had seen. He knew he had been a bishop of some sort in France, in the thirteen hundreds, and that an old woman had burst into his chambers and disrupted his dictation. The rest was still vague, but he remembered being a child locked in a room at the end. It stood in his mind like a vivid dream.

"There was a French Bishop born around 1330 named Nicole d'Oresme, a very respected and influential churchman of his day. You actually said the name Nicole. It has to be him."

"Hmm," muttered Mike. "Never heard of him. Cool. I'll have to look him up, see if I can learn anything."

"He's the one that coined the phrase, a 'Clockwork Universe'," she informed him.

"How about that, I'm famous," replied Mike, laughing.

He told Jessica about the recent problems everyone had been having, Judy's sickness, Sam's sore, Richard and Sara's fighting.

"Do you think it has anything to do with the house?" he asked. "It just seems like too much of a coincidence, all this happening after we went into that house. And the stuff with Hunter."

"I don't know Michael. It does seem strange that this all started happening right out of the blue, all at the same time. If I didn't know better, I'd think someone put a curse on all of you."

"You believe in that stuff?"

"I hate to break it to you, but there are all sorts of things out there that you and I don't even have an inkling of. There are far stranger things than you could imagine behind your everyday concept of the reality."

"I know, I've read the Castaneda books. I know that anything is possible within certain broad limits, but this whole thing about ghosts and spells, well it's just a little hard to swallow. It defies all commonsense experience."

"You heard that voice didn't you?"

"Sure, but that could have been anything."

"Like what?"

"Like the guy next door whispering through the wall, or Linda unconsciously throwing her voice. Either explanation is more likely than that it was a ghost talking to us."

"Yes, but neither explanation really works, does it? They leave you wondering still, don't they? Linda denies throwing her voice. Why would she lie? And do you really think you would hear someone whispering in the next apartment, as if he were in the room? I doubt it. And what about what happened when you went into the house? What was that about?"

"Mass hysteria. So, what's your point again?" Mike inquired, finding little to refute her arguments.

"We could be dealing with a real supernatural phenomenon here. Something none of us have experienced before. By supernatural I only mean we have no scientific explanation for it, but it's probably a rather natural thing as far as the universe goes."

"OK, OK, so I live next door to Casper the Ghost."

"It's not a joke, Michael. I'm concerned about your friends. Maybe you should talk to my friend Laura. Maybe she can help."

"Yeah, I remember you and Hanna talking about her. You said she was your teacher. What does she teach, or should I ask?"

"She's just a friend. She's into the occult, just like you and your friends. She's been doing it for a long time and everyone says she is very gifted."

"So she's a witch and so are you, but you're good witches like the one in the Wizard of Oz."

"Can't you take anything seriously?"

"Sure, like where I'm going to be living next month if I don't get a job."

"Still haven't found work yet?" she asked.

"Nope, it's a real drought out there."

"Have you tried working for someone else?"

"Yeah, but everyone's got all the help they need. I guess I started too late."

"Gee, you'd think someone could give you a job."

Mike agreed, and said it was almost as if he'd been blacklisted, the way he couldn't get work while everyone around him was working steady.

Mike confirmed the directions to the funeral parlor where Hanna's casket would be and what time to be there on Wednesday. Jessica thanked him again. They made plans to get together later in the week. Mike felt a little better after talking to her, although sad at Hanna's death.

Richard Kelly cruised the dark streets in his new Lexus sport coup looking for just the right one. He had bought the car despite his wife's strenuous objections and the fact that he couldn't afford it, taking a loss on the trade-in for his Saab. He needed a little diversion.

Life seemed to be getting harder to deal with lately, as if everything was closing in on him at once, his job, his finances, his wife, his friends. There were times when he thought he would explode. The new toy, all chrome and luxurious leather, was needed to raise his broken spirits.

If Richard had been able to recognize how different his inner dialog had become, he would have been shocked, for the calm humorous voice he had known all his life had become a raging, hate-filled, psychotic drill sergeant, barking out orders and ridiculing everything he did. Now the only thing that assuaged his burning anger and feelings of inadequacy was what he was doing tonight, cruising the streets and looking for women.

Richard had already used up most of his savings, and would soon be digging into his and Sara's retirement fund. But it didn't matter. All that mattered was the burning emptiness in his soul and the nervous need to fill it.

Richard spotted her on the next corner, on his side of the street, a cute little redhead in pink hot-pants, with big lips and long lashes. Her gold shiny halter-top was just big enough to cover her perky breasts, leaving most of her belly and all of her back and shoulders bare. He pulled over to the curb, his heart beating like Ginger Baker's double base drums, and rolled down the window.

"How much?" he asked.

"Twenty-five for a BJ. A hundred for the works," replied the redhead, smacking her gum.

"Get in," said Richard, opening the door.

Across town, things were not going well in the Kelly household. Judy was in the kitchen. She didn't sleep at night. Judy could only be up during the darkness. The glare of the sun and the brightness of the daylight hurt her eyes and head so much it blinded her. Even a soft lamp would send bolts of pain shooting to the back of her eyes. She spent the day in her room where the windows were covered with thick curtains and drapes. Here she stayed, like a creature of the night, in her chamber hiding from the light.

She had gone to the emergency room, but the doctors could find nothing wrong. They'd have to do more tests they told her. A lot of good they had done. She'd have to go back next week.

Judy sat at the kitchen table in the dark, with sunglasses on, eating a bowl of oatmeal. As she sat, she rocked back and forth, humming some long forgotten lullaby until the rays of the rising sun sent her scurrying back to her room again.

Sam was in the bathroom peering into the medicine cabinet mirror. Contrary to Judy, Sam had every light in the small room turned on - the overhead light, the reading lamp by the toilet, the fluorescent above the medicine cabinet. He was examining his nose in great detail, and what he saw there filled him with horror.

His nose had become a hideous thing, diseased and pus-filled, deformed with craters and sores that oozed and bled. Like with Judy, the doctors had been unable to diagnose the problem or discover the source of the malignancy. It was nothing like they had ever seen before, except in severe skin cancer patients. But Sam's tumor-like growths and sores were not cancerous.

He could not believe the thing staring back at him was his own face. He had always prided himself on his good looks and neat appearance. Now all he saw when he looked in the mirror was a hideous parody of a face, a deformed thing that filled him with disgust. Soon he would have no nose at all.

That same morning Mike was woken by the shrill ringing of his phone. It was 5:00 AM. He answered it with some trepidation.

"What?" exclaimed Mike after hearing Richard's story. "You got arrested for soliciting a prostitute? Are you nuts, Richard? What about Sara? I thought you wanted a family? What's got into you?"

"Look, if I wanted a lecture, I would have called Sara or Sam or my lawyer," replied Richard. "At this point all I want is some simple quiet help. I thought I could at least count on you for that. I'm going through some rough times. I don't want Sara to know."

"Well, I hope you don't expect me to lie to her for you? I just can't do that, Rich."

"I know, Mike. Just lend me the cash for bail and…."

"Richard, I'm out of work. I don't have enough to pay next month's rent. I can't help you."

There was silence on the other end of the line, as Richard digested this bit of information.

"I'll pay you back first thing," Richard said finally. "You're the only one I can turn to, Mike. I know you'll be discreet."

"I'd be glad to help if I could, but I just don't have the money. I don't have five hundred bucks to lend you, honest Richard. Why don't you just fess-up to having a problem and get the help you need?"

"Why you pretentious son-of-a-bitch," yelled Richard. Mike could hear the venom in his friend's voice. "After all we've done for you, you can't lend me a sticking hand when I need it? You ass-hole. You prick, you…"

Mike hung up the phone in shock after a further string of abuse. He couldn't remember Richard ever talking like that, let alone to him. What's come over his friend? Mike sat looking at the phone as if it were a bomb.

He was so upset by the call he couldn't get back to sleep. He wasn't sure what to do and started thinking about how he could get his hands on five hundred-dollars at this time of day, and even more importantly, should he. Was that really the best thing for his friend? He sure sounded like he needed help, but not the kind Michael could offer. Still, he couldn't just sit there while Richard sat in jail. That his friend would frequent prostitutes and resist arrest just didn't make sense. Something bizarre must be happening to him, something out of the ordinary.

Mike thought of calling Sam. He would understand Richard's predicament. He was certainly in a better position financially to help. Sam was Richard's best friend. But it was too early. In any case, Sam and Judy were having serious problems of their own. It sounded like they were the ones who needed help. Although he had gotten little sleep and felt as if his eyes were made of lead, he dragged himself out of bed and made some coffee. Then, as the sun began to flood through the front window, he paced the floor in front of it wondering how to help his friends.

Chapter 14

Wednesday morning at eleven, Mike drove to the funeral home where Hanna's body was lying in rest. He wore his best white shirt and his only blue suit. Jessica was there, along with a few other women. Hanna's three sons and their families were also present, seated around the casket. Jessica introduced Mike to everyone.

Mike paid his respects to Hanna. In death, she looked much as she had in life, with her broad face in repose and the crooked smile still playing on her lips. Soon he was walking behind Hanna's boys and grandsons, carrying her light casket to the waiting hearse. He drove to the cemetery with Jessica.

"I can't tell you how much this means to us," Jessica told him. "She would have been so pleased to know you were here. She liked you very much."

"Really?" answered Mike. "I'm honored. I only met her that one time."

They drove the rest of the way in silence. At the cemetery, Mike helped carry the casket to the gravesite, where the small group of mourners stood in a tiny cluster. There was no priest, but an older woman dressed all in white chanted something in a strange tongue, and said a few obscure words that might as well have been Greek rather than English.

While the small ceremony was taking place, a large black crow landed on a tree directly over the open grave and started cawing with a loud, raucous, hacking sound. It kept this up non-stop until Mike became so annoyed he wanted to throw a stone at it. Jessica gave the bird a long hard stare, but it kept cawing unabated all the same, as if laughing at their sorrow, until they left the gravesite. It was very disconcerting to say the least, and added to the dreary atmosphere of the dark, damp, overcast day.

On the way home, Mike almost told Jessica about Richard's phone call of the previous night, but thought better of it. He wanted to talk about it with someone, seek their advice as to what he should do, but he didn't want to compromise Richard's confidence.

When they arrived at Jessica's place, she invited Mike to a picnic the next day. The library was closed on Monday and since he wasn't working, she thought it would be an excellent time to get away. It was supposed to be a perfect summer day with no rain in sight. Mike accepted. Jessica asked if he'd mind if her friend Laura, who Mike had met at the cemetery, came along. Mike said, no, the more the merrier, slightly disappointed.

When he got home there was a phone message from Sam waiting for him. Mike hadn't heard from any of his friends in almost two weeks, except for the few disturbing phone conversations he'd had with Richard. He immediately sat down and dialed Sam's number. Sam answered on the first ring.

"Jesus, Mike!" he said as soon as Mike said hello. "I've been trying to get in touch with you all day."

"Why? What's up? Everything OK?" he asked.

"No, everything is terrible, just terrible. I don't know where to begin."

"Just take your time and tell me what's wrong? What can I do?"

"I don't even know how to say this. It's just so hard to believe."

"Go ahead, just say it," urged Mike, growing more concerned by the minute.

"Richard beat Sara up. He put her in the hospital. I guess it was really bad. The cops had to lock him up."

"What? How'd that happen? I talked to him just this morning. He was already in jail,"

"You talked to him? When?"

"Around five. He called me, wanted me to bail him out, but I didn't have the money. You know, I'm out of work."

"Well, I guess he ended up calling Sara. Told her to come down and bail him out. She came down and did as he asked, but you know how she can get. She must have got on his case, because when they got home he started whaling on her. They say he cut off her right index finger with a knife, messed her up real bad."

"Oh, my God!" shouted Mike over the phone, shocked at the news. "That's horrible."

"Yeah, and that ain't the half of it. Judy's awfully ill. She can't leave her bed. The light gives her horrible blinding headaches and the doctors can't do a thing about it."

"How are you doing? What can I do?"

"Not good I'm afraid. I have some more tests tomorrow morning, but, well I'm not doing too well. I should warn you, next time you see me get ready to be grossed out."

"It can't be that bad Sam. What is it, do they know?"

116

"Not really, but it's a lot like skin cancer from what I can tell. Look, the reason I called is someone has to pick up Sara at the hospital tomorrow and I can't make it. Could you come into town and pick her up? She's at Beth Israel. She's supposed to be released by two in the afternoon."

"Sure," said Mike. "I had tentative plans, but this certainly takes precedence. I'll do everything I can to help."

"Thanks Mike. I knew I could rely on you. I'll call you later. Got to go. Bye."

Mike got off the phone shaking his head and recriminating himself for not aiding Richard. After all, if he had helped him, none of this would have probably happened. Then again, it may have happened just the same and it would still be his fault.

He called Jessica and told her of his commitment. She said it was no problem, as they could picnic in the morning and he could go into town later in the afternoon. There was plenty of time to do everything.

The next morning Mike met Jessica and Laura at Jessica's house, and followed their directions as they rode together to the picnic site - along the highway, through a small town center with a general store and a drinking fountain, left at the post office, up the winding narrow country road to the base of a hill. They got out, grabbed the bags and baskets that comprised lunch, and hiked the rest of the way up the trail to the rocky summit.

Jessica had on kaki shorts and a sleeveless pink blouse. Her friend Laura, a statuesque woman with long brown hair and a fair complexion, looked like a Girl Scout troop leader, in dark green shorts and a brown, short-sleeve shirt. Mike wore his usual blue-jeans and T-shirt. They talked about the weather and the scenery as they strode leisurely up the hillside trail.

In the course of their walk, Mike told them about the troubles his friends were having and the seemingly overnight onslaught of the problem. Both Laura and Jessica said it sounded strange. Eventually the subject of the Stillman house came up. Laura said nothing, but nodded her head in understanding as Mike told her about the events of the past few months.

They reached the summit, a crescent of rock and cliff-face looking out over a sweeping valley to the east. A sea of green stretched into the distance as far as they could see, interspersed with gray ribbons of highway cutting this way and that across the land. The valley was dotted with farms and lakes, wide fields, and church steeples. In the farthest distance, barely visible in the haze, the sun sparkled off skyscraper windows in Boston like faint beacons.

They sat on the rocks and looked out at the stunning view as they ate the picnic lunch Jessica had made of humus, spinach bread, and rice cakes. Not exactly what Mike had in mind, but eatable nevertheless. After lunch, Laura rummaged around in the oversized handbag she had brought along, taking out a piece of chalk, some crystals, and a mirror.

"Let's play a little game," she suggested, as she started drawing a large circle on the rocks with the chalk.

"Michael," Jessica began, as if she and her teacher had rehearsed this. "This is just like your running, same idea. All you have to do is relax, breathe deeply, and clear your mind. Then follow Laura's instructions. OK? It'll be fun."

"And what are we doing?" asked Mike, not sure he liked what was going on.

"We're going to cast a protective spell over you," Jessica informed him, with an uncertain expression.

"Get in the circle," ordered Laura.

Mike did as he was told and sat in the middle of the chalk circle. Laura placed the crystals on the circle at the four points of the compass, placing the mirror against a rock so that it reflected the light of the sun onto one of the crystals. The reflected light seemed to bounce from crystal to crystal, surrounding him with a thin circle of light. Jessica and Laura sat in front of him, just outside the circle and clasped hands.

"Now, Mike," said Jessica, as Laura started chanting something unintelligible. "Just relax and clear your mind. Laura will tell you what to do. Just breathe deeply, relax. That's it."

Mike went quickly into a quiet alpha brain state. He sensed the wind pick up imperceptibly and change direction to blow from the east. The sounds of the woods, the birds and insects, seemed to amplify and grow stronger as he listened. Sunlight reflected and shimmered off the leaves and grass with intense brilliance and color. Soon there was a soft buzzing in his head.

A sense of peace and well-being came over him, a sense of serenity and calm. Suddenly, nothing mattered, not his job, not his dead dog, not even his own failings. His very insignificance in the scheme of things gave him comfort. He smiled conspiratorially, as if he had just been let in on a great secret, a smile of 'aha' recognition.

"No evil can touch thee," chanted Jessica and Laura in unison, as they held hands, swaying back and forth. "Thank Thee, Great Mother, for delivering your servant Michael from evil. Thank you for protecting him, for showering him with your bounty, for blessing him with your goodness. Thank you for giving him strength in his hour of adversity. Your Will, Great Mother, works through him. No evil can harm him. No harm can befall him. Protect him, oh Mother."

Mike sat in the circle, bathed in the glow of its light and security, though feeling a bit self-conscious and silly. He couldn't deny the good vibes, however. Maybe they had drugged the tea.

The chanting of the girls mingled with the soft sounds of the forest, with its steady drone, to almost lull Mike to sleep. The serenity was suddenly interrupted. A cloud had moved in from the west and quickly darkened the sky. A gust of wind blew up from the valley, scattering their paper wrappers and empty boxes, as it swept up the hillside in swirling eddies. It grew colder by several degrees. Dust and dirt blew in the girls' faces as they tried to turn away from it, first this way, then that. But each time they turned it changed direction as if by malicious intent, blowing more dust into their eyes.

They rose, clutching at the blowing objects around them, while Mike, who seemed to be untouched by the sudden gust and flying sand, stood up inside the circle in alarm. There was a crack of thunder and a simultaneous flash, as a bolt of lightning hit a tree directly above them, sending a large, smoking tree limb crashing to the ground only a few feet away. The sound was deafening. They jumped, and Laura screamed when the branch dropped. Mike's ears range like the bells of Notre Dame. Then the first large drops of rain started falling from the sky like soft marbles.

"Look's like the weatherman messed up again," observed Mike, shaken but still with his sense of humor intact. He helped Laura and Jessica pick up the remains of their picnic. "That was a close one, eh? Scared the hell out of me."

The women said nothing, but continued to pick up their possessions with ashen faces. They ran down the trail in the downpour to Mike's pickup. The path was a raging mudslide by the time they got to the bottom. Just at the end of the trail, Mike slipped and fell on his backside, covering himself with thick brown mud.

No one said a word as he drove the two women back to Jessica's house. The storm had stopped as abruptly as it began. He had planned to leave right from her place, but now he had to rush home to clean up and arrived at the hospital to pick up Sara an hour late. She had already checked herself out.

Mike was frantic. He searched the grounds extensively and repeatedly and had her paged, but there was no sign of her. He called Sam, but he too had heard nothing and was deeply disturbed that Mike had missed her. Sam was having troubles of his own. His condition was worsening, with still no explanation, while Judy was back in the hospital. She had woken up blind. Richard was still in jail.

"Blind?" Mike said in disbelief. "What do you mean?"

"I mean she can't see a thing. She woke up last night screaming. She's as blind as a bat."

"God!" Mike replied, stunned. The news was getting worse and worse. He told Sam he'd stop by as soon as he could.

After talking to Sam, Mike drove up and down the streets near and around the hospital, looking for Sara, crisscrossing the same intersections numerous times, going around the same block repeatedly, but she was nowhere to be found. He canvassed the entire area again on foot, but still no sign of her. Guessing she may have tried to walk home, he drove along the Fenway toward Jamaica Plain looking for her, back and forth, up and down, all day long, stopping at her house several times, but still he could not find her. Not knowing what else to do, frustrated and exhausted, he finally went to the Brookline police station and filed a report, explaining the situation to the duty officer. They told him nothing could be done for twenty-four hours, but put his name down on record and said they'd call him if she turned up.

It was well after midnight when Mike returned home, where there was a phone message waiting for him from the Brookline Police. Sara had been found walking up Boylston Street in her hospital gown talking to herself. She had been spotted by an acquaintance, who called her name. When she got a blank stare and dumb expression in response, she became alarmed and called 911. They brought Sara back to the hospital for observation. She couldn't remember a thing.

There wasn't much Mike could do at this hour. At least she wasn't dead by the side of the road somewhere, though it sounded like she was in rough shape all the same. He wondered if it had anything to do with the beating she had suffered at the hands of her husband. He felt terrible about missing her earlier that day and responsible for her present situation. His guilt weighed on him like an iron girdle around his chest.

Mike explained the situation to the police for the second time that night and said he would contact the family in the morning. He'd have to call Sam to get Sara's maiden name, although he hated to bother him. The full import of what Sam had told him earlier that day had finally hit him. Judy had gone blind!

It was late, but he called Jessica anyway. He had to talk to someone, and she was beginning to be the one he thought of more and more. To Mike's relief she was still awake.

"How'd it go with Sara?" she asked. "How is she?"

"I was late and missed her," replied Mike. "That damn freak storm and me falling in the mud like a jerk, messed me all up. I looked all over for her and couldn't find her. Finally, I went to the police and filed a report. When I got home they had called. She turned up earlier this evening, walking in the road babbling. She can't remember a thing. Like her mind's been wiped clean. Can that happen from getting hit?"

"Yeah, I guess" answered Jessica, although she had no idea. "But amnesia could be caused by many things."

"So what were you guys doing this morning?" he asked, remembering how cute she looked in her light pants and sleeveless shirt.

"Like I said, just putting a little protective spell on you."

"Did it work? Things got a little dicey there."

"You're still here aren't you," she replied.

"So what do you think happened today?"

"Nothing. Just a storm," she answered, noncommittally. "Happens all the time, though I told Laura we should have been in the circle too."

Mike didn't push it. The storm had come up suddenly and none of the weather stations had predicted it. Then again, the weather in New England was nothing if not unpredictable.

Mike's friends were in serious trouble. He had to help them. He told Jessica he was going into town the next day to see Sara in the hospital. He had to contact her parents and make arrangements for her care since Richard was indisposed at the moment. He supposed he should visit Richard in jail as well, although his friend's recent behavior had been unpardonable. He'd probably have to go over to their house and make sure everything was OK. Then he needed to stop by and see if Judy and Sam needed anything. He told Jessica about Judy's blindness. He was losing track of events. Things were moving too fast.

All the time, ticking in the back of his mind like a hidden fuse, was the knowledge that he was still out of work with no prospects in sight.

One thing at a time, he told himself. Jessica offered to help since she had the day off as well. Mike took her up on her offer and thanked his lucky stars he had met such a fine lady.

Chapter 15

The next day Mike picked Jessica up and drove into Boston.

"Here, Hanna wanted you to have this," she said as she got into Mike's pickup. "She gave it to you in her will. They read it yesterday afternoon. It was almost like she knew she was going to die and added it at the last minute. She had something for me too. Wasn't she just remarkable?"

She handed Mike a small silver spider medallion.

"Yeah, she sure was. What's this?" Mike asked.

"It's a charm from Cemaes in Anglesey. It's believed to have magical powers."

Michael put the small medallion in his pocket.

They drove to the hospital first. Mike hoped that Sara would be OK by now, recovered from whatever temporary bout of amnesia she may have had, but he was to be disappointed. There was no diagnosis yet, but Sara's short-term memory was gone. She would experience things in the present normally, but none of it made an impression on her memory. She would forget from one minute to the next what she had done.

"This happens in some stroke patients," the doctor in charge informed him, "or in brain damaged patients. But Mrs. Jenkins has not had a stroke nor does she have brain damage."

"What about the beating she took from her husband?" Mike still couldn't believe he was talking about his good friends, Richard and Sara, in such terrible terms.

"That was pretty bad," said the doctor, looking at the records. "Contusions, abrasions about the face and chest, a mutilated hand."

He looked up at Mike as if to say, what kind of friends do you have, and went on.

"But no injury that could account for her present condition. We'll just have to run more tests. Maybe it's a psychological reaction to the stress and trauma she's undergone."

"Can we see her?" asked Mike.

"Well normally I'd say no since neither of you are relatives, but under the present circumstances it may actually help."

He escorted them to Sara's room and showed them in. Sara was sitting up in bed, watching TV with the blank stare of one who has no understanding of what she is seeing. It could just as well have been white snow.

She turned toward them and smiled serenely as they entered the room. She was wearing a nondescript hospital gown. She looked terrible. Her eye was swollen half-shut where Richard had punched her and her lip was split. Her hair, usually neatly tied in a pony tail or clean and straight, was matted and tangled and sticking straight out in places. She had an empty mad stare that completely disconcerted Mike. Her hand was covered in a large mitten-like bandage of gauze.

"Hi, Sara," he said, trying to make conversation.

"Hi," said Sara back, smiling at him.

"Remember Jessica? She came by to say hi."

"Hi," said Sara, still smiling serenely.

She answered his questions in monosyllables, smiling the whole time, aware of him and his words, but somehow blank and empty all the same, as if none of it was registering with any permanence, as if it were literally going in one ear and out the other. Any hope of finding out what happened, or how to get in touch with her family was soon forgotten, as Mike's heart cracked more with each passing minute. This was not the friend he remembered, the vibrant, intelligent, challenging, sexy female he used to know.

He left the hospital in a depressed mood and called Sam. There was no answer, so they decided to stop there before going to see Richard. As they drove into Sam's yard, Mike noticed how long the grass had grown. Sam always kept it so neat and trim you could putt on it. Now it was long enough to lose a golf ball in. Sam's dog, Roland, came bounding around the corner as soon as they drove up. He seemed overly excited, jumping up and down, panting and barking. When he started jumping up on Jessica and nipping at her elbows, Mike chained it up on its runner.

All this time, no one had come out to greet them. It was a fine early August day, cloudless and in the mid-seventies, a perfect day to be out in the backyard. Yet there was no sign of anybody. Sam's Volvo was parked in the drive.

"Hello," called Mike, as he bounded up the steps to the rear porch. "Anybody here?"

There was no response. He tried the screen door and walked in, calling as he did so.

"Hello, Sam, you here? It's Mike and Jessica. Hello, anybody?"

He heard someone coughing deep in the house.

"Sam, buddy, is that you?" he yelled, going further inside. Jessica followed a few steps behind.

"Who is it?" called a voice, gruff and nasally, as if whoever was speaking had a bad head cold.

"Sam, it's me, Mike Russo. You OK?"

"Don't come in," croaked the voice. Something was missing, something that made it sound somehow inhuman. "Go away."

"Sam, we came to help. Is there anything we can do?"

"Go away," it hissed, like a reptilian thing with a human thorax.

Mike was uncertain what to do, and looked back at Jessica. When he turned back around, Sam was standing in the darkened hall at the top of the stairs. Even in the half-light and at the distance between them, the ravages wrought on Sam's face by the onslaught of his pitiless affliction were only too evident. What was left of his nose was black and bleeding, a hideous bulbous thing rent by fissures and crevices from which pus oozed. It hung like an overripe monstrous apple, ready to fall off his face.

"Can you help this?" Sam coughed, through clenched teeth, jabbing at his face. "Can you cure this? Can you make Judy see again? Get out!" he screamed. "Leave us alone."

Mike's first impulse on seeing his friend's shocking appearance and hearing his choking voice was to run out of the house and never turn around. But his loyalty to his friend won out over fear and revulsion.

"Sam, let us help you. Where's Judy? Can we help her? Do you need anything, food, medicine, anything at all?"

"Judy's at the hospital for the blind, learning to live all over again like a newborn baby. Every doctor in the country has been consulted in our cases and none of them know a thing. It's all unprecedented. So you see we're being well taken care of. As for food, well, I've kind of lost my appetite looking at myself in the mirror lately."

"Look, no matter how bad things are it doesn't mean you have to shun your friends."

"I can't bear to have anyone see me like this," Sam said in a choking voice, tears flowing down his cheeks. "Please go, please."

Mike couldn't stand the pain in his friend's voice, but didn't know what else he could do.

"If you need anything, anything at all, please call me."

They left Sam's house with heavy hearts. Mike was thankful for Jessica's quiet strength, without which he wasn't sure what he would have done, for this was just about the worst day in his life.

He still hadn't gotten any information on Sara's family. They decided to go and visit Richard at the city jail to see if he could shed any light on the situation.

Mike had a hard time tracking down his friend, who had been incarcerated in an old municipal jail under the Mystic River Bridge. He found his way there with difficulty and located a parking place with even more trouble. Visiting hours were almost over by the time they arrived, but Mike was able to spend fifteen minutes with Richard, talking through the thick Plexiglas partition using a phone set.

Richard looked sullen and unkempt, his usual clean face scruffy, his clothes disheveled. He still had a black eye and swollen lip from resisting arrest two nights before. Avoiding Mike's eyes, he looked down at the floor evasively as he told him his side of the story, reluctantly giving Mike Sara's maiden name and her parents' address. He didn't appear sorry for what he had done or that Sara was still in the hospital.

Mike told Richard he would go by and check on the house for him.

"You want Sara, don't you?" yelled Richard out of the blue through the Plexiglas. "You want to screw her?"

"What? No," stammered Mike, taken aback. "Richard, how can you say that? She's in the hospital. You put her there."

Richard's shouting had attracted the attention of the guards. He didn't seem to care.

"You tell that bitch the next time I see her screwing around, I'll kill her. You hear me, Michael? I'll kill her!" he yelled, as the guards pulled him away and out of the room.

Mike sat there in shock. His friends were disintegrating right before his eyes. What was going on?

Jessica was waiting for him in the truck. He told her what had happened. They decided not to stop at Richard's house and headed directly home. Mike could call Sara's family from there. All the way back, Mike wondered about his other friend, the remaining member of their little group, Linda. He hadn't heard from her in weeks and hoped she was faring better than the rest.

They got back to Jessica's place and had supper. Mike didn't have much of an appetite, but Jessica talked him into eating a little fresh garden salad, with some brown rice and a piece of trout, which she had picked up just that morning from the market. The good company and cozy kitchen cheered him up considerably.

"I can't believe all the bad things that are happening to my friends," said Mike after dinner, as they sat at the table in the big warm kitchen sipping wine. "It just doesn't make sense, Judy going blind, Sam's nose. And Richard, that's just crazy. He was so mild-mannered and good-natured. I just can't believe any of it."

"Someone has put a curse on them," Jessica said.

"What? A curse? How? Why?"

"Laura agrees," Jessica continued. "What happened the other day on the mountain wasn't just a fluke storm. It was a sign. Something was warning us, telling us not to meddle. Even Hanna sensed it. And I bet it has something to do with that house and Jeanette Stillman."

Mike couldn't disagree, but he couldn't believe it was true either. He sat there shaking his head from side to side. The wine was starting to create a dull glow behind his ears. He'd been too preoccupied and upset to notice it earlier, but now he began to appreciate the way Jessica's jeans hugged her hips and how her T-shirt followed the curve of her breasts. Her long blonde hair shimmered in the light of the wavering candles. Her nose, too long in the full light of day, looked just right in the forgiving shadow of the cozy kitchen, while her pursed lips were moist and inviting. He thought he saw a look of desire in her eyes, like she might not mind a kiss. He started to strategize how that might come about.

Jessica's mind was elsewhere.

"Hanna was right," she observed. "She knew Laura isn't experienced enough to handle whatever is happening to you, but she died before she could help us."

"I guess that means we're on our own," replied Mike.

"Not entirely," said Jessica. "Not entirely."

Linda put on the last of her make-up and smacked her lips in the mirror. Ever since moving back in with her roommate, she'd been on one long binge, playing harder and partying longer. She seemed filled with a hunger that couldn't be satisfied. She lost contact with most of her friends, Judy and her bizarre entourage included. She couldn't believe she had fallen for that hick, Mike Russo, a carpenter no less, and an out of work one to boot. What could she have been thinking of? Although he was a hunk, there were plenty of hunks out there bigger and better than Michael.

Linda couldn't believe the talent she was getting lately, each one better than the last. Men were just throwing themselves at her, not just any men, but quality men, rich good-looking men.

Tonight was no exception. She had a date with a dashing stranger at an exclusive private club at the top of one of Boston's skyscrapers, a high tower overlooking the harbor. She was dressed in an elegant black gown, bare at the shoulder, which showed plenty of tanned cleavage. Her flaring hairstyle looked ravishing. Her makeup was applied just right. She moved to answer the doorbell, which had just announced the arrival of her date. Her roommate had long since moved out, disgusted with the nightly whoring and the parade of deadbeats and two-timers Linda brought home. If she didn't get AIDS, her roommate complained, she'd surely get murdered.

The stranger at the door smiled down at her with stunning blue eyes, his mouth firm, his chin strong. He was dressed in a tuxedo with a white bow tie, his broad shoulders filling out the black fabric of the tux nicely.

"I thought we'd start out with this," he announced, handing her a bottle of Dom Perignon. "I tried to get some of the good stuff, but this is all they had on such short notice. You look ravishing, darling."

He wrapped his arm around her slim waist and pulled her to him, kissing her hard on the lips. Oh, this one's good, she thought, as she kissed him back. She liked the way he held her, like he wanted to crush her.

She got some champagne glasses out of the cupboard while he opened the bottle.

"To your beauty," he said, toasting her with his glass full of bubbly, "As fragile and empyreal as a rose."

She wasn't quiet sure she liked the toast, but she enjoyed the sparkling liquid that slid smoothly down her throat.

He looked at her from under dark smoldering eyebrows, his mouth taut and almost cruel.

"I have something for you," he said, putting down his glass and pulling out a medium-sized oblong box.

"I thought of you as soon as I saw it. I've been thinking about you since the day I first saw you." He started unwrapping the package. "I can't stop thinking about you. How you'd look naked, lying stiff and still, with your hands at your sides and your eyes closed, on a cold, hard, steel gurney, dead and frozen."

Linda looked at him, not sure she understood what he had just said. She gave her head a little shake, as if that would make the words rearrange themselves to something innocuous, anything but what she'd just heard.

Her date opened the box and pulled out her gift, a large, sharp, butcher knife.

"For some reason, when I saw it," he continued, standing up and pointing the knife at her. "I just had to buy it for you."

He was smiling. His teeth looked sharp and pointed in the shadows of the room. His eyes were glazed and bulging, as if his lids were being drawn back. Linda went to scream, but something punctured the pit of her stomach and stopped the sound dead. She started to object, but something flashing cut the chords in her throat. She went to put up her hand, but something sharp pierced her heart and her arms went limp.

The killer left the way he had come, taking the bloody knife with him. Brad, as his mother called him, had always been a little sadistic, a little cruel, but he had never gone this far before. He had violent sexual fantasies and enjoyed 'slasher' movies as much as the next guy, but he had never acted on his sick, demented impulses before. He probably would have remained on the borderline of psychosis, a thinker if not a doer of evil deeds, if he hadn't driven by that odd house in the country and been compelled to stop and take a few pictures. Being the amateur photographer that he was, Brad developed the pictures himself. It was then that he noticed the image of an old woman looking out from a rear window. It gave him a start, the way her eyes burned through the black and white photograph to stare at him. He thought the house was abandoned. He had even peered through the windows to see the empty interior of the place. He had not seen any old woman when he stood there snapping the pictures. It was after using a magnifying glass to study the image in more detail that he first started hearing the voices.

He had spotted Linda a few days later out clubbing with his friends. There was something about her, some vulnerable yet wicked quality that made him want to hurt her horribly. He became obsessed with her. He knew the minute he saw her he would have to kill her, the voices told him so.

Now that the deed was done, the incessant nagging in his head was finally silenced. Only a dark void of forgetfulness filled his mind.

He would remember nothing after closing the door of Linda's apartment, nothing except a vague flash of excitement. Now he had another strong urge to take a ride out to the country to a small town just west of the city.

Brad couldn't have told you why he was on Route 2 heading out of town, or where he was going. He just knew he had one more thing to do.

Chapter 16

One thing led to another and Mike ended up spending the night with Jessica. She surpassed all his fantasies. He left reluctantly early the next morning, exhilarated and exhausted all at the same time.

The days went by slowly with still no work. The rent would be due shortly and Mike's funds were running out. He thought of asking his mom for a hand, but she had all she could do on a fixed income to just squeak by. No, he'd have to find some other way to make ends meet. His daily visits to the union halls and work sites were an exercise in futility. His ads for odd jobs and carpentry work went unanswered. He contemplated moving back home, but the thought almost made him suicidal.

The condition of his friends remained unchanged. Judy was home now and totally blind. Sam's nose hadn't fallen off yet, but the rot had spread to his upper lip and right cheek. Sara, who lived in the present moment only, was under the care of her family in Springfield, and Richard was still in jail under the care of his lawyer, awaiting trial.

The shocking news of Linda's murder had been in all the papers. Mike heard it from Richard, who called him from the jail.

"I had her, you know," gloated Richard. "I screwed her good, right in the house with Sara there. Yeah, she was a real nice piece of ass. They say he sliced her right up the middle like a fish, like I'm going to do to Sara."

The news of Linda's gruesome murder along with the other revelations coming from the obscene mouth of Richard Jenkins was too much for Mike to bear. He just made it to the bathroom in time to lose his breakfast. Jessica had been very consoling.

Over the recent days, with not much to do, Mike had been thinking more about his past-life recall episode. The thoughts and images that returned to him slowly were so vivid and detailed that he couldn't help becoming curious about them and their import.

On a whim, Mike decided to visit his old friend, Neil Gibbons, an ex-Jesuit who lived a few towns over and now taught history at the local high school. Perhaps he could shed some light on Mike's past-life experience. Better yet, maybe Neil knew of some carpentry work.

Mike drove his pick-up along the back roads to his friend's house. Turning right off route 110 onto Mill Road, he followed the tarmac lane as it became more crowded with trees. Rounding a sharp turn, he passed an old saw mill. The smell of cut wood permeated the air.

He drove a quarter mile along the small rutted road, then turned into the circular driveway of a large, two-story white house. Two large willow trees stood in the overgrown front yard.

Mike followed the drive to the rear of the house and parked in the spacious dirt area that passed for a back yard. A large collie bounded up to the truck as he got out. To his left, behind the house, was a good-sized barn that now served as a combination workshop and office. The vacant field next to the house was choked with raspberry bushes.

Neil Gibbons lived in the house with his dog, Raven, and his girlfriend, Nelly. Mike had done some work for Neil refurbishing the barn and they had become good friends. Mike stopped and looked at the large red structure for a moment before going into the house. Nelly met him by the door.

"Hi, Mike, long time no see," she said. "Come over to look at your handiwork?"

"Hi, Nelly. No, just came by to see Neil. Is he around?"

"He went to the store. He'll be right back. Why don't you come in."

Mike waited in Neil's den, occupying the time looking through his friend's collection of philosophy and history books, while Nelly finished her chores. Mike was a personable guy and made friends easily, so it wasn't unusual for him to strike up a friendship with Neil. They found each other to be exceptionally interesting, and spent many long hours sitting over a brew or two discussing the finer points of philosophy and religion, something Mike didn't get a chance to do with many of his other friends, who were more interested in expressing their opinions than in the give and take of different ideas and viewpoints. Neil, being an ex-Jesuit, didn't care much for Mike's dabbling in the occult, while Mike thought the structure and formal dogma of the church stifled any real spiritual enlightenment. Their opposing views offered many hours of lively but good-natured debate.

Neil's reasons for leaving the order, just like his reasons for joining, were many and varied, not least among them the desire for a normal sex life. The stale platitudes and back-stabbing politics just added to the dissatisfaction, and he was soon soured to the priesthood for good, although he did not leave the church itself.

It didn't take long for Neil to return from the store. He came into the den and greeted Mike.

132

"Hey, Mike. How you doing? We haven't seen you in ages. Where you been keeping yourself?"

"Oh around. It's been a busy summer," Mike replied.

"To what do I owe this unexpected visit?" asked Neil.

"I was wondering if you knew anything about a medieval churchman, a bishop in France called Nicole something or other?"

"Nicole, Nicole? Hmm, could you mean Nicole d'Oresme? He's the guy that coined the phrase, a 'Clockwork Universe'?" said the ex-Jesuit.

"Yeah, that's the one," confirmed Mike.

"Yes, he was quite an influential thinker. Mathematician, natural philosopher, astronomer, a regular Renaissance man. Great Aristotelian scholar if my memory serves me right."

Mike was amazed at Neil's recall and breadth of knowledge. The Jesuits had trained him well.

"Let's see," said Gibbons, getting up and pulling a book from the shelf, a large, dark-green tome with black and gold lettering. He thumbed through the pages. "Ah, here he is. Nicole d'Oresme, Bishop of Lisieux in France in 1377. Born near Caen around 1325 or 1330, in Normandy. Why the sudden interest in medieval scholars?"

"Oh, we were doing some past-life recall and I morphed into this guy," explained Mike.

"You're not still messing around with that stuff?" said Neil, his disappointment obvious.

"Nothing serious," replied Mike. "Just a group of us fooling around. It's a good way to meet chicks. It sure is interesting, though. It's kind of like hypnosis. You go into a trance and see yourself as someone else."

"Sounds like a bunch of superstitious horse manure to me," observed the ex-Jesuit.

"Yeah, just like the Holy Ghost and exorcism."

"I'll be glad to explain it all to you someday, makes as much sense as reincarnation."

"Oh, then how do you explain the fact that I never heard of this guy before, but I knew his first name and that he was a Bishop in France in the 1300's?"

"I don't know. If you really did, then it is strange," admitted his friend, scratching his chin. "But there are several just as likely explanations, like you've heard of him and just forgot, or it's just a weird coincidence."

"What can you tell me about this guy? Maybe there's something I need to know."

"Well, let's see," said Neil, thumbing through the pages. "Like I said, he was quite a scholar. Taught art at the University of Paris in the 1340's and studied with the famous master, Jean Buridans, there as well. He held a scholarship of Philosophy at Paris and in theology at the College of Navarre there in 1348. He was in Paris when the plague hit. He continued to teach art and theology at Navarre through the 1350's. Became a close friend with the Dauphin of France, and when the boy became King Charles the V, d'Oresme was his chaplain and consular. He had much influence. They made him archdeacon of Bayeux, in Normandy, in 1361, and canon of Rouen the following year. It says here that he continued to receive top procurements throughout his life. He was elected canon at Sainte-Chapelle in Paris and Dean of the Cathedral at Rouen in 1364. He was finally chosen Bishop of Lisieux in 1377. He was translating certain Aristotelian text from Latin to French there when he died the following year."

"I'll be," said Mike in astonishment.

"What?" asked his friend.

"In my flashback, I mentioned the plague in my youth, and the long war between the French and English."

"Don't tell me you never heard of the Hundred Years War," replied Neil.

"Yeah, sure, now that you mention it, but I sure as hell couldn't have told you when it was, or about the plague. Neil, I'm just not into that stuff."

"I know you've done some reading, Mike. Heck, I've even lent you some of my books."

"Honest, Neil, I don't know anything about this guy. I remember being in a dark room with a secretary working on some book. It must have been the translation you mentioned."

Neil stared at him skeptically, then looked back down at the text and continued reading.

"Says here that he wrote over thirty works on philosophy, theology, mathematics, physics, astronomy, magic, economics, and politics. He was one of the most subtle and penetrating minds of the times. You're supposed to know so much, you tell me something about him."

"I don't remember much," admitted Mike honestly.

"Aha!" answered Neil, feeling he had scored a point.

"But I remember saying the universe is like a clock and God's the great clockmaker. And mind you I know nothing about this stuff, honest. I've never read or heard a thing about him. I mean where did I get the name Nicole from? For a man yet!"

"Do you remember anything else?" inquired his friend.

"Let's see," mused Mike. "I remember ranting against astrology for awhile, and saying God made the perfect universe, something about once put in motion it continued without needing intervention."

"Interesting," observed the ex-priest. "Sounds like you picked up something there, however you did it. d'Oresme was an opponent of astrology and a great populizer of science. He promoted the idea that the universe was like a great clock. He was also a believer in Aristotle's impetus theory, which said once put in motion, the heavenly bodies tended to stay in motion. It all seems to fit with what you remember saying. Very interesting, but I'm afraid you don't have much in common with this person. He was a great thinker."

Mike gave a mock look of offense and raised his shoulders in a shrug. "Hey, I resemble that remark," he joked in his best Groucho impersonation. They both laughed.

"Does that help?"

"Sure does, thanks Neil. I feel like I know the guy. Hey, you mentioned he wrote something on magic? I'm just curious." The word had popped out at him when he heard it mentioned nonchalantly in the list of d'Oresme's works. Maybe it was just what he needed to deal with the calamities surrounding him.

Neil looked up from the book and said, "Yeah, he wrote a treatise on Magic and the existence of demons called, the 'Questio Contra Divinatures'. d'Oresme died a hundred years before the invention of the printing press, so only a few copies of the original manuscripts exist. Anyway, you'd have to know Latin to read them."

"You read Latin, don't you?" asked Mike.

"Sure, umpje in the akele, ikeme," said Neil laughing.

"Thanks, Neil."

The conversation turned to Mike's present situation. He told Neil he'd been out of work for over a month, with still none in sight. Neil told him he'd ask around the school. In the meantime, he was thinking of putting an addition on the house. He had intended waiting until next spring, but maybe, since there was such an able and talented carpenter available, he just might do it now. The prospect of work gave Mike some hope, although it would hardly be enough to keep him going for long. He told Neil about his friends, who Neil only knew through previous conversations he'd had with Mike. He didn't approve of their dabbling in the occult.

"Put your faith in Jesus, Michael," Neil counseled. "He's the only hope for mankind. Without Him we're like children lost in the night, helpless and open to all sorts of evil. Put your trust in the Lord. Pray to Jesus."

Mike didn't like it when Neil went religious on him. Sometimes Neil sounded more like a Born Again Christian than a Roman Catholic. But then that was probably why he left the priesthood in the first place, even if he hadn't left the church. Neil practiced his own brand of Catholicism.

Mike had once been a Catholic as well, growing up in East Boston. But the church had done little to help him when his father died. The words seemed empty and meaningless, offering neither solace nor understanding. He didn't think they would help any more now than they did then, and he and his friends were in a heap of trouble.

Mike was saying goodbye at the screen door of the back porch, when Nelly, Neil's girlfriend, gave a yell of pain. She had been preparing vegetables over the kitchen sink, and had cut herself with a knife. She was bleeding profusely.

"Nelly!" yelled Neil, seeing her wound. "You practically cut your finger off!"

They wrapped her hand in a towel and jumped in the car. Mike followed them down the road in his pickup to the small hospital in the next town. It took six stitches to sew her up. Mike stayed until he was sure things were OK, then thanked Neil for the information on Bishop d'Oresme and made his way home. He knew it was probably just a coincidence, but he couldn't help wondering if Nellie's accident had something to do with his current troubles and the curse that seemed to be following him around like a leering drunk.

Mike drove home trying to put all of the pieces of the puzzle together, still not fully convinced there was a puzzle to put together. Did all this really have something to do with the house? Was there something in his past-life recall that could help him? Would he be out on the streets come winter? These and other questions flittered through his mind like moths through a closet.

The horror of what had happened to his friends kept reemerging to consciousness, persistent and annoying. It made it all but impossible to eat or relax. He hated his apartment now that it was empty of companionship. Everyone who had lived there except him - Linda, his dog - had died a violent death. Was he next?

He wrote down what he remembered of Neil's exposition on the medieval bishop, circling the fact that he had written books on magic and demons. Maybe there was something there. But if there was, Mike had no idea of what it might be.

He thought about what Neil had said about putting one's faith in Jesus. He wished he had that kind of faith, but no matter how many times he read the Bible or listened to a sermon, it just didn't happen. He seemed to need something more pertinent, something more immediate.

He thought about some of the things Jessica had said concerning her religion, magic, a craft practiced by people who wanted a more organic, earthly interpretation for their spiritual yearnings, who sought the power of the female, the motherly principal rather than a male dominated fatherly one.

He looked out his front window onto the light of the dying day. The old house crouched and spread itself across the yard as if it were stretching. It seemed to soak up the fading light, to suck it into itself like a smoker inhaling his last cigarette, so that it seemed darker than anything around it, menacing and brooding.

Mike was no longer twenty-six years old and no longer standing in his apartment looking out the front window. He was seventeen again and looking at his future as it came tumbling down around his ears.

His first three years in high school had been dismal failures. He had barely passed his freshman and sophomore years, and had to take both algebra and geometry over again. His junior year had been little better. He had finally buckled down during his senior year, more due to a fear of being drafted than his mother's insistent pleading.

His friends were all going to college and had student deferments. His only hope of going to college and avoiding the draft was getting a scholarship, and he had just about doomed any chance of that after his sophomore year. When he finally did decide to buckle-down and study, under the naive assumption he could turn around three years of academic failure with a single year of effort, it was too late. It just wasn't going to happen no matter how hard he worked. Mike Russo, of fourteen Windsor Street in Boston's east side was not going to go to college.

He stared at his tenth and last rejection letter. His overall grades just weren't good enough. Sorry, but there were far more deserving disadvantaged children who had tried a lot harder than he had. They had to be considered first. Maybe, if

enough people dropped out of the program, there might be a chance for him, but it
was very unlikely. Had he tried trade school? Mike knew he was going to learn a
trade all right, in the fields of Viet Nam.

If only his father hadn't died five years earlier. If only his dad had lived, he
surely would have been able to afford to go to college like his other friends. If only he
hadn't crashed his car on the way home. It had been Michael's twelfth birthday. He
had been waiting for his father to bring him his present, a brand-new bike. His
father never arrived. Now, because of that, Mike's future was ruined. He'd be lucky
if he didn't die in the jungle somewhere, far from home.

In his daydream, Mike was sitting in his senior homeroom, waiting for class to
end. They had just been informed that everyone sitting on his side of the room had to
leave via the back door, while the other side of the class was to leave by the front. He
did as he was told, and followed the others on his side of the classroom out the rear
door. It gave out directly onto a dense jungle.

He was running through a jumble of trees and ferns. This is what he got for
not doing well in school. If they had only told him, only given him some sort of
warning, he would have tried harder, worked harder. Now it was too late.

The Viet Cong were chasing him. He was running barefoot through the lush
underbrush, dressed in only his green shorts and undershirt. He had to get away.
Everyone knew what the enemy did to prisoners. He had to get away. They were
right behind him. He heard them laughing all around him in the night, laughing at
him like crows.

Mike was again staring at the old house. A large, black crow was
sitting on the roof of the building cawing at him like a barking dog,
angry and persistent. Mike blinked once or twice and rubbed his eyes.
He looked at his watch. Thirty minutes had gone by. There was no way
of denying it this time. He had checked the clock before looking out
the window. It had been 7:45, fifteen minutes before the show he
wanted to watch. It was now quarter after eight. What had happened to
the last thirty-minutes? Had he blacked out again?

He went into the living room and tried to lose himself in the bad
movie he had missed the first fifteen minutes of, but couldn't
concentrate on the show for fear he was slowly going insane. He'd
have to call a doctor if he had any more blackouts. He resolved to give
Jessica a call in the morning. She seemed to be the only ray of light in
this whole dismal affair that had become his life.

Mike generally never thought much about his war experiences,
although they really weren't that bad compared to some. Basic training
at Paris Island was worse, although he hadn't buried anybody in boot

camp. But tonight, now, after his little flashback while looking out the window, all he could think about was the war - the horror of seeing friends blown to bits; the bloated bodies of the dead enemy; the hog-tied corpses of young girls accused of fraternizing. No, Mike may not have had it as bad as some, but war is hell no matter which way you look at it. He had put enough of his friends in body bags to last him a lifetime.

He thought of the hardships and discomfort he'd endured, days without food, sleeping unprotected on the ground in the freezing cold and the pouring rain. He had crawled on his belly in snake-infested swamps and marched through the stifling heat of a jungle bristling with booby-traps and enemy solders, and he had survived.

Instead of defeating him, instead of causing him to shrink from his trouble, these thoughts gave him courage. After all, he had seen a lot worse than this. He had lived and fought through things that most people only read about. He had faced death and stared it down. Some stinking, little haunted house or curse, or whatever it was, wasn't going to defeat him, not private first class Mike Russo, pride of the East End, not by a long shot.

Chapter 17

Jessica stepped from her bath and poured a few drops of lavender and sandalwood oil over her body. Several large white candles provided a warm golden light. She moved to the bedroom and slipped on a pair of soft pajama bottoms and a small white pullover that left her arms bare. Her long blonde hair flowed to the small of her back.

She turned on the hall light and walked up the six ladder steps to the small attic space over her apartment, where she had her tools and materials laid out on a low rectangular table made of oak - her crystals, her candles, her incense, her wand and salt shaker.

She lit the incense and sprinkled the sea salt to the four corners of the room and over all her implements. Then she placed the colored candles on the floor, the green one in the north, the yellow one in the east, the red one in the south, and the blue one in the west, and lit them with a white candle made of beeswax. Using her ash wood wand, she made an outline of a circle around her, connecting each arch of the circle to one of the colored candles. While she did this, she imagined a golden thread circling the area and extending from the floor to the ceiling, completely enclosing her in its protective boundary.

Jessica held Hanna's gift in her left hand, an ancient piece of uncut amethyst with the stone still in it, and invoked the protection of the heavenly Goddess, and a blessing of Light and Benevolence, to help guard her and aid her in her purpose. She had not eaten in several hours and had no alcohol that day. More importantly for her concentration and energy level, she had not had sex with Michael in twenty-four hours, the absence of which was becoming rarer as their relationship grew.

She was performing a protective banishing spell to drive away the negative spirits that seemed to be assailing Michael, and to protect him from their evil influence. She made her symbolic offering of flowers and herbs and called on the archangels Michael, Gabriel, Raphael, and Zadkiel to aid and protect her.

"Michael, angel of the south, sun warrior, protect me," she intoned. "Gabriel, angel of the west, messenger of the gods, defend me. Raphael, traveler of the north, watch over me. Zadkiel, seer and wisest council, guide me."

Her crystals were arrayed on the low alter in front of her, her healing stone, her brown and yellow citrine for strength, her clear quartz for energy, her sparkling citrine wish-crystal. It was the night of the full moon, a time of peak power.

She took one of Mike's shoes and placed it in the center of the alter. Then she took a piece of his hair and dropped it on the white candle, where it sizzled into nothingness.

"Banish all evil from this man," she said, holding Hanna's stone and her ash wand. "Protect him, oh Mother. Shield him with your healing power. Deliver him from the dark forces that besiege him. Give him succor and strength, dear Mother, dear Goddess."

A feeling of intense well-being washed over her. She was filled with peace.

"Thank you, oh guardians, for answering my call."

She tried to imagine the guardians as pillars of fire standing in each corner of the room. Suddenly, her concentration was disrupted as the trapdoor to the attic closed with a bang, slamming against the floor and blowing out all but the center white candle, plunging the room into semi-darkness. The bang seemed to reverberate through the house like a gunshot in a hollow cave. Jessica instinctively imagined a bright white light over her head, and laughed at her own fear, which was rising in her gut like a suffocating tide. She experienced the same sensation of whirling dust and flying sand that she had felt on the summit that day with Mike and Laura, although the room was free of dirt and dust of any kind. She transferred the amethyst to her right hand, her power hand, and held it tight, as she held her arms in front of her, calling on her guardian spirits for protection. The single candle flickered and went out. The loud knocking continued to echo throughout the house like the handclaps of a giant.

The day was cloudy and gray, but the clouds promised to burn off by noon. Mike drove down the road to Jessica's house smiling in anticipation. He had been spending more time there as the summer wore on. Jessica was the kind of girl a fellow could get used to. The heavy thoughts and memories of the night before were completely dispelled by the light of day and the prospect of seeing her. However, all was not a bed of roses.

Mike's rent was due and he still didn't have steady work. Although the job for Neil would help, if something else didn't come up soon it would be a long, cold winter.

Jessica had suggested he stay with her to help his rent worries. She had already OK'd it with the people who owned the place, who might even have some work for him around the estate. It was an offer he was thinking more seriously about with each passing day, especially since his landlord was not going to hold him to his lease. Although he still had a bad taste in his mouth after his last experience living with someone, he was optimistic things would be different with Jessica. The thought of Linda lying in the cold ground, her young body being eaten by worms and decay, almost made him go off the road. Life just wasn't fair. At least Jessica was safe.

He turned the corner onto her road and then into the long drive to the estate. Parking his truck next to Jessica's secondhand Gremlin, he went to the door. No one answered his rather loud knocks, so he tried it. Maybe she was in the shower and couldn't hear him. The door was open.

"Hi, Jessica. It's Mike. You decent?"

No answer. He walked further into the house, getting more uncomfortable the deeper he went. "Hi, Jessica? You here?"

He searched the downstairs rooms. There was no sign of her. He poked his head up the stairs and called her name softly. Maybe she was still in bed, although she usually didn't sleep this late. Creeping up the stairs, he called her name again. He walked down the creaking hallway to her room and peeked in. It was empty. Her bed had not been slept in. He stood there in confusion. Where could she be?

Suddenly, there was knocking in the hallway. It sounded like it was coming from the ceiling. Mike walked out and looked up. Seeing the trap door above his head for the first time, he walked over to it.

"Jessica, you up there?" he called.

"Michael, is that you? Thank God someone showed up," she yelled back, as he pulled open the trap door.

"Here you are," he declared, going up the short ladder and poking his head through the entrance.

"I've been up here all night," she informed him. "It's the darnest thing. The door was locked tight. It must have gotten stuck when it slammed closed."

"It wasn't stuck when I tried it," observed Mike, looking around the room curiously. "What's all this?"

"Nothing, just a hobby," she answered, pushing past him down the ladder stairs and shutting the trapdoor in his face. She seemed perturbed about something. Mike figured that she was just miffed at being shut up in the attic all night, but what really upset her was that her protective spell had been so rudely interrupted.

Mike couldn't take his eyes off her in her sheer, armless top.

Jessica mentioned nothing about the events of the previous evening, as they went back down to the kitchen. Her little ritual had been ruined, just like the one on the hilltop. She had gone through the ending ceremony despite the interruption, removing each candle counter-clockwise and anointing it with salt and oil, waving the pendulum over each crystal nine times and throwing all the disposable material in a plain paper bag. She had eaten a light meal of rice cakes, which she had brought to the attic with her. This gave closure to the ceremony and guaranteed that any good that came out of the spell would endure.

"So what was going on last night?" asked Mike from the kitchen table as Jessica made breakfast. "What were you doing, practicing witchcraft up there?"

"I was performing some white magic," she explained, as she sat down at the table opposite him, taking a piece of toast. "Magic can give focus to our energies and form the impetus for good things to cling to. It can calm your mind and give you energy. It's a natural power we all have within us. It's in the elements of nature, the sun and moon and stars, in trees and streams and rocks."

Mike had known she dabbled in witchcraft for some time, but had never heard her talk about it to such length. Other than the little ceremony he witnessed on the hilltop, he'd had no exposure to her beliefs. He did his thing and she did hers, and they rarely talked about it. In any case, Mike was trying to forget about his involvement in the occult and get his life back to normal.

"I think we're going to need more than a little hocus pocus to help me," he said. Jessica agreed.

When she returned from her shower, Mike broached the subject of his moving in and asked if the offer still stood. She said yes. She was wearing a pair of gray cloth workout pants that hung low on her hips, and a gray athletic bra. She looked trim and fit, not an ounce of fat on her. Mike looked her over admiringly. Just then, there was a knock at the door. Jessica went to answer it, unconcerned about her state of dress.

"Oh, hi Jim," she said, opening the door to a large, crew-cut man dressed in the dark and light-blue uniform of the sheriff's office. "Come in."

"Hi, Jessica," said the bull-necked deputy, stepping into the house. "Where you been? Haven't seen much of you lately. You're hardly ever home when I call. I even went down to the library, but they told me you took the week off. Why didn't you return my calls?"

Jim Boone was Jessica's old boyfriend. They had been introduced by mutual friends soon after her arrival in town. He was a big, good-natured boy, but found it hard to understand that Jessica didn't want to go out with him any longer. She'd been ignoring him on purpose, hoping he'd get the idea without her having to spell it out for him. Evidently it hadn't worked. He stared at Mike with undisguised dislike, narrowing his eyes as he looked back and forth between the stranger, who was sitting at the kitchen table, and his skimpily-clad ex-girlfriend.

"What's he doing here?" the deputy inquired.

"Jim, I thought we discussed this," she replied. "I don't need to explain my guests to you. Now be nice. This is Mike Russo. He built the new Davis house up on old Post Road. Know anyone looking for a good carpenter?"

"No," he said, not bothering to say hi to Michael and not taking the seat she offered him. "I just wanted to stop by and see how you were doing. Can't stay. I'm on duty. Just wanted to say hi, be sociable. I see you have company. I'll see you later."

He turned and started for the door, then stopped and turned around.

"Is that your truck out there, mister?" he said, in a formal tone.

"Yes," said Mike, feeling a bit uncomfortable. This was the first he'd heard about Jessica's old boyfriend.

"Well, you better get your windshield fixed before you get a ticket."

He turned and walked out. Mike's windshield had a small hairline fracture that had slowly turned into a large crack as the summer progressed. He had put off fixing it until it became too large to ignore. Unfortunately, the law had noticed it, now when he was out of work.

"A friend of yours?" Mike asked her, once they were alone again. The mood had been ruined.

"Yes, my old boyfriend."

"Gee, a man of the law yet. You could have mentioned it."

"He's made it very difficult to meet people. I thought he had dropped out of my life for good. I guess I was wrong."

"Great," said Mike, irritated.

"Forget him. I want to go in that house," announced Jessica, suddenly changing the subject.

"No way," replied Mike. "Everyone who's gone in there, including my dog, has come to no good. Forget it."

"Michael, I can't help if I don't know what we're up against, and I won't know what we're up against until I visit that house."

"Forget it, Jessica. The best thing we can do is get as far away from that place as possible."

"What about Richard and Judy and Linda? They got far away and look what's happening to them. No, Michael, remember what Hanna said. Have confidence in your power. Together we can fight this thing. All you need is a little knowledge to make you very powerful, I know it."

"Now you're really talking crazy."

They argued back and forth like this for some time. Mike finally agreed to consider it some more before ruling it out entirely.

"The best defense is a strong offense," she told him. "You have something very strong hidden within you. I could sense it on the mountain. Something wanted to hurt you, but couldn't. We may be the only hope your friends have. They've tried all the normal ways, all the doctors and all the priests. Now it's time to try a different approach, a magical approach. We're going to kick some butt."

"I wish I had your confidence," he said.

"That's the first thing we're going to start building. Here, read this," she said, handing him a small paperback book titled, 'Using Magic to Heal your Life'. "Lesson One, know you have power, more power than any spirit or negative force."

Judy lived in blackness. For one so image oriented, so visual, it was a doubly hard burden to bear, a burden she had to shoulder alone. For Sam was embroiled in his own living nightmare. What kind of life was this, she asked. A life not worth living, she answered.

She had withdrawn into the black cocoon of her blindness as if it were a second skin, avoiding her therapy appointments and Braille lessons, her friends and relatives. Her time was spent contemplating how best to kill herself. She wanted something sure and quick, silent and painless. She oscillated between a razor in the bathtub and hanging herself from the second story landing. Both thoughts gave her comfort, and she was moving toward them with methodical certainty, like a frail boat over the falls.

Any strength she may have had from the occult had long ago left her. She was ill-prepared to face this double catastrophe. Sam had quit his job and been out of work for weeks now and their savings were being devoured by their medical expenses, which helped them not at all. But Judy didn't care. She didn't plan to be around long enough for it to matter.

The slow onslaught of the sickness, with the excruciating headaches and the strong aversion to light, and the eventual blindness, were a complete mystery to the doctors and medical experts familiar with her case. It was like nothing they had ever seen before. There was no physical or physiological damage that could account for her blindness, although a psychosomatic cause had still not been ruled out.

After the doctors, Judy had tried her own methods, spiritual healers and Christian Scientists, but nothing worked, nothing could stop the onslaught of her affliction. She had prayed and she had pleaded, but still her sight did not return.

Nothing in her past lives, nothing in the spirit-world could help her, for she, like the others, was in the grip of an unseen, malignant force that was slowly smothering her.

She groped her way to the bathroom to see if she could find a razor.

If someone like Jessica, with the power to see auras, had been looking at the old house at that moment, as it sat like a spreading fungus on the front yard of Mike's apartment, they would have seen long, black, shimmering tendrils of vapor, floating away in thin empyreal wisps in all directions, like missile-trails searching out their targets. Wherever they went, death and misery would follow.

The spirit animating this house was no ordinary one, no lost soul or reluctant apparition. This was a powerful spirit, who in life had been dedicated to evil. It had been somehow disturbed and had freed itself from the shackles of forgetfulness, to become aware of its own identity. And because of this, it had become powerful and dangerous. Once woken, it would not go gently back into the peaceful slumber of the grave.

Chapter 18

Slowly, over the next few weeks, Jessica taught Michael the secrets of her craft, though only as much as he was ready and willing to accept. She found him an apt pupil, skeptical and rational, while at the same time perceptive and intuitive. He seemed to know just what to do and say, as if he had performed the rituals and spells before. He was open to new experiences and ideas, and he seemed to draw on a deep innate reserve of inner strength and wisdom. It appeared that he could amplify whatever power she possessed, power she was still unsure of. She had no doubt that Michael had tremendous potential, if only that natural talent could be tapped and directed. After all, their futures might depend on it. Mike took the whole thing with a healthy grain of salt.

He was moving his belongings to Jessica's house, loading the last of it into the bed of his pickup. He had started working on a new addition to Neil Gibbons' house, and was still doing some work for the people who owned the estate where Jessica lived. Slowly but surely, things were getting better, although his friends' situations had not improved.

Mike looked forward to setting up housekeeping with Jessica. He certainly wouldn't miss living near the old house, although Jessica still wanted to go there. In the meantime, she was initiating him into the secrets of her craft, gradually building up his confidence and power through a series of exercises and spiritual calisthenics.

As he was getting into his truck, a brown and white sheriff's car drove up the driveway. Mike recognized Jessica's big friend as he got out of the car and walked over. For some reason it appeared he wanted to see Mike. He wondered what it was about.

"Hello, Mister Russo," said the deputy, keeping on his sunglasses and not smiling.

"Hi, Jim. What can I do for you?" Mike replied sociably.

"You knew that Reynolds girl didn't you?" asked the officer, not wasting time with pleasantries. "The one that was murdered. Didn't she live with you for awhile?"

Mike hesitated in answering, not sure what the deputy was after. This certainly couldn't be an official inquiry. The homicide took place outside of his jurisdiction. Things just didn't work this way, did they?

"Yes," he said, finally, seeing no reason to deny it, since it was easily verifiable from a number of sources, including Jessica.

"She moved out about a month ago, right?"

"What's this all about, officer?" Mike asked. "I'm late for an appointment."

"Wouldn't be going to visit Jessica would you?" said the deputy, looking over at Mike's truck. "What you doing, moving in?"

"I don't mean any disrespect, but I don't see how that's any business of yours."

"That may be, but murder is my business," he said. "Your neighbors say you and this Linda Reynolds, that well, you two used to argue quite a bit, loud yelling and swearing. Is that true, Mister Russo?"

"Well, as I remember it, she did most of the yelling and swearing."

"Easy to blame her now that she's dead, eh Mister Russo? You own a knife?"

"Is this an official investigation, officer?" Michael inquired.

"Does this look official enough for you," answered the deputy, patting his badge and gun.

"Well, in that case, I'll have to call my lawyer."

"You do that, Mister Russo, and I hope you have a good expensive one too. Good day." The big deputy turned and got back into his vehicle. Mike had a sinking feeling in his stomach as he watched the car exit the drive and go down the highway. This could certainly bode no good.

He told Jessica about his encounter with her old boyfriend.

"I think the guy's out to get me," he told her. "He was questioning me about Linda Reynolds, the girl I used to live with, the one who was murdered not too long ago. They still haven't caught the person who did it."

"Don't worry, Mike. He's just trying to rile you, intimidate you so you'll back off. He's harmless, really, just a lot of bark with no bite."

"I wish I could be so sure. He seems dangerous enough to me."

"You were with me that night, remember. You have an alibi, so don't worry. Jimbo's not too bright. Give him enough rope and he'll hang himself for sure."

"OK, you're obviously the expert where Jimbo is concerned."

"Good, now take me to the house," she demanded.

"What, today? It's such a dreary day."

"Doesn't matter, time is wasting. We have a lot to do. I think you're ready, at least for an initial foray. I just want to make a reconnaissance in force, just to get the lay of the land. I want to feel its power in its home base. Don't worry, we won't probe too far and we'll have protection."

"Like what?" asked Mike, skeptically.

"Like that talisman," she answered, pointing to the small silver pendent shaped like a spider that sat on the windowsill where Mike had put it on moving in. "Hanna gave that to you in her will. It's an item of great power. It will protect us."

Mike closed his eyes and pursed his lips. He hadn't forgotten what had happened to his friends. "It's too dangerous," he said finally.

"Doing nothing is more dangerous," she countered. "Whatever it is that's doing this, the longer we wait the more strength and confidence it builds, the more malignant its influence over your friends becomes."

They ate a light brunch, after which Mike unloaded his truck and moved in the rest of his clothes and possessions. Jessica prepped him with last minute instructions. Then they drove back to Mike's apartment building. As predicted, the sun had burned off the morning clouds. It was now hot and hazy, with little wind to move around the humid air. Jessica wore loose comfortable clothing, while Mike had on his customary jeans and T-shirt.

He led her to the window where he had entered previously twice before. It was locked, as were all the windows at the front of the house, much to his relief. The old domicile stood as ominous and sinister as ever, sitting in the stifling heat like a white peeling beast, all watching eyes and leering mouths. Silent and menacing, it waited to devour any who passed near.

"I'm afraid it's locked. Too bad," he said, ready to give up.

"You're not going to get out of this so easy," she replied, moving along the side of the house.

Mike followed as they walked down the side of the building, past his ex-apartment. The shadows appeared thicker and deeper, as if the sun was reluctant to cast its rays here. None of the windows opened. Finally, they stood before the half-closed entrance of the rear shed.

The door was opened just wide enough for a dog to squeeze through, but Mike could only get his arm and shoulder in. He tried pushing it wider, but it was nailed and boarded-up on the inside. At Jessica's insistence, he went back to his truck and got a hammer, which he used to pry away the few boards holding it closed. Still, he had to push hard to open it a few inches, scraping it against the hard dirt-covered floor.

When he had it opened wide enough to pass through, he peeked around into the darkness. A flock of crows suddenly came wheeling out of the doorway, their wings flapping and squeaking like hinges, startling both Mike and Jessica.

"Look's like a bunch of birds were nesting in here," he observed.

"Highly unusual, wouldn't you say?" replied Jessica. "I would expect pigeons or barn swallows maybe, but crows? They don't nest indoors."

"I see your point," said Mike. "And that crow at the cemetery."

"Yeah, familiars more likely," she answered.

"Familiars?" echoed Mike.

"Never mind. You ready? Let's go."

They pushed through the narrow opening and entered what looked like a shed or storeroom. The floor was bare and covered with debris. The walls were grimy and shorn of covering. The small windows were boarded up, letting in a minimal amount of light. Broken glass and grit crunched beneath their feet as they walked across a dirty floor that seemed to slant in three different directions at once. They made for a small door in the far side of the room.

"This is the shed," observed Mike. "It traverses the back side of the house to the kitchen from what I can tell. This should be the kitchen right here."

He tried the white porcelain door knob, which turned easily in his hand, and opened the door onto the long narrow kitchen. It looked just like before, as if set for breakfast, with paper and magazines strewn across the floor, a grease-stained counter squatting along the wall.

Jessica took it all in. "Looks like someone left in a hurry."

"We had the same thought. Look at the dates on the magazines. Latest one is 1966, the year the murders that Hanna told us about took place."

They moved to the doorway leading to the rest of the house. To the left was the original part of the building built by old Max Stillman. To the right was the sinister hallway leading to the macabre rear of the house, Jeanette's rooms.

Jessica wanted to go to the right, through the dark hallway.

"This way, Jessica," suggested Mike. "You don't want to see that. There's nothing interesting back there, just cobwebs and dirt. Up front is where the good stuff is."

"I didn't come here to admire the architecture," she replied. "I came to get acquainted with Jeanette. She's back here. Come on."

Mike looked wistfully toward the front of the house with its finely-crafted tiles and polished hardwood floors, where it was sunny and warm. With a sigh, he turned and followed Jessica into the dank rear hallway.

Mike was struck anew by the bizarreness of the place, how the roof sagged in spots and the floor slanted and bulged. Everything was distorted and out of kilter.

"I see what everyone was talking about," observed Jessica. "It's weird."

They moved along the corridor to the first room on the left, the children's bedroom with the three bare cots. Torn shades still hung from the windows like flaking skin. Jessica walked into the room and turned in a clockwise direction slowly in a circle three times. Mike noticed she had the spider scarab in her right hand and a piece of rough amethyst in her left. She raised her arms and said something he didn't quite catch. Then she left the room.

"What are you doing?" he asked, as they entered the next one directly across the hall.

"Just getting to know the place," she answered. "Laying the groundwork, finding the spot where the force emanates."

"Sorry I asked."

"Quiet. Open your mind, look, listen."

The next room had been closed the last time he was in the house, and the door locked. Now it stood opened, as if inviting them to enter. It was filled with dusty mirrors. Some were long and standing, others round and hanging. A few leaned against the walls. Reflecting each other, they provided a depth and dimension that seemed to go on forever, disorienting the onlooker. Mike had the distinct impression they were mirrors into another world, each one reflecting an endless series of repeating images stretching beyond the confines of the room. There were no windows. Only the faint illumination from the doorway filtered in. A light fixture swung where a bulb once hung, the empty socket staring out from the high ceiling. Something flittered just out of Mike's view from mirror to mirror, as if moving behind the glass, something small and dark.

Jessica ignored the sensation and surveyed the room three times like a rotating lighthouse, then went to the next room. Mike remained transfixed in the doorway. He was no longer following Jessica through the house.

Mike was standing in the dark, still as stone, staring with horror into the mirrors.

A dark form was slowly crawling toward him from the back of the image, too faint at first to see clearly. It slowly moved closer. Then the form was reflected in another mirror, then another, until he was surrounded by them. As they crept closer, he began to make them out - children, with long wet hair and menacing dark eyes. The form before him began to crawl out of the frame and slithered to the ground. Looking up at him, it began to move forward. Closer and closer it came until it was almost upon him. Mike was rooted to the spot, terror overwhelming him. Other forms began to crawl out of the mirrors toward him. The first one grabbed his leg. It opened its mouth and called his name.

"Michael, Michael," said Jessica, shaking him and shouting, her face just inches from his. He had gone still and silent the moment she left the room, and stood there staring blankly. She had been trying to get a response out of him ever since.

Moving the silver scarab over his head in a circular motion, she concentrated her thoughts and said his name again.

"Michael, you are enclosed in the protection of The Mother. It protects you from the floor to the top of your head. You are enclosed in it, enclosed in heavenly light."

She concentrated her mind and imagined the light she was describing. As she did this, Mike slowly seemed to regain his senses and looked about him.

"What happened?" he said. "Did I black out again?"

"Just for a few moments. Are you OK?"

"Yeah, I am now," said Mike. "For a moment there I lost it. There were children crawling out of the mirrors, coming for me."

"Sounds like a hallucination. I can guess what brought it on. Now that we know what can happen in here, we'll be better able to handle it."

"I hope so," said Mike, not so sure. "It caught me unaware."

"Don't let it happen again. Focus your thoughts. Feel your power."

Jessica insisted on continuing her reconnaissance of the rest of the house, despite Mike's weak protests. He followed close behind, holding the spider talisman that Jessica returned to him tightly in his right hand as they made their way along the dark slanting hallway to the last door on the left.

They stood staring into the black pit of the cellar. A chill permeated the atmosphere, making their breath visible. Mike shivered involuntarily.

"There's a powerful presence emanating from this place," Jessica informed him, looking down the stone stairwell.

"Yeah, it's real creepy. We're not going down there are we?"

"Whatever spirit is haunting this house is coming from the basement. It's poisoning the whole place."

Suddenly, something started tugging at Mike's shirt, pulling it out where he had it tucked in. It felt like tiny hands were plucking at it, first in front, then in back. Jessica could distinctly see something pulling the fabric of his t-shirt. They looked at each other in surprise. A chill grabbed at Mike's heart, making his hair stand on end. He imagined a bright light over his head and laughed. Both efforts failed miserably with the realization that a half dozen invisible tiny hands were grabbing at him. This time Jessica saw it too.

"Just ignore it," she counseled.

It took every ounce of self control to keep from running out of the building. Instead, he stood his ground and calmed his breathing. The basement door suddenly slammed shut in their faces, making them both jump back. Soon every door in the house was opening and closing, one after the other, like a string of pistol shots. Jessica and Mike looked at each other in alarm.

"Impressive," said Jessica, laughing out loud. Mike laughed too, emboldened by his companion's bold, hearty voice.

The doors continued to open and shut, making the light in the hallway blink and sounding like tiny explosions.

A blast of frigid air rushed up the stairwell as the door swung open one final time, blowing Jessica's hair back. They continued to laugh boisterously, while the house became silent.

Then they heard the howling, soft at first but slowly building. The wind blowing from the basement rose as well. Mike tried to pull the cellar door closed, but something held it tight. The sound was growing louder now, drowning out their laughter.

Mike made his legs be still, although he felt like running headlong from the house. He remembered Hanna's words, and called on the God-Head to protect him. Jessica held her amethyst high over her head.

"It's time to go," she advised.

They calmly walked back up the hallway toward the front of the house. The warped doorway at the end of the hall started flapping back and forth again like a gate in a pinball machine, but they easily passed through and made their way back through the kitchen to the shed.

As they approached the back shed, a small furry animal jumped in front of them and bared its teeth. It growled and chattered, darting back and forth as the doors began to bang open and shut behind them. The rabid animal was not going to let them pass.

Grabbing an old broom handle that was leaning against the wall, Mike jabbed it at the animal just as it attacked, jamming the stick into its tiny teeth-filled mouth. The badger clamped its jaws on the wood with a loud snap, digging his canines into the broom handle. As it did, Mike flipped the end of the broom with a jerk and tossed the rodent hard against the opposite wall where it landed on the floor dazed. Mike and Jessica scrambled to the door and slipped out.

As soon they were out of the house, Jessica performed a binding spell, holding whatever spirit had been disturbed within the confines of the building, imagining the entire structure enclosed in a cone of light. They could still hear doors banging angrily inside.

"That's one pissed off ghost," observed Mike, looking at the house.

"Whatever it is, it's very powerful," said Jessica. "That's no ordinary spirit."

"What do we do now?" he asked.

"I don't know," replied Jessica, staring at the building as if it were the very gates of hell itself. "But we'll have to think of something and fast."

Richard pulled his car off the highway into the rest area. His two-bit court-appointed lawyer had finally gotten him out of jail. It had taken all his and Sara's retirement fund and then some to post bail, but he had done it. Now he was on a mission, or at least had been on a mission until a few minutes ago. Now he sat in his car trying to remember exactly what it was that was so important it had him steaming up the Mass Turnpike twenty-five miles over the speed limit.

Until about ten minutes ago, his every waking moment had been taken up with thoughts of his unfaithful wife and what he was going to do to her. In his mind's eye, he could see her doing it with everyone, his friends, his peers, his boss, their doctor, his god-damned little lawyer, everybody. But most of all he saw her screwing his friend Mike Russo. He had even driven to Michael's apartment looking for him, but his friend no longer lived there.

They had told him about Sara's problem, her sudden memory loss, but he hadn't believed them. It was only a lie to get him out of the way. He would show them it didn't pay to lie to Richard Kelly.

He finally remembered what he had been doing. He had been on his way to Sara's parents' house, where she was supposed to be staying. He dredged his frazzled memory for his purpose, so strong and hot only moments before, something about teaching her a lesson.

The sexual and violent fantasies that had been driving him to a frenzy only moments before were now nothing but dull flickers of memory with no power to motivate or anger. Maybe if he just kept going along this highway he'd remember what was so urgent by the time he got there. That thought fueled his body enough for him to pull out of the rest stop and proceed down the Mass Pike.

Whatever it was that had been driving him had been momentarily distracted, but the lapse would not last long. Even now it was reaching out to him from beyond the grave.

Chapter 19

Mike sat at the kitchen table thinking about the events of the day while Jessica showered upstairs. She had been preoccupied with her own musings after their return from the old house.

He replayed the scene in his mind. He was now convinced that there was indeed an evil power emanating from the place and infecting his friends. There was no use denying what his senses were proclaiming, the place was haunted and whoever went in there was cursed. Even though he was not a true believer, he was glad Jessica knew something about magic and casting protective spells, though she had not said a word since coming home.

Mike sipped his tea and looked up. She was standing at the doorway staring at him with a strange expression.

"It's coming!" she informed him. "It got out of the barricade I erected around the house and it's coming for me."

There was fear in her voice. Mike heard the wind pick up outside as it whipped tree limbs and shook shutters. He felt a cold chill down his spine, like slimy wet seaweed being dragged across his back. Jessica stood looking at him with a funny gleam in her eye.

"What's wrong?" he asked. He didn't like the way she was staring at him.

Standing in the doorway, she started making a deep humming sound, as if someone had cut off her tongue and she was trying to scream. Her pupils rolled back showing the whites of her eyes. If Mike wasn't mistaken, she was gnashing her teeth. Her rigid stance was highly disturbing. She appeared to be agitated, as if she was fighting some deep internal battle. Mike instinctively sat up and looked at her in alarm.

Making a series of guttural sounds, she walked into the room. She had a slight limp. Her body was crooked and stiff. Mike tried to stammer a few words, but his tongue stuck to the roof of his mouth so that only a muffled croak came out.

She walked toward him with a frightening expression, her breath coming in harsh, hissing gasps. She spit out a howl that made Mike's teeth chatter.

As close as he was to panicking, he forced himself to remain calm, evaluating the situation and watching her every move.

Jessica's large, clear quartz crystal was on the table, as was her white beeswax candle, which was burning brightly in its silver holder. The reflection of the candle flashed within the crystal. Despite his terror, Mike slowed his breathing and imagined that he was increasing the brilliance of the light with each exhale.

Months of practice and training with his friends - the silly exercises and mind control experiments they used to do for hours and which he thought were a total waste of time - came in handy now that his body was pumping adrenaline and his heart was beating wildly in his chest. He could feel his knees knocking beneath the table. Still, he concentrated on his breathing and imagined the bright light from the crystal filling the room.

He saw Jessica move toward him out of the corner of his eye, but blocked her out of his mind. Exhaling, he breathed out with an audible sigh, and with it, discharged all his doubts and negative emotions. With each breath he imagined his power growing with the light, believing it to be so.

The light from the crystal started to spread and rise in the air, spiraling in a tight circle like a twirling beacon, spreading higher with each exhale. At this point, Mike was unable to distinguish between his inner world and the world around him. It all blurred in a hazy mixture of dream and reality so that he no longer knew what was his imagination and what was real.

The light flashed from the crystal, which was now spinning on the table, faster and faster, splashing light around the room. Soon a radiant pillar of iridescent, mother-of-pearl shell-light, brilliant and hard, began to pierce the darkness. Golden sparks flew outward from its corners and edges like flares, flashing over Jessica like a flickering strobe-light.

He raised his arms over his head and shouted in a commanding voice.

"Your light protects us all from harm, Lord. It gives us strength in our time of need. Your radiance repels all evil. Your brilliance dispels the darkness and fear."

Mike continued chanting until the spinning light filled the room. Jessica stood near him by the table not moving, silently staring at him. Suddenly, she shook her head.

"What happened?" she asked, as the light slowly began to dissipate. Soon it was gone as mysteriously as it appeared. Jessica looked around confused, knitting her brows. "Last thing I remember is getting out of the shower and throwing this on. Next thing I know I'm down here in the kitchen watching some weird light show."

"You don't remember anything?" Mike inquired.

"Only the light. Did you do that? I saw a revolving pillar of light."

"Eh, I guess," said Mike. "You saw that?"

She nodded her head.

"You said something funny before you wigged out," he continued, "about someone coming for you, getting by your barrier. Then you just started to spaz out. I thought you were sleepwalking or something. It was horrible. It's that house."

"She must have possessed me, Jeanette I mean. She must be a powerful spirit to break my binding spell and come here like that. No ordinary ghost could do that. It has to be a witch's spirit."

Only a few moments before, Mike would have scoffed at the whole idea of possession and witchcraft, but he couldn't deny what he had just seen. Nor could he deny what he had done.

"Did you just do what I think you did?" she asked him again.

"I think so," he replied slowly. "I used your crystal and concentrated on the candlelight reflected in it just like you showed me. Then it sort of took off by itself."

"It's all supposed to be inner visualizations, you know, imagined. I've never known anyone to actually create real light like that. You really are a warlock. That was magic."

Mike just smiled at her with a stupid grin. He really didn't know what to believe at this point. So much had happened, so many inexplicable things, that anything was possible.

The next day, while Mike was putting up some siding for Jessica's landlord, a state police car drove up the drive. They were looking for Mike and wanted to ask him some questions down at the station. As he followed them in his truck, that all too familiar sinking feeling began to churn in his stomach again. What could they want? Were they going to question him about Linda? Had Jim Boone voiced his suspicions to the staties?

He pulled into the state police barracks in Concord and parked. The tall gray walls and watchtowers of a state prison for juvenile defenders frowned down on him from across the highway. He followed the officers inside and waited in a conference room until two plain-clothed detectives walked in. The smaller man introduced himself as Captain Gary Holmes. The tall, husky one said nothing. Captain

Holmes was about Mike's size, with neat, prematurely gray hair and a rosy, youthful complexion. His eyes smiled as he looked at Mike.

"Mister Russo, we'd like to ask you some routine questions concerning Linda Reynolds. We understand you knew the deceased?"

"That's right. I met her late last year through some mutual friends."

"Can you give me the names and phone numbers of these mutual friends?"

"Sure, but you may have trouble getting in touch with some of them," said Mike, uneasily.

"Oh, why is that?" asked the detective.

"Well, the person who introduced us, Judy Kelly, has gone blind and her husband has been diagnosed with some sort of bad skin cancer."

"Is there anyone else who can tell us about your relations with Linda Reynolds?" asked the detective.

"Yes, Richard and Sara Jenkins." Mike gave their phone number and address to the officers. "But Sara has gone to live with her parents." He explained the situation. Captain Holmes wrote it all down and looked at Mike pleasantly.

"How well did you know Linda Reynolds?" inquired the detective. "Tell us about your relationship."

"Like I said, I knew her a few months. We went out."

"Is it true she lived with you at 1523 Main, apartment 22, at the Carriage House?"

"Yes, we lived together for a couple of months."

"Not very long." Holmes left the statement dangling, as well as any implications it might have attached to it.

"It was a difficult time," answered Mike. "My dog ran away and died soon after we found him. I lost my job. I think she was expecting things to be different and decided to move back to town. There were no hard feelings. We were still friends."

"You got along well with the deceased then?"

"Yes," answered Mike. "We were good friends. Living together just didn't work out."

"Did you two argue a lot?" asked the state trooper.

Mike thought about the question before answering.

"We had our share of disagreements. Like I said, it was a difficult time for both of us. But we didn't fight anymore than most people, and

159

there certainly wasn't any violence or anything like that, if that's what you're getting at."

"I'm not trying to insinuate anything," replied the policeman. "We just want to know how well you knew her and if you might know anything that can help us solve her murder."

"I wish there were something I could tell you," Mike told him. "I didn't really talk to her much after she moved out. My friends were closer to her than I was, but they're all having problems of their own. I'm afraid I really can't tell you much more."

"Was she seeing anyone else?" asked detective Holmes.

"Not that I know of," answered Mike. "You'd have to ask her roommate."

"We did. She said Mrs. Reynolds saw lots of men, one even fitting your description."

"Well, that may be, but I didn't see her after she moved out."

Officer Holmes checked his notes for a few minutes.

"We have information from Sam Kelly that states you saw Linda Reynolds at his house on July 10th. She moved out before the fourth, is that right, Mister Russo?"

Mike was getting confused. They had already talked to Judy and Sam. He didn't like the way this was going. He felt like he was being ambushed.

"Am I a suspect in Linda's murder?" he asked incredulously.

"At this point, Mister Russo, everybody's a suspect."

Mike felt it advisable not to say anything more until he could see a lawyer. The state police captain didn't think that would be necessary, but asked him to let them know if he was planning on leaving town. They might want to ask him a few more questions. They were working with the Boston Police on this case and wanted to hold up their end of the investigation. Before Mike left, detective Holmes asked him another question.

"You're living with Jessica Wilson now, aren't you? Get around, don't you?"

Mike didn't answer, and left the building feeling very upset.

Jessica was home from the library when he got back. He told her what had happened.

"Do they really think you have anything to do with Linda's murder?" she asked.

"I don't know, but they asked me about our relationship and whether we fought. The guy who interrogated me seemed to twist

160

everything I said around. It was very uncomfortable. When I asked if I was a suspect, they said everyone was a suspect. Then why aren't they hassling anybody else?"

"Don't worry, Michael," said Jessica. "You have a good alibi - me." She hugged him and kissed him on the cheek. "We've got to stay focused on the real danger, that witch-spirit of Jeanette Stillman. If she thinks she can mess with my head and get away with it, she's got another thought coming. We're going to jam our next spell right down her throat." Jessica was obviously taking the whole thing personally.

"You're not thinking of going back in that house again, are you?" Mike asked.

"I'm not only going there, I'm going right down into that basement and driving her back to hell where she belongs."

"I don't know," objected Mike. "After what just happened I think we should be careful. You should have heard yourself. It was downright creepy."

"No, Michael," replied Jessica, sticking to her guns. "That won't happen again. I'm ready for her now."

Mike did not share Jessica's confidence. He remembered how she looked under the influence of that other entity. Whoever it had been, it had not been Jessica, not the Jessica he knew. He remembered her words.

"No," Mike insisted finally. "Whatever's going on here, I want no part of it."

"Mike, you don't have a choice. Neither do your friends. Something has latched onto all of you and it isn't going to let go until you're all dead, and even then it might not!"

Deep down, as much as he didn't want to admit it, Mike knew she was right. He couldn't run. He couldn't hide. He had to face his demons or perish trying. Well, Mike Russo told himself, he had faced a lot worse.

Jessica looked hard at him, as if to penetrate his soul.

"Michael, remember what you did, right here in this room," she reminded him. "That wasn't a dream. That was the most incredible thing I've ever seen. You pulled me back with your light. Remember what Hanna told you, and Judy's teacher. You have a great power, perhaps the greatest anyone has ever seen. I know I never saw anything like what you did. Whatever spirit is haunting us, it's afraid of you, but it's drawn to you at the same time, like a moth to the light. That's why all your friends are sick but you remain unharmed."

"I don't know about that," Mike replied, although he had to admit, what had happened to him thus far was highly unusual. But it was nothing compared to what was plaguing Sam and Judy and Sara and Richard. Mike shuddered. There was still plenty of time for something terrible to happen to him.

"Michael!" she fumed. "Don't wimp out on me now. Your friends need you. Please."

"OK," he said, unable to resist her pleading eyes. "But I hope you know what you're doing."

Sam no longer looked in the mirror. Like his wife Judy, he shunned the light, not because it hurt his eyes, but because seeing his face distressed him so. What had once been his nose was now no more than a huge, scab-covered cavity where cartilage and fluid sat under two dark, pinprick eyes. The cancer had spread to his upper lip and cheeks, so that his face had become a hideous mask of sores. Not even the doctors could look at him without dread.

His recent phone conversation with the state police about Mike's relationship with Linda had taken his mind off his immediate troubles for awhile, but not long enough. Even speculating on whether Mike had anything to do with Linda's murder couldn't keep him from thinking about his terrible affliction for long.

A black pit of pestilence was devouring him face first. He was sinking into the void a little more each day. Before long he would be gone. And who was to blame? Whose fault was it? Who had done this to them? Sam didn't know, but he was beginning to get the germ of an idea.

It was only a matter of using his reason and a little common sense deduction, of putting two and two together. Everything had been fine one minute, then horrible the next. That moment had come after visiting Mike Russo's apartment. He had done something to him. Sam didn't know what and he didn't know how, but it was a conclusion he could no longer escape. Mike had killed Linda, just like he had in a previous life. Now he was doing something to the rest of them as well.

Now that Sam knew what was happening and who was doing it, he asked himself what he was going to do about it.

Chapter 20

Jessica had been collecting every protective crystal she could lay her hands on. She had black agates and amethysts, bloodstones and garnets, Lapis Lazuli and tiger's eye, topaz and turquoise, rose and smoky quartz. She hung bouquets of herbs around the house and in every room, agrimony and alyssum, bay and blackthorn, clove and clover, cumin and curry, even thistle and holly.

She kept the crystals in a dark silk purse, and washed them every day under running water. She sprinkled salt over them, and passed them over lavender incense three times a day, preparing her instruments like a surgeon for the time of battle. She also readied her secret weapon, Michael.

Mike had listened to Jessica's pronouncements with little enthusiasm. There was something manic and fearful in her boasts, as if they were meant more to boost her courage than to formulate an actual plan. There was much too much emotion and bravado and not enough thought and judgment to make Mike feel comfortable or confident the plan would work. In spite of all her precautions and tools, Mike felt they needed something more to succeed, knowledge that could only come from someone like Hanna, or perhaps, a medieval churchman who had written treatises on magic and demons.

"I've got an idea," he said, explaining what he had in mind to Jessica. As farfetched as it sounded, she could think of no reason to object.

He called his friend Neil Gibbons, who happened to be home.

"Hi Neil," Mike said. "Remember that guy Nicole we were talking about, that medieval bishop. You said he wrote a book about the existence of demons and magic."

"Yes, the Questio Contra Divinatores," replied the ex-Jesuit. "It was all very intriguing. I've been thinking about that."

"Well, I was wondering if you could maybe get a copy of it somewhere, perhaps in a museum or library or something."

"Yeah, they might have it in the Vatican Archives," laughed Neil. "But I doubt they'd let us see it."

"Very funny. Why don't you ask your friend the Pope if we can borrow it."

"All kidding aside, Mike, there may be copies of some of his works available locally, but it might be hard to find that particular one. It is probably very rare."

"Well, it happens to be very important to us."

"This doesn't have anything to do with your dabbling in the occult, does it?"

"No, Neil. It's way beyond that. People's lives may be at stake."

"That sounds pretty serious. This isn't a case of demonic possession, is it? You should leave that stuff to the profession. The church has special priests to handle that."

"Now you're sounding like one of us dabblers in the occult. No, nothing like that, at least I don't think so."

"OK, it sounds intriguing. I'll do a little research and see what I can turn up. Maybe Harvard Library will have a copy. They have a good archive of medieval books. I'll look around and let you know."

"Try to write it down and translate it, well you. I'll do the rest of the work on your extension for cost. My time will be your time."

"You got yourself a deal."

"Thanks, buddy," replied Mike. "You're the greatest."

The short time later, Neil called to tell Mike he had found something.

"I will work on it the rest of the day," Neil informed him. "Why don't you and your girlfriend come over for dinner. I'll get Nelly to cook up your favorite dish. I'm making photocopies of the book and will tell you all about it."

Mike and Jessica arrived at the Gibbons residence at six o'clock that evening.

Neil didn't waste any time and had it all laid out on the dining room table waiting. While Jessica helped Nelly in the kitchen, Mike and Neil talked.

"I found it in the archives at the McMullen Museum in Boston College. I tried the Boston Library and Harvard's medieval archives, but no luck. Each of them had works of d'Oresme, but none had the one you're interested in. I contacted an old friend at BC, who teaches there, to see who might have a copy. He told me about the one they have at the college, published in 1566 in Germany. It's in Latin. Luckily it's not that long and was easy to copy. I have the photocopies here."

He sprayed out the printed sheets on the table.

"The Questio Contra Divinatores in Qual lib eta Annexo of Nicole d'Oresme," announced Neal. "I've been translating it for you."

"Neil, you're the greatest. That's fantastic."

The ex-Jesuit started reading the text.

"Et reducite ad metuendas Dcemonis violentias," he said in Latin, continuing on for some time. Both Nelly and Jessica came in to listen. It reminded Mike of the priests saying mass when he was a kid.

When Neil Finished, Mike asked, "What the heck does it mean?"

"It says something like, 'Send back to the demon three-fold what it exudes. Send back the evil to the one who brings it'. Look's like some kind of exorcism. You should be careful with this stuff. Forget whatever you're thinking of and put your faith in Jesus Christ."

"That's amazing," said Mike, ignoring his friend's admonition. "That's it! Send back the evil like a boomerang."

Later that evening, after a meal of Lasagna and garlic bread, where Neil entertained them with funny stories from his days in the seminary, Mike and Jessica discussed what Neil had showed them. Neither of them had had any wine, which Neil and Nelly made copious use of.

"That makes sense," said Jessica. "Any spell strong enough to affect this thing would certainly come back upon the person who spoke it. This way we just turn the spirit's malignancy back on it with no harm to ourselves. Perfect," she announced. "I think we're ready. Let's go back and finish this once and for all. It's a propitious time, the night of the waning moon."

"Why not do it in the light of day?" Mike asked, "It's late."

"No," she insisted. "It has to be tonight." She looked out the window. "Tonight the moon will be perfect. Now's the time."

It was midnight.

Jessica collected her purse of crystals and packets of protective herbs, together with the other material and left the house with Mike.

It was dark and windy as they walked to his truck. An overcast sky blocked out the stars. The small stones of the driveway crunched beneath their feet. As they were getting in the pickup, they heard someone approaching behind them. A light was flashed into Mike's face as he turned toward the sound.

"Where you two going?" demanded a voice behind the glare.

"Jim, is that you?" asked Jessica. "What are you doing back here?"

"Never mind that," answered the deputy, moving closer and keeping the beam on Mike. "I'll ask the questions around here. Now where are you going with him?"

"That's none of your business," replied Jessica, angrily.

"You better stay away from him, Jessica," cautioned the deputy. "He's no good. Don't you know, he's being investigated for the murder of Linda Reynolds? Do you want to end up like this?"

He thrust a morgue shot of the dead girl into Jessica's face. She was nude and covered with dark, inch-wide slits where the knife had penetrated her skin. Jessica turned her head away.

"Oh, Jim! Take that away," she pleaded in distress.

"There's no call for this," said Mike. "It's a state police matter. If you don't leave us alone, I'll call and tell them you're harassing us and interfering with their case."

"You do that, wise ass," urged Jim. "If you know what's good for you, you'll leave Jessica alone or you'll have me to deal with."

"You'd better leave, Jim, before I call your boss," said Jessica. "Bye."

The deputy lingered a few moments more before swinging the flashlight beam away from Mike's face and treading back down the drive to his car. Mike walked over to Jessica.

"I'm sorry," she said.

"It's not your fault," replied Mike.

"He's not going to leave us alone until this whole thing is cleared up," said Jessica. "I don't know what his problem is. I told him you were with me the night Linda was murdered. Maybe he thinks I'm lying to cover up for you."

"He's just jealous," said Mike. "And I don't blame him. I'd be jealous too if you took up with someone else."

"Don't get cute, Michael," she replied blushing. "He has no call to carry on like that. I'll have to tell Sheriff McGuire about him. Then maybe he'll leave you alone. I can use the typewriter at the library and write a letter to the state police explaining you were with me the night of the murder."

"I'm not sure you should involve yourself at this point," cautioned Mike. "Why don't we wait and see if they question me some more. In the meantime, just make sure the sheriff gets the word about Jimbo."

"Yeah," agreed Jessica. "I'll see him tomorrow. The real problem is in that house."

"I was hoping you'd forget that," said Mike.

* * * * *

Richard took the exit off the Mass Turnpike to the outskirts of Springfield, stopping in the center of a suburban shopping mall to get his bearing. He hadn't been there in a few years, but after awhile he recognized where he was. Following the road over a bridge, he turned left down a country lane, around a bend, along the river, then left, into the first driveway after the large maple tree. He recognized Sara's parents' house with no difficulty. He sat in the idling rental car and surveyed the yard.

There was a Honda mini-van sitting in the driveway in front of him. No one was about. He got out and walked around to the back of the house.

Richard's plan, which had faded on him halfway here, was now back with a vengeance, guiding his every step. The violent sexual fantasies that had plagued him like a hoard of hungry wolves, now hounded out all other thoughts. The images came unbidden, and when they did his temples pounded and his fist clenched, and all he saw was blood.

He peeked through a rear window of the house into an old-fashion kitchen. It was empty. Moving to the next window, he looked onto a dining area. There she was in the next room, just visible on a corner of the couch, watching cartoons on TV.

He tried the window. It was unlocked. He opened it and climbed in.

Judy contemplated her death with morbid anticipation. She thought of it each hour of the day and night. Her thoughts of suicide had turned into a steel-willed obsession. Sam was shut in his room, too locked in his own concerns to notice his wife's cries for help, such as they were. They had not spoken to each other in weeks. None of it mattered anymore. It would all be over soon.

She thought about the children she would never have, the family she would never raise. Now none of it would ever be. This line of the family was going to come to a screeching halt. Well, so be it.

It wasn't so much the blindness she couldn't live with as the creeping despair in her heart, the endless void her life had become. Ending it all was the only choice, her only way out.

She had come to a decision on the final solution, selecting a razor in the bathtub – quick, painless, and clean. The thought was her only consolation in her dark despair.

While Judy languished in darkness with thoughts of suicide, Sam lay in the darkness of the next room, contemplating his revenge. It burned in his brain like cocaine. The whole conspiracy lay transparent to his mind. It had started long before their visit to Mike. Mike had been stalking them for a very long time. Yes, Mike had been sent to kill them. Maybe it was one of their enemies. Maybe it was someone they had once offended. Or perhaps it had something to do with reincarnation, some force reaching out from the past. Whatever or whoever it was, they had sent Michael to do their dirty work for them. Mike had connived his way into their circle, feigning friendship until he was a trusted member of the group. Then, when their guard was down, he had invited them to his house where he had poisoned them. He must have slipped something into Judy's eye drops and given something to Sara to make her lose her memory. He remembered feeling funny after using his nose spray that evening. Mike must have spiked it with something as well. He had a little more trouble explaining Richard's problems, but knew that Mike was behind it.

Of course, Mike had killed Linda. That much was obvious. Perhaps Mike was simply crazy. Whatever the case, he had to be stopped. But how? That's what Sam was concentrating on now, or at least trying to concentrate on. But thinking on any one subject for long was becoming more difficult as his face slowly disintegrated before his eyes. The thought that someone had done this to them intentionally made him angry beyond words. He vowed out loud to get revenge. Mike would pay.

Chapter 21

Mike and Jessica drove up the highway toward the old white house. The night seemed to grow darker the closer they got. Mike had the spider amulet Hanna had given him around his neck. He felt confident, although still afraid. His mouth was dry, his heart beating fast. Jessica sat stone still by his side.

They drove past the small center of town, past Jessica's library, silent and lightless in the dark windy night, up the highway toward the unknown. They turned at a slight bend in the road and there it was, as if it had pounced in front of them - the Stillman house.

Mike turned off the highway into the building parking lot. A few lights were on in the apartments. A single street lamp shed a faint glow from the corner across the street. Just the faint outline of the house could be seen from the parking lot. Mike could sense it watching them as they approached, waiting silently for them to enter.

Mike had Jessica's large clear quartz in his right hand, the same one he had used in her kitchen a few nights before. Jessica carried the special materials that the mysterious Latin text translated by his friend Neil had called for. Their only light was from a small flashlight Mike carried. They came to the rear shed door, still half-ajar, and entered boldly, without hesitation. Any spirit watching their boisterous sure movements would have been given pause at their confidence and audacity.

They entered the dark storeroom. Mike's light cast a narrow beam that hardly penetrated the darkness. The sound of growling and the chatter of sharp, pointed teeth started abruptly from the corner. Mike could hear tiny claws scurrying across the dirt-encrusted floor.

Jessica lit the first of her candles, the large white one in the silver holder, and held it aloft. In the flickering light that filled the room with darting shadows, Mike could make out a small furry creature crouching by the far door. Jessica lit the red candle and handed it to Mike. He placed it on the floor in the middle of the room and held the clear quartz crystal in front of it. Immediately, the space was filled with a blinding light. The small creature stood frozen to the spot, staring blindly. Without stopping, Mike and Jessica continued through the door into the kitchen, and from there to the foyer and the rear of the house, to Jeanette's rooms.

They moved with such speed and determination they seemed unstoppable. As fast as you can take a breath, they had traversed the crooked hallway and stood staring into the dark void of the cellar, a black shadow in the darkness more sensed than seen. Even the light of their brilliant candle hardly penetrated the gloom of the yawning hole.

As they moved down the stone steps into the flag-stone basement, the spirit of the house woke with a vengeance. A cold wind swept up the stairs and slammed the door shut behind them. Their candle suddenly blew out, plunging them into darkness. The slender beam of Mike's flashlight was swallowed in the black emptiness of the cellar. The shadows closed in around them, caressing their faces with icy fingers.

Mike felt his way across the uneven floor, imagining a bright light above his head. It didn't matter that the candles were out. The inner light would protect him. He laughed boisterously.

The cellar door started slamming violently back and forth. Soon all the doors in the house were banging as well. He flashed his light on Jessica to make sure she was OK, and was instantly sorry he had done so. Her long blonde hair was pulled out in all directions, as if a gang of misbehaved kids were playing a prank. She looked at him with resignation and told him to ignore what he saw and heard. Something was pulling at his own hair and clothes. He had the distinct impression a dozen small hands were reaching out of the darkness for him, tugging at him. It drove him mad, but he concentrated on the task at hand.

They clasped hands firmly in the darkness. More hands groped them in the blackness. They were becoming frantic now, clutching at their clothing. Still he ignored them.

Holding the spider-talisman in his right hand, Mike spoke the words from the text he had brought back from the fourteenth century.

"May your hatred and venom coil back on you like a snake," he intoned in Latin as tutored by Neil, the ex-Jesuit. "May the vicious malignancy you spew forth recoil upon you."

There was not a part of him not being pulled or pitched by a dozen tiny invisible fingers. Still he went on.

Again following the mysterious text translated from Latin by his friend, Mike sprinkled Holy Water and salt around the room. As he did, he spoke again.

"Pain and misery flow back to you. All your evil flows back on you like light dust against the wind, threefold, back to thee from whence it sprang. All falls back on you. All falls back on you."

Mike repeated these last words, his voice rising in decibels and power with each utterance. Something tried to rip Hanna's spider pendant from his hand, but he held the charm tightly in his fist and continued.

At the climax of his chant, he threw the bottle of Holy Water and salt that he had been holding down onto the concrete floor of the cellar, smashing it to bits. As he did so he cried in a loud voice, raising the candle, now lit again, above his head.

"The pain returns to you. The evil returns to you. The suffering returns to you. The fear returns to you. I call on the Eternal Light. Send it back to you!"

The pulling fingers stopped. All was silent.

A low rumbling noise slowly began to emanate from deep within the earth, growing louder. The ground began to shake. Dust and debris snowed down upon them.

"I think it's time to go," suggested Mike. "The place is falling down."

He flashed his light at Jessica, who stood motionless, staring at the ceiling in horror. The house shook on its foundation, raining more dust and debris on their heads.

Mike looked up and saw a black shadow rising in the darkness like a giant wave. It threatened to engulf them, swallowing what was left of the light. The building shook, the ground roared as if bellowing in rage. Mike, blocking the terrible image from his sight, stood his ground and cried loudly over the den.

"Send it back! Send it back from where it came!"

There was a loud crack and the stone foundation split around them.

The rumbling increased. Rock and wood splintered and shuddered. The whole house swayed violently.

Mike's first instinct was to rush up the stairs and out of the cellar, but the door was shut tight and he knew there was no time. Instead, he grabbed Jessica by the arm and pulled her underneath the staircase, where they huddled for protection.

The store shed in the rear collapsed in on itself with a loud crash, taking part of the kitchen wall with it. The foundation shuddered, shifting the house an inch to the side with a creaking moan.

As they crouched in the darkness beneath the stairs, Mike held Hanna's spider-amulet in his right hand and called on her and all the other kindred souls he had known. He didn't trust the dilapidated stairs

171

to protect them from the tons of stone and wood about to come down on them. Instead, he concentrated his mind, imagining a barrier above them, while he exhaled his fear and doubt.

A pale blue shaft began to glow over their heads, so ephemeral he was not sure it wasn't some trick his eyes were playing on him in the darkness. Not caring whether it was real or not, he focused his mind on sustaining the illusion, imagining it was holding up the stairs. As he did, he saw Hanna in his mind's eye, sitting in her rocker smiling at him. Then the whole building collapsed.

Miraculously, the staircase held as the ceiling caved in around them, showering the basement with floorboards and plaster from the rooms above. Somehow they remained unhurt amid the avalanche of stone and wood. The destruction around him was tremendous, as if the very place itself was being swallowed by earth. Soon only the chimneys remained standing, as smoke and dust rose thirty feet in the air.

As the dirt and debris settled, and the rumbling began to subside, lights flickered on from the apartment house next door as people were woken by the commotion. Mike and Jessica crouched in a cubby-hole beneath the stairs covered with grit and dust, clutching each other tightly, hardly able to breathe.

Soon all was still and silent except for the howling of the wind through the ruins. A light drizzle had begun to fall. Mike could see sky above him through a small peephole in the rubble, which he quickly enlarged by moving some boards.

The cellar stairs had miraculously protected them from being crushed by the tons of debris. Or had it been something else? The way was blocked with large beams and stones, but Mike was able to push some floorboards aside and crawl out of the cubbyhole, helping Jessica as he did. Using a large wooden ceiling beam, they shimmied up and out of the basement. Soon they stood with the gathering crowd, staring into the heap of wreckage as the town fire truck roared up the driveway, its siren howling. No one noticed them among the onlookers.

They said nothing as they drove back to Jessica's house, neither daring to utter their thoughts, neither fully believing what had occurred. Had they done it? Had they brought the curse down around the ears of that old witch?

It was all too weird for Mike, who kept trying to find a rational explanation for the evening's events and kept coming up empty. There was no rational explanation. He had to believe what was occurring around him, like a hapless Castaneda in the hands of an old Indian shaman. His life and sanity depended on it.

He tried to calm the rising sense of exhilaration bubbling up in his gut. He wanted to slap Jessica a high-five and yell football cheers, but she sat stiff and silent beside him, deep in thought, staring out the window at the passing night. He decided to adopt a wait and see attitude, even though his every instinct told him they had done it, they had sent whatever demon was haunting the place back to hell where it belonged.

The next morning, bright and early, after only a couple of hours sleep, Mike was on the highway again, heading back to the old house. The sun had not yet risen. It would cast little light on this cold, damp, cloudy day. Jessica stayed home. She seemed preoccupied with something, saying little and lost in thought.

When Mike arrived at the ruins, only a single fire truck and a few bystanders remained. He parked his pickup where it had been the night before and joined the knot of onlookers.

"What happened?" Mike asked feigning ignorance.

"Place fell down last night," replied a middle-aged woman in a red robe. "Made a heck of a racket."

"What are they doing?" he inquired, watching a few men in fire hats and rubber boots inspecting the basement walls.

"I don't know," answered the woman. "Look's like they found something."

Another man standing next to them, holding his dog by the leash, added further information.

"I think they found some bones, a bunch of them in the cellar wall there."

As they watched, another official car pulled up and the county coroner stepped out. Walking to the side of the ruins, he consulted with the fire chief and sheriff. Then he took his bag and descended down a ladder into the basement where they were moving what looked like bones from the wall and covering them with white sheets. News travels fast in a small town, and before eight the place was crowded with onlookers and the curious.

Bodies had indeed been discovered in the cellar of the old house. While some citizens of long standing knew about the incident of ten years before, few knew that the bodies of the seven murdered children had been left buried in the basement of the old house. It was the town's dirty little secret. So what if seven children lay in unconsecrated ground with their bones intermingled and their arms intertwined, left as Jeanette had interred them. The good name of the town had to be protected. The secret had to be kept. To most inhabitants of the community, however, the discovery came as a gruesome shock. Mike, however, knew the truth, as hard to believe as it was.

Judy sat in her room, in a silk kimono, relieved for the moment from the overpowering depression that had been smothering her these past weeks. She was still blind, but no longer had a burning need to kill herself.

Sam lay in his bed, his eyes closed, next to a table full of ointments and salves prescribed to sooth his sores and blisters. They finally seemed to be having some effect. He still suffered from his mysterious malady, but its spread had abated during the night. He had actually been able to lose his pain and thoughts of vengeance in forgetful sleep.

Richard slept in the back seat of his car, where he had dropped off after eluding capture. He had been spotted almost as soon as he stepped into the house by his wife's brother who was home for the weekend from college. He was in the kitchen right beside the window when Richard crawled through. The brother made a grab for him, but was thrown to the ground as Richard turned and clambered back out of the house. He made his getaway while the hysterical family called the police. They thought it was a burglar, Richard's brother-in-law not recognizing him. A sweep of the area failed to turn up anything.

Sara had no idea what had happened. Her parents told her nothing, not wanting to agitate her fragile condition, especially now that she was making a recovery. For the first time in weeks she actually knew her own name. They had no idea that the intruder might be her estranged husband, who was trying to kill her.

It was as if a weight had lifted from all of them, as if some smothering, pox-ridden blanket had been removed from over their heads. Although the curse may have been lifted, however, it still lingered in the air like the threat of impending storm, looming in dark nearby clouds that won't go away.

Chapter 22

Mike was exhausted the first few days after their ordeal. The whole thing was beginning to fade from his memory, so that it was hard to determine what had actually happened and what was imagined. The main thing was that it was over.

Whatever he might have thought or believed previously, he was now a firm believer in magic. He preferred to think of it as the power of concentrated thought, the focusing of the creative life-force within us, a realization of the loving sustaining principle of the universe.

Jessica had remained quiet and aloof since their ordeal. She hardly registered any emotion at all when he returned to tell her the news of the grisly discoveries. Over the next few days they spent less time together. They hadn't had sex since before that night. Mike wondered if this pattern was destined to recur whenever he tried to live with someone.

He had expected he'd feel better once the house was destroyed, and he did at first, but over the next week, as his initial elation wore off, he went into a deep funk. He still hadn't heard from his friends. At first, he thought it was just the results of that strenuous night. As the days wore on, however, he realized it was something else. He felt drained and depressed, as if the weight of the house had descended on him when it fell. It was not the relief and jubilation he thought he would feel.

He had been thinking more about his father lately, and how he missed him; about all the things he wanted to say to him, all the things he wanted to show him. Would he be proud of his son now, of what Mike had made of his life? Out of work, living off a woman, involved in God knows what nonsense. No, Mike had to face it. His father would probably not have approved of what he had done with his life so far.

In a funk, he made the mistake of calling his mother, who still lived in East Boston.

"Why didn't you tell me you moved?" she said, after he told her where he was. "What if I had to get in touch with you for an emergency? Then what would I have done?"

"I wanted to get settled in before I called you," he replied sheepishly. "I wasn't sure where I'd be."

"You could have come home you know, if you're out of work. Your room is still like it used to be."

"I know, Ma. I'm established out here now. It'd be too hard to get set up there."

"Your brother calls me every night and he lives in California."

"He has a job."

"Well, it doesn't sound like you're doing all that well where you are. After what happened with your last girlfriend, I'm surprised you're in such a hurry to shack up with another one."

"Ma, it's not like that. Jessica saved my butt. I didn't have a place to go."

There was a stony silence at the other end of the line.

"You could've moved back home," she said again. "You know the police came and asked me a lot of questions about that girl who was murdered."

"What did you tell them?" Mike asked. He was sick to hear the police had asked his mother questions about the murder.

"That I didn't know anything about your love life, since you seldom called your poor old mother."

"Thanks. I'm sure that was a big help."

"Are you in trouble?" she asked.

"No, Ma, of course not. As a matter of fact, thanks to Jessica, I have an alibi."

"Some alibi," she replied.

"Do you ever think about Dad?" he said. For some reason they seldom talked about his father. It had been too painful at first. Then it just never seemed appropriate. She kept his picture on the TV and their wedding photos on the bureau in her room, but they never reminisced much about the good times they all had together.

"Of course, Michael. What a silly question. All the time. Why?"

"Oh, I don't know. I miss him, that's all," answered Mike, feeling depressed and vulnerable.

"It's been fourteen years, Michael. We have to get on with our lives."

"I know, Ma. I just wish he was still around. I need his advice."

"If it's good advice you want, listen to your mother. Come home."

"I'm fine, Ma, don't worry," he lied.

"You don't sound fine to me," she observed. "You sound downright awful. Now, what's wrong?"

"Nothing. My friends, Sam and Judy, and Richard and Sara, you met them a couple Christmases ago, they're not doing too well. I'm just worried about them, that's all."

He told his mother about Judy's blindness and Sam's cancer, and about the domestic problems Richard and Sara were having. Being a consummate gossip, this information enthralled her and she kept Mike on the phone for another twenty minutes with her questions. When Mike hung up a little while later, he was even more exhausted and drained than before.

Jessica was at work, trying to drive her concentration back to the task at hand, but her mind kept darting away like a wary cat, always back to those dark thoughts. She had no idea where they came from, out of what corner of her mind, but they were sinister and full of hate, nothing like she had ever had before.

She stared at the card catalog and tried to force her brain to decipher the words she was seeing. Why was she having so much trouble keeping her mind on track? She'd always had such good concentration. It was if she was waging an internal war with herself.

She couldn't bear the thought of going home. She loathed being with him. Why had she let him stay with her? Why had she gotten involved with him? She couldn't remember. All she knew was she couldn't stand being in his presence. As a matter of fact, she found it difficult to be with anyone. Even the children, with whom she had always been so patient and helpful, filled her with disgust. She had all she could do not to strangle them as they sat reading their stupid little books.

She decided not to go home. She could get a room at a motel or stay with a friend, but she could not spend another night in that place. Something about him revolted her. His very maleness offended her. His masculinity was a threatening menace. She couldn't explain it, but she was filled with such fear and loathing it was hard to contain. She moved like an automaton to the front desk, a robot without emotion, under the influence of some alien force.

Telling her assistant she was going into Boston to do some research, she left the building. Pondering where she could go, she drove around aimlessly along the darkening country roads. It was as if some inner conflict were raging within her. She had to find a secluded spot where no one could observe her.

It was getting late, long past the time she'd normally be home. Something was happening to her. She didn't know what or why, but something was happening. She tried to fight whatever it was, the inner voice that was taken over her own familiar dialog, but it kept drowning her out. Soon there would be nothing of Jessica left.

She thought of Hanna in her distress and tried to remember what she had said. Suddenly the strange inner voice took over.

Yes, good old Hanna; Hanna my old girlfriend; old white-trash Hanna. Yes, Hanna's old home will do nicely.

Mike looked at the clock over the kitchen stove as he tossed the stir-fried vegetables in the pan. Jessica had been getting home later each night, ever since that last episode in the old house. It was almost 8:30 and she still wasn't home. Mike was more than concerned. She should have shown up hours ago.

She hadn't been herself since that night when he thought it had ended. Instead of the cheerful, pleasant, affectionate girl he knew, she had become caustic, sullen, and angry. That is when she spoke at all. It was as if she blamed him for all the trouble in the world, from AIDS to the Middle East.

He had called the library earlier, around four, but she had already left. The assistant said that she had gone into Boston to do some research. That was all they'd say. Mike wondered what kind of research she was doing and if it had anything to do with her current mood. Despite their victory of a few nights ago, Mike had the disquieting feeling that nothing had really been resolved, although there was a definite relaxing of the evil influence, if that's what you could call it.

Mike didn't know what to do. He had waited as late as he could without word from her then started dinner, hoping she'd be home by eight to eat it with him. He pulled the chicken out of the oven and spooned some veggies onto his plate. The clock above the stove said 8:45 and there was still no Jessica. He uncorked the half-empty bottle of wine and poured most of it into his glass. The food looked and smelt delicious, and he hadn't eaten since early morning, but for some reason he just wasn't hungry. The chicken tasted like cardboard in his dry mouth. He could hardly swallow anything down his fear-constricted throat. After a futile attempt to eat, he decided to go out and look for her. He left a note, put away the rest of the food, and went out to his truck.

It was already dark outside, a bright, clear, moonlit night full of stars. Crickets were chirping loudly in the bushes and trees surrounding Jessica's house. Mike got in his Ford and headed to the library.

All was quiet in the square. He walked up to the building and looked inside. It was dark and empty. He knocked and tried the door, but it was locked and no one answered. After a while he went back to the truck and sat in the cab trying to figure out what to do next.

He drove into town and asked around - the general store, the pizza shop, the corner garage, and the schoolhouse where night classes were being held - but no one had seen her. A few gave him suspicious looks and asked him if anything was wrong. He must have appeared a bit disturbed. He certainly felt that way. His hands shook and his voice wavered as he asked everyone he met about her.

He drove back to her house, but she hadn't returned. He was beginning to panic, imagining all the terrible things men do to women happening to her. It just wasn't like Jessica to be missing like this without letting him know where she was. Perhaps it wouldn't be a bad idea to call the police. It was almost 9:30. Instead, on a whim, he decided to drive by the ruins of the old house.

The moon was peeking over large cumulus clouds, bright and round, as Mike drove into the parking lot of his old apartment. The beams, half-walls, and roofing of the collapsed house stood slanting like skeletons in the moonlight. The mist was creeping in out of the woods behind the house like a living thing. Mike wished he had brought a jacket to fight off the night chill.

Walking slowly around the ruins, he surveyed the twisted rubble. Then, out of nowhere, he heard a low and barely audible whisper right behind his ear. He turned quickly, but there was no one there. Then he heard it again further away, the whispering of children, as if a dozen of them were calling for him. It was coming from the woods behind his old apartment building.

Thinking it might have something to do with Jessica he followed the voices, which were fading as if moving away. He ran behind the apartment house to a small path leading into the woods where he and the dog used to go for runs. The whispering was coming from this direction. He heard it distinctly, but was starting to doubt his own senses. He followed them anyway, and plunged into the darkness of the trail where only the dimmest of moonlight penetrated.

As he made his way through the woods, Mike wondered if he was going crazy, but the sound was all around him. It seemed so real. It couldn't be his imagination. Maybe they were trying to tell him something about Jessica. What has happened to her?

Soon he was hopelessly lost, stumbling along in the darkness like a blind man. He went on like this for some time before his survival training kicked in and he got himself under control. He had been through a whole lot worse than this in basic training. These thoughts gave him courage. He calmed his breathing. Was the house or whatever inhabited it still playing with him?

He wondered this as he climbed a tree to get his bearings. At some point the whispering had stopped. Mike had never noticed. As he looked out over the swaying treetops, bathed in the silver glow of the moon, he heard nothing but the sound of the leaves rustling in the wind. He saw the highway several hundred yards to the west.

Descending the tree, he headed in that direction. After another half-hour of pushing through tree branches and bushes in the dark, he stumbled onto the road a couple of miles above his truck. He started down the highway in that direction.

Mike wondered if it had been a hallucination, but his recent experiences made anything seem possible. As he was pondering this a car drove up behind him and pulled off the road. Mike turned. Jim Boone was behind the wheel. He put on his wide-brimmed hat and got out of the vehicle.

"Hold it right there, Russo," he yelled, even though Mike had turned and stopped. "What are you doing out here?"

"I'm walking. What does it look like I'm doing?" Mike answered in no mood to be interrogated.

"Don't give me any of your lip," growled the deputy, walking quickly over to Mike and jutting his jaw three inches from his nose. "What are you doing, walking out here this time of night?"

"Last I heard it wasn't illegal to take a walk at night. It was a nice evening. I came up to look at the old house. It fell down a couple nights ago. Then I decided to take a walk."

"What's this?" asked the deputy, pointing to the scratches on Mike's cheek.

"Nothing," replied Mike, feeling his cheeks. "I must have scratched myself in the woods there." As Mike felt his face, Jim noticed the scratches on the backs of his hands as well.

"What were you doing in the woods?" he asked, getting more suspicious by the minute.

"I thought I heard someone crying back there and went to investigate. I know it sounds weird. It was probably just an animal or something, but it sounded so human. I just went in a little way, but I got kind of lost. I'm heading back to my truck now."

The sheriff's deputy looked at Mike like a cat looks at a canary.

"Here, I'll give you a lift," he offered.

"That's OK. I'd prefer walking if you don't mind."

"I do mind. You don't belong wandering out here in the woods at night. You'll cause an accident or something. Come on."

Mike followed Jim to the car and got in.

"How's Jessica doing?" asked the deputy casually, as they drove down the highway.

"Fine," said Mike.

"Where is she?" Jim inquired.

"Home, I suppose," answered Mike.

"I was just there," the deputy informed him. "I didn't see her."

"Well, I don't know then. I haven't seen her either. I was actually out looking for her before I heard the noises. She's been very busy lately. She must still be in Boston."

"She always stay out this late?"

"She's a big girl, Jim, as I'm sure you know. She comes and goes as she likes. She doesn't have to consult me, but no, this isn't like her."

They arrived at Mike's ex-apartment building. The mist had closed in and filled up the clearing, making the collapsed ruins look like a smoking bombed-out crater.

"Thanks," said Mike, getting out of the car hastily.

"I'll follow you up to Jessica's cottage, if you don't mind," said Jim.

"Be my guest," replied Mike, getting in his pickup and pulling out of the drive. He drove as slow as he could all the way back to Jessica's house. After about ten minutes, the deputy passed him and disappeared down the road. He was there waiting for Mike when he arrived a short time later. Jessica's car was not in the drive. She was still not home. It was almost eleven.

"Doesn't look like she's home yet," observed Jim, stating the obvious.

"This isn't like her, Jim. I'm worried."

"Oh, now you're getting worried," said deputy, looking at his watch. "You should have reported this. Why don't you come with me."

"Am I under arrest?" asked Mike.

"No, but that could be arranged," replied the Jim. "We can look for Jessica together."

"I told you, she went to Boston tonight. She'll probably be home any minute. Maybe she called but didn't leave a message."

"We'll leave her a note and tell her to phone the station. Come on."

"No, I should stay here in case she returns or calls. You don't need me."

"Yes I do, come on," demanded the deputy.

Mike didn't see that he had any choice, so he went with Jim down to the sheriff's office, where he answered more questions. Jim went out a short time later telling Mike to wait there. He spent the rest of the time looking at the mug-shots on the wall and waiting for word about Jessica. A short time later Jim returned and rushed into the office flushed and excited.

"Call Sheriff McGuire!" he ordered the dispatcher.

"At home? Are you nuts?" answered the girl on duty.

"Call him, pronto! Tell him to get down here as soon as he can. I've got something he's got to see."

The way the deputy kept glancing in Mike's direction with a knowing look made him nervous.

"Can I get a lift home?" Mike asked.

Jim ignored him and strode into an adjoining room, leaving Mike to cool his heels for another twenty minutes until the sheriff arrived.

"What's got Jim so riled-up, Louis, that it can't wait until morning?" asked Sheriff McGuire as he walked into the squad room. He gave Mike an inquiring glance.

"He wants to show you something," the female deputy informed him. "He's in the evidence room."

Mike was tired of waiting and concerned at the commotion. He wondered if it had something to do with him. He wasn't going to wait around to find out. When the desk clerk disappeared into the adjoining room to see what was going on, Mike slipped out of the building unobserved and started jogging back down the highway. He didn't plan on stopping until he got to Boston.

Chapter 23

The sheriff had put an all points bulletin out on Mike Russo, who was wanted in connection with the murder of Linda Reynolds of Newton, Massachusetts. A knife with the victim's blood, and matching the wounds on the victim's body, had been found under the seat of the suspect's pickup truck.

The sheriff couldn't believe Russo had been in custody and had simply walked out of the station. It would be hell to pay if the state police or the media got wind of what happened. After berating his deputy for not locking Mike Russo up after discovering the murder weapon in his possession, he sent out every available car to scour the area. It wasn't his fault but he would get the blame. By the time he had realized what was going on, Russo had disappeared into the night. He notified the staties and Boston cops, but did not mention his office's error.

If the suspect was on foot or in his vehicle anywhere within a fifty-mile radius, they would find him.

Mike had left the Sheriff's office with intentions of hitching all the way into Boston, but realized he wouldn't get far hiking on the road. He had no place to go. His old apartment had already been rented and they would certainly look for him at Jessica's. He thought of Richard's and Sam's, but even if he could somehow get there, they'd probably call the cops as soon as they saw him. After all, they all heard Linda say he had killed her in a previous life. Then she turns up dead. Mike doubted whether any of them would believe he wasn't the killer.

No, he couldn't drag any of his friends into this. He had to handle it alone. He had to find Jessica. She was his only alibi. He remembered her room in the attic and the trap door in the ceiling. Perhaps that would be a good place to hide until he could figure out what to do. He cut across a couple fields and an orchard, following wooded trails until he was peeking over a hedge in back of Jessica's small carriage house. It was quiet and dark. Her car was still nowhere in sight.

He crawled across the yard on his belly. Making sure no one was inside waiting for him, he climbed through a rear window into the house. He knew all that combat training would come in handy someday. He just never thought it would be like this.

Grabbing Hanna's silver spider pendent from the kitchen table, he made his way up to the second floor and studied the inconspicuous door in the hallway ceiling. With any luck at all they wouldn't see it. After all, he had never noticed it before Jessica got stuck up there. He pulled down the trapdoor and slipped up the wooden ladder, closing it tight behind him.

Groping his way in the darkness to Jessica's small oak altar, he fumbled around until he had one of the candles lit. It cast a flickering glow on the steep paneling of the ceiling. Her bags of protective crystals and herbs were on the small alter, along with her other tools and material. Mike felt a sudden surge of adrenalin when he remembered what had happened in the kitchen with Jessica. Had it been real or was it all a dream? Did these magical implements really have such power? Did he really do what he thought he had with the rotating pillar of light? Was it real or just his imagination, a hallucination or a fact? His musings were interrupted by the sound of someone entering the house. He blew out the candle and lay on the floor in the darkness listening.

Sheriff McGuire decided to visit Jessica's residence himself since Russo was currently living there, bringing along the errant deputy, Jim Boone.

"You say she hasn't been home tonight?" asked the sheriff. They had been talking about Jessica and her whereabouts.

"No. Russo said she went into Boston and would be home late, but it's after midnight now. I'm worried about her. That guy was acting really strange tonight."

"And where'd you say you found him?"

"He was walking down one-eleven about two miles from the Carriage House apartments."

"Near where the old Stillman house used to be?"

"Right, until a couple of nights ago."

"Hmm," said the sheriff, scratching behind his ear. "We'd better have some of the boys check the woods back behind there in the morning."

They arrived at Jessica's house and pulled into the drive. Walking up the gravel path, they knocked on the door. No one answered. After knocking a few more times, they let themselves in. Jim pushed the door shut behind him too hard, and it closed with a loud bang.

"Damn it, Jim!" said the Sheriff. "Why don't you announce to the whole neighborhood we're here. Be careful, will you."

"Sorry, Chief," said the bumbling deputy. "I didn't realize how easy it'd close."

"Well, keep it down," ordered McGuire.

He called out softly, "Hello, Miss Wilson. Are you here? It's Sheriff McGuire."

"Doesn't seem to be anyone home," he whispered to his deputy. "Why don't you take a look around outside, check the grounds. I'll look around in here."

He turned on all the lights and went through each room one by one, making notes. He took special note of the magical paraphernalia he found in the kitchen. Jim returned from outside as the sheriff was heading up the stairs.

"Nothing out there," said the deputy. "Find anything in here?"

"No. Look's like they're into witchcraft or something." The sheriff pointed to the objects on the table.

"Must be that Russo character," said Jim. "Jessica wasn't into anything like that when I knew her. Come to think of it, some of his friends said he was into the occult. You don't suppose he's done anything to her, do you?"

"I hope not," replied McGuire. "I sure as hell hope not."

They moved through the rest of the house. Jim Boone helped search the upstairs rooms, lingering longer than necessary near Jessica's bureau where some of her finer undergarments peeked out of the opened drawer. He missed the trapdoor to the attic, absorbed as he was in thoughts of Jessica in her underwear.

Hanna's old house had been deserted a little over a year, ever since Hanna was moved to the rest home. It had been on the market most of this time, but the realtor was having trouble selling it. Even as a fixer-upper it left a lot to be desired. A sagging porch, peeling walls, and a leaking roof were the least of its problems. It needed plumbing and a new well as badly as it needed windows and a paint job. Small furry things had long since made their home in the attic.

Hanna's house was no longer unoccupied, however, although the real-estate agent, had she known, would have been surprised. Its new occupant sat by the front window in a straight-backed chair staring out at the silent night. She would have preferred her old rocker, the one her granddaddy made, with its slow, rhythmic back and forth motion. But one did the best one could with what one had on hand.

Hanna's front porch, covered with lilacs and overhanging willow trees, was hardly visible from the street. A small stream ran behind the place to meander in a field full of tall, yellow grass before disappearing into a wood of young birch. Behind the stream, neat rows of squat apple trees marched in line up a round hill. Jessica's stomach growled, but she ignored it.

Something had changed. It had not happened all at once, but slowly, one thought at a time until the thoughts were those of another. The 'I' she held in her mind now referred to a different identity, one who did not yet have a name, but was certainly no longer Jessica Wilson.

The silent struggle raging in her soul had ended, as all traces of Jessica were snuffed out. Her eyes became hard and narrow. Her lips tightened in a thin, cruel smile. Her bony hands gripped the arms of the chair until her knuckles turned white like her hair now was. She stared out the window, projecting her mind far beyond the confines of the small patch of lawn she looked on, out to where her victims waited.

Richard hadn't washed or shaved in days. He had woken up in the back of his car disorientated and drowsy after trying to break into his wife's parent's house. He couldn't remember exactly what had happened since then, but he had managed to get away in any case. At first, the attempted break-in caused a bee-hive of activity, as busy cops and eager state troopers arrived on the scene, but soon things quieted down. No one suspected it was him and he had managed to stay out of sight.

A few days later, he parked his car in the train depot at the other end of town and walked to Sara's parents' neighborhood about a mile away. He knew the area from the many summer weekends they had spent visiting. They used to wade in the river by the side of the house. It was a secluded, wooded neighborhood with the houses wide apart and few between. Richard could easily observe the place from the woods across the street or at the back of the house without being seen.

He found a sheltered spot on the opposite side of the road and staked-out the place. His caution was well founded, for a state police car showed up while he was watching. He wondered vaguely if he had been recognized, though it really didn't matter. He couldn't have cared less if the whole state was after him. His only concern was to get his hands on his wife's throat. He'd sit here as long as necessary to teach her a lesson, and no power on earth could stop him.

Several cars came and went while he sat there, focused on the object of his intent. No longer forgetful or wavering, no longer doubtful or confused, he was full of purpose.

All that day, no one left or entered the house. As night fell, another state police car pulled up in front of the home and parked. For some reason, they decided to stay all night, and were uncomfortably close to his hiding place. Crawling deeper into the woods, he succeeded in crossing the street unseen several yards behind them. Then he moved through the woods to the back of the house where the river flowed through a patch of trees. There he stayed, observing the house through the night.

Richard was unaware of the passing hours, or the discomfort and hunger that would have normally distracted him. His eyes didn't grow tired. He hardly blinked. An energy and focus he had never known before possessed him. His eyes were riveted on the backdoor of his in-laws' house as if he wanted to burn holes in the white-painted siding.

He hadn't eaten in days. The last full night's rest he had was his last night in jail. Shortly after daybreak, he curled up in a ball and fell asleep, more animal than human, a primitive carnivore hunting its prey with cunning patience and single-minded purpose, like a raptor.

Sarah was again oblivious of her surroundings. She sat in her room and stared at the wall. What lucidity she'd had, had not lasted long. By the time the doctor arrived to verify her miraculous recovery, she had already lapsed into a catatonic state even more severe than her prior condition. There was nothing they could do but wait and see if things would improve on their own. They had no idea what was wrong with her, or that it was her husband who had tried to break in, and was only a few hundred yards away.

Miles away in his Jamaica Plain's home, Sam was back in the throes of his personal agony. His medications no longer worked. Whatever temporary relief the drugs had given him from his affliction had long since ceased. Now he lay in his filthy covers and alternated between bouts of the shivers and rounds of the sweats, as his face was being eaten before his eyes. With his renewed discomfort came the terrible thoughts of vengeance.

In his delirium he again sought the cause of his malady, the source of his sickness, someone to blame it on. Again, Sam played back the events of the past few months. Again, all fingers pointed at Mike. It all began after seeing Mike. It got worse on each visit with Mike. All of them who had visited him were either sick or dead. There was no other explanation. Mike had to be the cause of their problems. He and that witch, his new girlfriend, must have put a curse on them. The thought made Sam's blood boil. He was not normally a violent person, but he wasn't going to stand by and watch Mike Russo kill them all one by one. No, he was going to do something about it if it was the last thing he did. But not now. Now all he could do now was roll over and vomit onto the floor, moaning like a dying dog while his blind wife lay in darkness in a tub of warm water.

Chapter 24

Mike was twelve years old again. He knew he was twelve because he was waiting for his father to come home with his brand new red Schwinn, 3-speed bike. His dad had promised it to him for his birthday if his grades were good this year in school, and Mike had gotten all A's and B's, his best grades ever.

He had forgone a party with his friends so he could have a new bike, which he had been anxiously anticipating for days. His dad called from the store to say he was on his way. That had been an hour ago. Where could he be?

He looked out the window and watched the cars go by, waiting for the familiar profile of his father's secondhand Buick to pull up. The passersby, who all seemed strange, with sharp features and black beady eyes, stared in at him as they walked by in groups and alone. The cars zoomed back and forth at incredible speeds, despite of the number of people walking along the side of the road as if to a fair.

Suddenly, he saw his dad's big black Buick come around the corner and head up the street, going impossibly fast, much too fast for the road. He'll never stop in time, worried Mike. He watched in frozen horror as his dad's car slammed into another vehicle as he tried to turn and stop at the last minute. The pre-owned Buick drove up the back of the other car and flipped over on its side, sliding down the highway in a shower of sparks. It then turned over on its top and burst into flames. Mike watched in dismay as the driver, a man who looked ridiculously like his father, waved to him as the flames consumed him. Mike waved back through the window. Suddenly the car exploded and was blown twenty feet straight up in the air.

Mike woke with a start, lying on the attic floor, his heart beating rapidly, drenched in sweat. It took him a moment to remember where he was. In his exhaustion, he had fallen asleep while listening to the men below. He recalled just enough of the dream to plunge him into deep depression. He seldom thought about the day his father died. It hadn't happened exactly like in the dream, right before his eyes, but he had been waiting for his father to bring his present when he died in a car accident. His mother and relatives had shielded him from most of it, but he knew enough to realize it had changed his life forever.

Mike listened intently with his ear to the floor, but could hear nothing. All was quiet. The house appeared to be empty. He heard what sounded like doors shutting and engines starting outside. They must just be leaving, he realized.

He assumed it was the police. Luckily, no one noticed the trapdoor in the ceiling. It was still night outside. Mike lay in the dark, listening. Suddenly the phone started ringing and didn't stop.

The ringing was incessant. Whoever it was, wasn't taking no for an answer. Mike wondered if it could be Jessica. That thought motivated him to open the trapdoor an inch and peek out. All was quiet except the persistent sound of the phone. He opened the door a little wider and waited - still nothing. The phone continued to clamor. Gaining courage, Mike opened the door all the way and descended the small ladder. The phone hadn't stopped ringing for the past ten minutes. Whoever it was wasn't going to hang-up until someone answered.

Mike went into Jessica's bedroom and picked it up.

"Hello," he said, hesitantly.

There was heavy static on the other end of the line, as if it were a short-wave radio rather than a modern telephone. Mike could just make out a man's voice through the white noise, a voice at once familiar and odd at the same time.

"I've got it," said the voice, in a loud whisper, which kept fading in and out. "I've got your bike, Mike. I'll be home shortly. I'm on my way. I've got your bike. Happy birthday."

Then the voice became conspiratorial, hardly audible over the static. "Careful son. Be careful. Look for the meadowlark," it whispered.

Mike tried to gulp in air but none came. He tried to speak but had no voice. He tried to move, but stood frozen to the spot. It was his father's voice coming through the headset. Faint, disjointed, drowned out by hissing, but his dad's voice all the same, distant and fading. He was stunned to tears. Finally, he was able to choke out something between sobs.

"Dad! Dad! Is that you?"

"No, it's me, you snot rag," said another voice over the phone, this one harsh and feminine, grating like fingers on a chalkboard. "You can't stop me. I'm going to get your friends one by one, then I'm going to come for you, and there's nothing you can do about it."

"Who is this?" Mike yelled into phone. "What do you want?"

"Why don't you ..."

White noise swallowed the terrible voice then turned to a dial tone. Mike took the receiver away from his ear and looked at it as if it were a loaded weapon. Was he going crazy? Hadn't the phone just rung steady for twenty minutes? Hadn't he just heard his father's voice? And whose was that last one?

He sat on the side of Jessica's bed trying to decide what to do. Jessica obviously wasn't coming home. He was safe here for the time being, but couldn't hide out forever. He was sure they were looking for him. The only person who could clear him of Linda's murder was missing herself. He had to concentrate. He had to assume that what was going on was real, the voices, the apparitions, all of it. He had to find a way out of this nightmare back to the world of the sane.

He peeked out of the bedroom window down onto the rear drive. The sun was just coming up on a gray drizzling day. He could see the sheriff's car parked across the road. What had the voices said? Was his father trying to tell him something, warn him? How seriously could he take that? Be careful. Why sure, don't need to tell me that. What about a meadowlark? Look for the meadowlark? What is that about? Riddles upon riddles and Michael hated riddles.

The second voice, was that the voice of Jeanette Stillman, talking to him like his father from beyond the grave, on the phone no less?

Mike had heard stories of the recently deceased calling loved ones soon after they'd departed. He had always chalked it up to malicious pranksters with a sadistic streak. Is there something about telephone wires and electrons that facilitate communication with the dead? Was it true what the psychics say, that to understand the living you had to talk to the dead? Mike pondered all these thoughts as he sat alone in the gloom.

After creeping down to the kitchen and grabbing a few items and some food, he went back up to the attic. He had made a peanut butter and jam sandwich, which he ate as he strode about the attic room looking at things of interest. In one corner of the room was an old roller desk. There were letters and envelopes stacked neatly in its nooks and crannies. One of them caught his attention. On further inspection he discovered it was from Hanna, Jessica's old friend. It must have been a few years old, because the return address wasn't the Rosebud Retirement Home where she had lived when she died, but her family home on 737 Meadowlark Lane, in the next town over. Meadowlark Lane!

Mike stared at the envelope in disbelief, bringing it nearer, then farther, to verify his eyes weren't playing tricks on him. What a coincidence. That's the last word his father had said to him over the phone. He brought the envelope to Jessica's low oak table and studied it under the light. By lunchtime he had found Meadowlark lane on a local roadmap and formed his plan.

Sam was living in his own private hell. It consumed his every waking moment. It made noxious his every breath. Life had become a horrible thing to be shunned each morning for as long as possible. He laid in bed doped up on mega-doses of pain pills and nerve medication for as long as possible, not bothering to move for most of his bodily functions. But even he could stand the stench no longer.

He slithered out of bed like a legless creature and rolled across the floor to his hands and knees. It took an eternity for him to raise the rest of the way to his feet, where he stood swaying for a full minute.

The disease was spreading again. He could see it on his mouth and cheeks, the pestilent sores and decaying flesh; feel it creeping under his skin. He had it in him. It swam in his blood.

Well, he wasn't going to go without a fight. The son of Stanley P. Kelly was not going to just lie down and die. No, he'd take a few with him, beginning with the one who started it all, the conniving little murderer, Mike Russo.

He dressed himself haphazardly in sweatpants and a pull-over, and stole out of the house to his Volvo, which had sat in the drive, unused for weeks.

As he pulled into the street, he thought about what he was going to do. He visualized both he and Mike going off a bridge into the river, or over a cliff to die together in a fiery crash. It was the only thing that gave him comfort. He almost smiled to himself until he happened to glance in the rearview mirror and saw his hideously mutilated face. Wincing and shuddering, he quickly tore his gaze from the image. Tears of anguish welled-up in his eyes so that he could barely see as he drove out of the city westward towards Route 2.

Jeanette looked out at the dismal day. Her back was sore. Her legs were cramped and fallen asleep, but she didn't care. She was concentrating. She hadn't felt this good, this strong in years, ten years to be exact.

She had lain so long undisturbed, so long without knowing, that she had forgotten what it felt like to be alive. Something had tugged her back from the void and she found herself running in the woods again. Then next thing she knew, she was among a group of strangers. Young punks is what they were, thinking they could fool around with spirits and such, so close to her home, the house she and her granddaddy built.

If only those darned town folk hadn't gone and meddled things could have gone on the way they'd done for years. She needed young'uns to perform her evil rites and spells, their blood and innards, their eyes and tongues. She'd birth 'em, raise 'em, and kill 'em, just like chickens, with no one the wiser. That was up until that last time with Maxine and her seven little piglets.

That wasn't bad enough, but these young fools insisted on violating her home, her sanctuary, first their mangy dog, then one alone, then the whole lot of them. Well, she showed them. She hadn't forgotten how to curse and conger, even if she had no corporeal form. She still had Mind and plenty of Identity to keep her going for some time yet. Now she had a body as well and it felt wonderful.

Granted it was pretty near a full time job keeping this one in line. Damn, this girl was rebellious. Not like young women in her day. No, this one would make a terrible wife. However, she made an excellent receptacle, young and healthy. She could do quite a bit to this body and it would keep on ticking. Now, however, Jeanette was just sitting and concentrating.

While she was controlling this form she was not able to affect the others as she had done before, all of them at the same time. That is except for that Russo character. Most of his problems were his own doing, not like the others. Now she had all she could do to control this one and reach out to the others one at a time.

She sat by the window, concentrating on her eating-away spell, summoning her victim to her. She held an oddly human-shaped piece of wax in her left hand, which she was whittling away at with the large knife. As she did, she sang softly to herself.

"Come to me with your pretty face.
Follow me into disgrace.
For to me you come in haste.
So I can eat your lovely face."

She chuckled to herself hoarsely and spat on the floor as she looked at her work with a satisfied grin. She dug the knife's sharp point into the middle of the humanlike figure's face and spoke again.

"Come to me, Sammy? I have something for you."

"No, sir, we haven't heard anything yet," said the sheriff to the chief inspector of the state police, who was yelling at him over the phone. "Yes, sir, I understand that, but we... I... Yes, sir, I'll... Yes, sir, I'll get right on it."

He hung up by banging the receiver down, and turned to his deputy.

"Well, Jim, you've really done it this time. My ass is grass because of your stupidity. But I'll tell you what. I'm not going down alone. You're going down with me."

"Aw, chief, it wasn't my fault. I tried to tell you all along that he was involved in that girl's murder. I was the first one to question him. I brought him in. I found the murder weapon."

"And you let him get away!" The sheriff went on, thinking out loud. "The Boston cops say the blood on the knife you found matches the murdered woman's, but they haven't found any of Russo's prints at the murder scene."

"So, all that proves is he wore gloves or wiped his prints clean. We've got the murder weapon."

"Yeah, that's another thing that bothers me," mused the sheriff. "Why would he just stash the knife like that under his seat? He had plenty of chances to get rid of it. For Christ's sake, he could have ditched it in the woods the night you found him. Instead, he conveniently leaves it in his truck for you to find."

"Maybe he's not too smart. Have you heard anything about Jessica Wilson yet?" the deputy inquired. "I'm very concerned about her."

"We've got an all points bulletin out for her. We've questioned all her friends and relatives, but there's still no word."

"I hope he hasn't done anything to her," said Jim, voicing his worst fears.

"Let's hope not. In the meantime, just keep your mind on your job and find Russo."

"Where do you suppose he could be?" asked the deputy.

"I don't know. They're keeping an eye on his mother's place in Boston, as well as his friends, although they don't seem that keen on him any more. We're watching Jessica's house and his old apartment. We've done a thorough sweep of the woods behind the place. So here's what I want you to do, Jim. Get a list of the guys he used to work with, and anybody he's worked for recently, and start asking around if they've seen him. If you get a hunch, let me know and we can check it out. We can make deputies if we need them. OK, you think you can handle that?"

"Sure," said the deputy. "Sure I can." Deputy Jim Boone could do that and a whole lot more. He was nothing if not tenacious, as his ex-girlfriend would attest. Now he had his sights on Mike Russo, escaped murderer – and he would find him if he had to search every country lane and backwoods trail in the county.

Richard woke up from time to time to stare sullenly at the farmhouse across the road. Every now and then he'd forget where he was and why he was there. Then it'd come back to him, like a half forgotten thought will bubble up and be gone again. At this moment, he could not quite remember.

He knew it had something to do with his wife and that he had to be careful, but that was all. He was dirty and unshaven, the area around him littered with his waste. He hadn't eaten a real meal in days, yet he was loath to leave his spot. All he knew was that he had to wait, and that his waiting would be rewarded. So he waited.

The dampness of the ground seeped up his back and down his legs. The drizzling rain soaked his hair and trousers. He hunched down under his thin jacket and closed his eyes. Then he pictured killing Sarah and it all came back to him.

Chapter 25

Mike waited until darkness before sneaking out of the rear window of Jessica's house, the same way he had entered the night before. He knew the general direction he needed to go and had worked out how to get there, but first he had to get off the property and down the road without being seen.

The ground was wet, the air damp. He hadn't crawled ten feet through the grass and bushes before he was soaking wet. He didn't worry about the chill night air, however. He knew he'd warm up soon enough.

Flipping over the low stone wall that abutted the property, he moved on his hands and knees along the fence through the newly fallen leaves toward the highway, which he crossed some way below the parked sheriff's car. Then he made his way along the highway in the direction of Meadowlark Lane, staying well off the road.

There would be no moon this night. Thick, dark storm clouds, which threatened to unload their contents at any minute, hid whatever light there was. Mike moved at a slow trot, double-time up the highway. He jogged across fields and small patches of woods, through backyards and along country roads, in a southwesterly direction for some time.

It was getting late, close to ten. He had long since burned off the chill and was now working up a sweat. He stopped to take a drink of water from his canteen and looked at his watch with his penlight. He wasn't sure where Meadowlark Lane was, but he knew the area. He'd find it if it took him all night. His main concern was that no one found him first.

Mike got lost several times and had to backtrack across some farmer's field more than once during the long evening. Finally, around two AM, he found the street he was looking for. The sky still hadn't unleashed its pending storm, but it was threatening.

Finding the house at the end of the lane, he observed it carefully from behind a fence. The fence enclosed what used to be a well-groomed backyard, but was now a field of long grass and overgrown hedges. A small stream meandered and bubbled behind him. Trees and shrubs engulfed the house like moss covering a rock. As far as Mike could tell, the place was deserted. A lonely 'For Sale' sign was stuck crookedly by the side of the road in front of the drive.

There was something obviously important about this place, important enough for his father to mention it from beyond the grave, or at least that's how Mike figured it following the bizarre logic of the day.

Perhaps Jessica was hiding here. After all, it was Hanna's old home. Mike pondered these and many other thoughts as he surveyed the house and surroundings from his hiding place. As he did, the sky opened up in a steady downpour of large, straight drops that fell like lead pellets. After he was sure there was no one around, he decided to go in. If there was something here, he certainly wouldn't find it standing out in the rain.

Darting across the overgrown yard, he crouched in the shadows behind the building. In just that short sprint across the uncut grass, he got drenched, his clothes soaked through to the skin. Pressing himself against the house, as far under the eve as he could go, he looked around for a way in.

He moved along the back, trying one window after another, while the rain pelted his face, but they were all locked. Wiping the water from his eyes, he peered into the darkness and continued his search for a way in. He moved to the side of the house, where he noticed a small, ankle-high window partially covered with grass, leading to the basement. It was slightly ajar. Bending down, he pushed it wider, swinging it down to create an opening just large enough for him to squeeze through.

He stepped onto a cement floor, which was cluttered with old furniture and boxes. Only the faintest light filtered in through the small, slanted window. Mike wished he had Jessica's crystals or the spider scarab, anything, but he had brought no protection, just the damp clothes clinging to his back. He'd forgotten all about magic and witchcraft, as if he had never known it existed. He hadn't been doing it that long. It wasn't yet a part of his nature. In his moment of trial he fell back on those lessons he had learned in the Marines, in the jungles of Nam, those years of training and drilling and fighting. That's what he was doing now, marching into battle, crawling into harm's way. He understood that. His body responded to that. There was no doubt or uncertainty in the hard reality of war. But who was the enemy?

He felt his way across the cluttered basement to the stairs and moved up them softly, feeling his way as he did. Each footfall echoed and creaked through the house like a public announcement. He stopped and listened after each one. Except for the splash of water on the awnings outside, there was not a sound.

He inched open the cellar door. What was he looking for? What did he hope to find by coming here? At a minimum, it might turn out to be a good place to hide, at least until the real-estate agent stopped by. He stepped from the basement into what had once been a kitchen. An old stove and empty ice-box stood along the wall. A rusted sink crouched in the dark, glinting faintly in a light of unknown origin. Looking around the room, he began to edge along the wall toward another door leading to the front of the house.

Going through the door, he walked into a long, low room. The old hardwood floors shined in the half-light with a gloss only years of repeated waxing could create. Hanna had raised three boys in this house and met the needs of a demanding man. She hadn't entertained much, but she kept that house immaculate. It was still fragrant with the scent of pine and lemon even after all these years.

The floor moaned beneath him as he inched along the wall, moving toward the wide entrance to the next room, ever closer to the front of the house, which he could not quite see. He tried to keep his mind clear and free of thoughts, focused on the moment, breathing slowly and evenly. The rain sizzled and popped on the sidings and windowpanes. That and the sound of his heartbeat were the only things he heard.

He moved to the archway and peered in. The faint glow of a street lamp illuminated the scene with a diffused light. Near the far wall, silhouetted in the center window, was a woman seated in a straight-back chair with her back to him. She had long hair and looked familiar. It was Jessica. She sat there stiffly.

Mike let out a cry of recognition and stepped into the room.

"Jessica, what are you doing here?" he exclaimed. "I've been looking all over for you. Are you OK?"

The figure didn't move, but continued to stare out the window at the night. Maybe she didn't hear him. He walked across the room softly, as if afraid to wake her.

"Jessica?" he said, walking up to her. He could see her profile in the light of the window, only three feet away. She sat rigid and motionless. Mike became alarmed.

"Jessica," he said again, and reached out his hand tentatively to touch her shoulder.

Standing up suddenly, she flung back the chair, which fell over with a crash and slid across the floor. Mike jumped back in fright and would have fallen backward if he hadn't hit the wall. He yelled.

"Jesus, Jessica! What are you doing?"

The person staring back at him in the half-light of the window looked like a caricature of his friend. She had Jessica's general features, build, and eyes, same recognizable appearance, but it was altered somehow, gaunter and drawn, meaner. Her hair appeared to have turned white. Mike stood against the wall in shock.

Her thin lips curled back in a wide, malicious grin, below cruel predatory eyes.

She tried to talk, but only a hoarse croak came out, as if she were just learning how to use her vocal chords. She moved toward him threateningly.

"Meddler," she croaked out.

The voice coming out of Jessica's mouth was raspy and harsh, like someone who hadn't talked in a dozen years. It sounded as if she were throwing her words across the floor at him. Mike stood frozen to the spot. He didn't know what he had expected to find, but it certainly wasn't this. He regretted that he had brought no talisman or weapon.

"Fool," she hissed, finally gaining full control of her host's vocal apparatus. "To think you could tangle with me with your trinkets and common-knowledge spells, I who have shed so much innocent blood for the dark lord!"

Mike started edging along the wall toward the far door.

She started speaking to him in another tongue that he didn't recognize. It sounded ancient and malevolent.

"She's mine now," she said finally in English.

When she said this, the door Mike had been inching toward slammed shut with a bang.

Gaining his courage, he laughed and said, "Banging doors again? That's about as old as you are, you hag."

She hissed and snarled back at him, moving menacingly in his direction.

Suddenly, a tall figure ran down the staircase that descended along the far wall. With a rush, it ran across the room right at Michael, a large knife in its hand. The hard soles of its shoes clamored against the polished wood floor.

Mike barely had time to put up his hands before the figure was on him. Even in the dark, Mike's quick reflexes allowed him to catch his attacker's arm as he flailed the sharp knife at his head. Holding the assailant at bay, he stared into his face, or what was left of it - cavernous nose, hollow cheeks, sore-covered lips. Pitted eyes stared back at him. It was a hideous deformity even a monster would abhor. Mike screamed in terror and the shock of recognition. It was his friend, Sam.

Without thinking, Mike hooked his leg behind the attacker's and pushed - an old trick he had learned in basic training. Sam stumbled backward and fell onto his back. Mike ran past him and out the slamming door. As he ran, he could hear the thing that was no longer Jessica cackling after him like an angry crow.

"Run, fool. You can't hide."

Mike bolted out of the house and down the road as fast as he could. He didn't care if the whole police force found him. He wanted to get as far from Meadowlark Lane as possible. Sprinting across the same fields and yards he had come through earlier that night, he ran back toward Jessica's house, shivering with fear.

He wasn't sure what he had just witnessed. Jessica possessed by an evil spirit? Sam horribly deformed and trying to kill him? Was any of this real? Maybe he needed a double dose of Thorazine and a nice padded cell.

Mike ran until he could run no more, throwing caution to the wind. He could feel the hot breath of his pursuers' right behind him, that hideous faceless thing that used to be Sam and the thing that was no longer Jessica. When he finally collapsed gasping for breath by the side of the road and looked behind him, there was nothing but the empty highway and the wind.

As he lay in dirt trying to get his breath back, a pair of headlights flashed behind him. To Mike's dismay, someone shined a search-light on him. Too spent and far-gone to respond, he crouched there helpless as an injured animal. A flashing blue light told him his luck had run out. By sheer dumb luck Jim Boone had found him again, emerging on the side of the road just as suddenly as he had disappeared.

The deputy could hardly believe his good fortune. A whole day and night had gone by without a word about Jessica or the suspect. Everyone had given up, figuring Russo had somehow left the area, but Jim knew better. He knew he was somewhere close by. Now he turns up not far from where he found him the night before.

He got out of the car and drew his magnum from its holster.

"Stay where you are," he barked in a voice edged with panic. "Get down on your stomach. Now!"

Mike did as he was told.

"Put your arms behind your back," yelled the deputy. "Now! Do it!"

Mike complied. He was rewarded with a foot in the back of the neck and a knee in the small of his back. Then his arms were yanked behind him with such force it almost dislocated his shoulder.

"Easy Jim," he huffed in pain. "I haven't done anything. Sam Kelly just attacked me. He and Jessica are back at Hanna's old house."

Jim, having about all he could take of this creep's whining, brought the butt of his gun down on the back of the suspect's head with a crack. When he finished cuffing the half-conscious fugitive, he called the office for backup. He would redeem himself and then some with this one. He'd be the hero of the day for sure.

As he started back toward his prisoner, Jessica suddenly appeared out of nowhere.

"Hi, Jimbo," she said seductively. "How you doing, big boy?"

"Jessica! What are you doing here?" he answered in surprise. "We've been looking all over for you."

Before he had time to utter another word, Sam came up behind him and slugged him over the head with a rock. The deputy went down hard.

"Kill him," hissed the thing that was no longer Jessica, pointing to the fallen deputy. "Kill him. Now!"

Sam, who no longer had a mind of his own, picked up the deputy's gun and without hesitating shot him twice in the head, point blank. It felt good to pull the trigger, to put someone out of their miserable existence. What he was about to do would feel even better. He turned the gun on Michael who still lay semi-conscious and handcuffed by the side of the road, and was about to shoot, when Jessica stepped in front him.

"No, Samuel! You don't want to shoot him. You want to shoot yourself. You want to put yourself out of your misery. You want to die. You long for death!"

Sam blinked at the forms lying around him with a blank expression and put the gun to his head. All he could hear was Jeanette's voice telling him what to do. He had no will but her words. He pulled the trigger.

Jeanette looked at the two dead bodies with satisfaction. This would work out better than she could have hoped. With the fool wanted for a double homicide and killing an officer, he wouldn't be bothering her any more. She'd be able to concentrate on the others without further interruption. She could hear sirens approaching in the distance. Pulling the keys to the handcuffs from the dead deputy's pocket, she un-cuffed the fugitive, placing the gun in his hand. Then she disappeared into the woods.

The depression that had been Judy's constant companion for the last three months returned like a familiar house guest. Her blindness wasn't a passive thing. It was a living scourge that devoured her very soul. She could bear it no longer, the pain, the loneliness, the sorrow. She would end it tonight.

She had called for Sam in her distress, but he hadn't answered. She was totally alone. She couldn't call on God. She had put all her faith in the occult and it had turned out to be a fragile crutch. Not even Madame Zarloff had been able to help her. 'One must live out one's karma, dear,' was all the old woman would say. Well, here's one to karma, thought Judy, downing the shot of whiskey. She wouldn't stop this time until the bath flow red with her blood.

Hot water filled the tub as she got undressed. She felt it occasionally with her toes, adjusting the taps as necessary to keep it just hot enough to tolerate. She pinched the razor lovingly between her fingertips as she felt her way into the scalding water.

Sleep, she thought, forgetful sleep, not the black terror-filled void she had been closing her eyes to these past weeks, dreading to open them again; the exhausted half-sleep of the battlefield. She sank back in the tub and closed her eyes.

Almost falling to sleep, she shook her head and sat up quickly, splashing water as she did. Her head was spinning. She wanted to die in peace. Now she had all she could do not to get sick. When she got her equilibrium back, she realized she had dropped the razor and the water was starting to overflow. She shut off the faucet and felt for the blade at the bottom of the bath. She almost had to laugh at her blundering attempt at suicide, but she wasn't exactly in a laughing mood. Instead, she gritted her teeth and searched the bottom of the tub with deadly determination.

Halfway across the state, Richard was on the move. The dark night and rain would cover him. He no longer had any doubts about what he had to do. It didn't matter if he had to kill her whole family and the entire police force he was going to take care of the cheating whore once and for all.

He stole across the street. He still had the knife he had taken four days ago from his own kitchen, a large one for carving meat that his in-laws had given them one Christmas. Richard's clothes were torn and filthy. His face was haggard and bearded. His eyes looked bloodshot and sunken, but he moved with a purpose, silent and deadly.

Making his way to the back of the house, he tried the rear entrance. It was locked. He listened carefully with his ear to the door. All was dark and quiet. Nothing stirred inside. The lights had been off for hours. The brother had gone back to school days ago.

Rain hissed and pinged off every conceivable object - the porch, the roof, windowpanes, car hoods and lawn chairs, the trees - making a sound that could have drowned out a rifle shot. He jimmied the long blade of the knife up and down between the latch and the door frame. Within minutes he had it open, and slipped into the small kitchen. Standing in the shadows, he waited for someone to scream or turn on the light, but everything was still.

He knew her room was the first one at the top of the stairs, and that her parents slept downstairs off one of the front rooms. There was no one else in the house. He crept along the hallway toward the stairs, the knife tight in his hand, a mad glint in his eyes.

Richard's purpose blazed before him like a burning bush, his future as clear as a mountain view. Suddenly, he knew just what he had to do. The stiffness and fatigue in his bones and muscles left him as he moved quietly up the stairs. Thoughts of sexual infidelity and righteous vengeance coursed through his mind like torpedoes. Slowly, inexorably, he crept toward Sara's room, his knife quivering before him as if it had a life of its own.

Chapter 26

Mike woke up lying on his face in the rain. The terrible blinding pain in the back of his head made him sick to his stomach. It took him a few moments to remember what had happened and to realize his hands were no longer cuffed behind him. He tried raising his head and looking around, but the pain almost made him pass out again. Steadying himself, he brought his breathing under control. The rain splattering on his temple helped to bring him to. Again, he tried raising his head just enough to look around. What he saw made him sick to his stomach.

Jim Boone was lying on his back, his mouth and eyes open grotesquely wide. There were two gaping holes in his skull running red with blood. Mike swore in shock. Sitting up, he took in the scene. It was then that he noticed the second body, the faceless corpse of his friend Sam. He heard the sirens approaching up the highway. It only took him a few seconds to realize what had happened when he noticed the deputy's gun dangling from his own right hand. He threw it down and stumbled into the woods only moments before the sheriff and his men arrived.

Sprinting through the trees as fast as he could run, Mike ducked and dodged branches as they slapped and scratched his face. He could hear what sounded like a hundred men crashing through the woods after him. The sizzling rain came down so hard it penetrated the trees like bullets, turning the ground Mike ran on into a muddy quagmire.

This part of the woods was familiar to Mike, even in the darkness, and he was able to stay somewhat on the trails and ahead of his pursuers, but he had no idea exactly where he was going. All he knew was that he had to get out of these woods and away from the police. Mike was sure they would think he was a serial murderer and cop killer. They would probably shoot him on sight. He didn't want to find out, and ran with another burst of speed through the trees.

Mike ran with his knees bent, his arms pumping at his sides, at a good clip. He could hear them a short distance behind. The rain pelted his face with large watery drops, hard as hail. It churned up the ground beneath his feet, making him slip and slide with each turn.

Hearing the crashing of tree branches somewhere ahead, and the yelling of determined men, he turned off the trail to his left. He moved through the underbrush, holding his arms in front of him for protection from the branches. He was running blindly. The thunder and lightning cracked around him like whiplashes.

Suddenly, he broke through the trees into a clearing and ran headlong into a low iron fence. At that moment, a brilliant flash of lightening lit the scene with an iridescent glaze. Mike recognized the place in the brief instant of light. It was the small family plot he had stumbled upon the last time he went walking with Hunter - the Stillman cemetery.

He stood in the torrential rain, staring at the small gravesite, which flickered into existence every minute or so when another lightning bolt jolted the air. The rain tore at the ground like claws, churning it into mire.

Jim Boone had not been one of Sheriff McGuire's favorite people, but the sight of the deputy lying there, so grievously murdered while doing his duty, almost made him want to scream. His men had never seen him this angry before as he organized them to hunt the fugitive down. He didn't have to tell them that they were to get the killer dead or alive. Jimbo lying opened-eyed in the rain said it all. Now they were moving through the woods with their pistols drawn and shotguns pumped, in teams of two, with vengeance in their hearts, searching through the torrential rains.

McGuire had separated from the rest of his men. He knew these woods better than anybody, having grown up not far from here. He had hiked, camped, and hunted in them long before any of these boys had been weaned. He knew exactly where the fugitive was heading. He decided to play his hunch and cut him off. Now Russo stood right in front of him like a prized buck. For a moment he considered just blowing him away, but knew how difficult it would be to explain a bullet in the back at point blank range.

The suspect didn't hear a thing as Sheriff McGuire crept up behind him, his gun drawn.

"Hold it right there," he yelled with a voice shaking with venom and rage. He couldn't get the picture of his dead deputy out of his mind.

Mike turned around slowly.

"Sheriff, it wasn't me," he said. "Sam Jenkins grabbed the gun. They struggled. It went off." Mike knew he couldn't tell him Jessica had ordered Sam to kill the deputy and then himself. They were going to have enough trouble believing his made up version, let alone the bizarre unbelievable truth.

"Shut up!" ordered the sheriff. "Jim had two bullets in the back of his head. You killed him execution style. Don't you dare move."

Just as he reached for his cuffs, a bolt of lighting zapped through the air to crash into a tree branch directly above them. The sound was deafening. There was a blinding flash and the limb came crashing down almost hitting the sheriff, who dodged away at the last moment, dropping his gun. Without thinking, Mike dove for the weapon.

McGuire, seeing Mike's intention, jumped toward it as well. They collided, tumbling over the low, wrought-iron fence into the small cemetery. The lightning cracked. The rain came down in torrents. They struggled amongst the lonely gravestones churning up the mud around them.

Mike tried to punch and beat the burly sheriff off of him, while the lawman clawed and choked and elbowed his opponent like a dirty wrestler. They rolled around in the mud as each strove against the other, digging deeper into the soggy ground cut with troughs and channels.

Soon both men were spent, but Mike, a bit younger, was starting to get the upper hand. He spun the larger man over onto his back and held him down. To his shock, another pair of arms was suddenly engulfing them. Bony, skinless arms were coming out of the ground. Then a skeletal head appeared with empty holes where eyes and nose should have been, a scraggly skull with long, flaring white hair and wide toothless jaws.

Mike jumped up in horror as a flash of lightning revealed the ghastly scene in all its grisly detail. Out of the ground, right beneath them, a body was rising and clinging to them as they fought. It still gripped the sheriff as Mike struggled away, and seemed to be pulling him down. For a moment he watched in fascinated horror, weighing the pros and cons of helping his adversary. But the dread of seeing someone being pulled under the mud by the skeletal arms was too much. Reaching down at the last moment, he grabbed McGuire's hand and pulled with all his might.

Back and forth he battled for the sheriff, who was now shrieking with terror as the bony hands clutched and pulled him. Finally, using the fence for leverage, Mike was able to yank the rotund man out of the mud, pulling the remains of Jeanette Stillman out with him. At that moment, the ground opened up into a huge sinkhole, swallowing everything within the confines of the small fence with a loud sucking sound, including Mike and the sheriff.

Jeanette sat in the attic of Jessica's cottage apartment, whose body she was occupying. A single red wax candle lit the room. She had a bloodstone in one hand and a sharp obsidian blade in the other. She was chanting, calling upon the dark spirits and malformed demons of the netherworld to do her bidding, calling on the souls of all the dead children she had sacrificed to the dark lord, to aid her.

She cut her host's thumb and pinched the blood into a bowl. It dripped in huge red droplets. Her power was rising with each fleeting minute, getting stronger, reaching out further. Already two of the meddlers were dead. One was at this moment sitting in a tub getting ready to slit her wrists. Another was dragging his screaming wife out of her bed by the hair, a butcher knife to her throat. The worst of the lot was at this moment a fugitive from the law, being chased through the woods by armed men and dogs, wanted for multiple homicides.

Not a bad night's work. But she wasn't done yet. She had plenty left to do, plenty of bodies to inhabit, children to murder, souls to steal. The thing that was no longer Jessica licked her lips and smiled a toothy grin. Yes, she had a lot left to do now that she was back.

Jessica's mind still fought her, but Jeanette's power was not to be denied. Jessica was now no more than a single compartment tucked away in the back of Jeanette's mind, almost out of conscious sight. Still, it was an effort to control her, and made it difficult for Jeanette to concentrate on the others. She moved her mind from one to the next like a time-sharing computer. In this way, she kept them all going inexorably toward their fates, all that is except Mike Russo. That fool was protected somehow. She didn't know how or by who, but someone or thing was sheltering him. Or was it something from within? She couldn't tell. Her curses and spells held no power over that one. Not that it mattered. He was his own worst curse, destined to self-destruct with no help at all.

She drew a large pentagram on the floor and raised her blood-bowl.

"Demons of the underworld," she intoned. "I bind you to my purpose. As lovers you will come to me. As suitors you will do my bidding. Like slaves, will you obey me! I bind you to me. I tie you to me!"

Dark storm clouds whirled above the house building to a great black towering height. The rain beat sideways against the windowpanes. The sound of the wind was like a wounded beast, howling in mortal pain. Jeanette spoke her curse into the night. Faster and faster came the words.

"Pull them down into the void. Engulf them in the pit, oh mighty one. Your power is mine! Oh great one. Oh Tammaz! oh Akitu! oh Zag! Ancient ones and demon masters, pull them down into the pit."

She saw the two men struggling in the mud and envisioned a swirling whirlpool sucking down all in its path, a twisting vortex that would swallow her enemies and drag them to her dark master. But something was fighting her. Something was striving against her as she fought to concentrate her spell, distracting her just enough to give someone a fighting chance.

Richard pulled Sara by the arm behind him, dragging her through the wet underbrush and bushes in the woods across from her parents' house. He had crept up to her room and snatched her before anyone in the house could stop him. Now he had her and they weren't ever going to get her back.

Sara had lapsed back into total forgetfulness, stuck in the ignorance of the moment with no past or future. She wasn't sure what was happening to her, but she knew she didn't like it. She thrashed about trying to get away from the mean man who was dragging her behind him. He was hurting her.

Richard, on the other hand, knew exactly what he had to do, but he needed privacy. What he was about to do had to be done far from the prying eyes of strangers. She had made surprisingly little noise, luckily for her parents, who had they woken up would have surely been murdered. They would know soon enough, however, that their daughter had been taken. The police would be notified, and all hell would break loose. He wanted to be far away by then.

Richard couldn't have articulated any of this. All he knew was that he wanted to teach the bitch a lesson. She was putting up more of a struggle the farther they got from the house. He stopped and slapped her hard across the face, then grabbed her by the hair and continued to pull her after him. Sara screamed and held his arm with both hands, trying to keep up with him. Tears streamed down her cheeks. At least she was spared the foreknowledge of what he was about to do to her.

"You think you can screw around on me and get away with it, you little whore?" Richard railed at her as he dragged her along behind him. "You think you can cheat on me without me finding out about it? I saw what you were doing. I saw you screwing him just as plain as day. You can't fool me. You'll pay, you tramp, you'll pay!"

The rage was overflowing, overcoming his ability even to speak. He flung her to the side of the trail and stood feet apart looking down at her with the knife trembling in his hand.

"Now you're going to pay. Tell me. Confess your sins before you die!"

Sara looked up at the crazed man. She knew enough to be afraid of the large blade pointing at her, but she was aware of little else. She couldn't understand what he was saying or where she was or why she was here. She just knew it wasn't very nice and she didn't want to be there. She cried and screamed, looking about frantically for a place to run, as the rain and Jeanette's curse bore down on them.

Judy had found the razorblade at the bottom of the tub, and refilled it with hot water. The near scalding water soothed her. She luxuriated for a moment in the hot bath, until her despair hit her again. She steeled herself for the act. She would do it right this time, she vowed.

Chapter 27

Mike felt himself sliding down a steep, mud-filled hole. He had let go of the sheriff's hand when the ground opened up. Now they were frantically grabbing each other to arrest their downward fall. McGuire clung to his leg. Grasping for roots and branches, Mike reached for what he thought was a root, but which turned out to be a shinbone. It snapped off the rest of the leg, sending Mike and the sheriff sliding down the slope to the bottom of the pit, which was filled with muddy water and floating bones. Screaming on the way down, they splashed into knee-deep cold muck. Oozing out of the mud on all sides of them were the fleshless bodies of Jeanette's interred grandchildren, the bones and remains of those she had sacrificed to her dark lord over the years.

The rain continued to batter them. Mike felt as if he was drowning in it. As they splashed around in the murky water, trying to get to their feet and out of the pit, a flash of lightning revealed a dozen rotting corpses creeping toward them.

"Oh, my God!" screamed the sheriff. "This pit is full of bodies."

"Yes," said Mike through the downpour and peals of thunder, "the children of Jeanette Stillman. She must have been killing and burying them out here for years. They've come back!"

A peal of thunder shattered the stillness. Each flash of light brought the mud-covered corpses closer until they were upon them. Their fleshless arms clutched them. Mike felt bony fingers pulling his hair. A skeletal figure crept up his leg. Hands of bone grabbed the back of his neck. He spun around, knocking the hands away, kicking out at the creeping things slithering toward him. He stifled a scream. Doubting his senses, he defended himself anyway, punching and pushing the decaying forms away. The sheriff cried in terror as well, his arms swinging like windmills, warding off the clinging dead.

Suddenly, a dark form rose out of the mud. It was black except for the whites of its eyes, which seemed to burn with hatred as they glared at Mike. Small like a child, it had long mud-plastered hair. Its mouth opened in a wide, soundless scream, a darker blackness gaping out of its shadowy face. It floated like a skater toward him, and was on him before he could move. He was sure it had come to take his soul. He was helpless before it as it swooped at him as if it wanted to get inside of him.

He raised his hand to strike it knowing it would have no effect. Then something unexpected happened. A bright, dazzling light appeared and a bolt of lightning struck the bottom of pit. It felt to Mike as if he had thrown it in a moment of blind terror, but he knew such things weren't possible. It passed right over his shoulder to spear the specter dead center, knocking Mike down as well. Thunder cracked and shook the earth. Then all was still. For a brief moment the image of Hanna flashed in his mind.

Staggering to his feet, Mike grabbed a tree root, then another, and pulled himself and the sheriff out of the pit. Once at the top, they lay panting on the ground exhausted. Lights appeared at the edge of the clearing. Dogs and men could be heard rushing to the scene. Soon they were surrounded.

"You OK, Sheriff?" asked one of the men behind a flashlight beam. No one answered.

Men rushed forward to help their chief. Others threw Mike roughly to the ground on his face and handcuffed him.

"Take it easy, boys," said Sheriff McGuire, sitting up and pushing people away. "No need to rough him up like that."

"He killed Jimbo," one of them replied, voicing the feelings of the others, who would just as soon have shot the suspect as arrest him.

"That may be, we'll have to see. But he sure as hell saved me when he could have let me go and gotten away."

"What do you mean?" asked a deputy.

Sheriff McGuire was not quite sure what he meant, or what had happened. Had a pair of bony arms really been pulling him into the ground? He couldn't say for sure, but couldn't get the image of those hands clutching at him out of his brain. Had Mike actually saved him from being dragged into the pit?

Mike was handcuffed with his arms behind him and roughly jerked to his feet. It was a long painful walk back to the highway, where the coroner was just taking the bodies of the unfortunate deputy and Mike's friend away. There were more hostile glances directed in Mike's direction.

He was put in the back of the sheriff's car, where he waited to be taken to jail. As dazed and exhausted as he was, he tried to put things together, everything that had happened to him from that day of the first get-together in his apartment until this very moment. He was doing a good job of it, all the pieces falling into place in his mind like a simple ball-in-the-hole game.

It started that first day of past-life recall when Richard had the bad run. They must have somehow disturbed the spirit. Maybe it was because they were all in such a bad mood, or perhaps it was because they were so close to the house, fooling around with the occult and spirits. He didn't know, but they attracted something's attention that day, something sinister and evil.

That something had to be the ghost of Jeanette Stillman. Her spirit haunted the old farmhouse as sure as Mike was an ex-marine. In life she had built the sagging, malformed, bizarre rear of the building, and her malignant presence still dwelt there.

According to Jessica, Jeanette's spirit was no ordinary lost soul, but a powerful witch who in life had murdered her own children and grandchildren to perform her hideous rites, the blackest of magic. What magic was she performing now from the grave?

While Mike waited handcuffed in the back of the sheriff's car the rain started to let up. Policemen in assorted uniforms eyed him with obvious thoughts of justifiable homicide. Mike was starting to wonder if they were going to take him back or just shoot him in the woods and leave his carcass to the dogs.

He concentrated his thoughts on the problem as if his life depended on it. It must be the spirit of Jeanette that was hurting his friends. Everyone who had ever stepped foot in that house, including his dog, had come to harm. Seeing Sam together with Jessica tonight just confirmed it.

Jessica was obviously being possessed by Jeanette's spirit. Mike would have never thought such a thing possible, but he couldn't deny his senses. He had seen her with his own eyes, heard her with his own ears. It was Jessica all right, but driven by someone else, someone totally alien.

He remembered what she looked like when he first encountered her in Hanna's old house, as if the skin of her face were being pulled or stretched to fit another countenance, a bigger-boned, longer face that wasn't Jessica's face at all.

Mike hoped she was fighting a strong enough inner battle to keep Jeanette preoccupied. It might be the only chance they had. He thought he knew where to find her, not that the knowledge appeared to be of much use to him at the moment.

He wondered about what had happened at the gravesite, the corpse coming out of the ground; the sinkhole opening up to swallow them; skeletons creeping out of the mud; that black hideous thing from the pit. The Light.

Were those the corpses of Jeanette Stillman and her demon brood, the ones she had killed over the years? God, there must have been dozens of them. She must have been doing it for decades - having the children, bringing them up, breeding them, only to kill them and sacrifice them to some long forgotten demon god. As bizarre as it sounded, it was the only thing that made sense. It had to be true.

That's the key, he realized with a start. Jeanette's body had been interred in the family plot after she killed herself. The authorities hadn't even bothered to cart her out of the woods. They just shoveled her into the ground right where she hung herself, right over her grandfather and her mother's graves.

Unfortunately, that's where Jeanette had buried all of her prior victims, in the ground with Grandpa and Mama. It only stood to reason that the spirits of the murdered children would object to such a mingling and wail to high heaven. Could anybody wonder that heaven could remain unmoved?

Their cries certainly disturbed the peace of Mike and his friends, who happened to stumble upon the old place. This realization came suddenly to Mike and with it its implications. At this moment the sheriff opened the front door of the car and got in. Starting the vehicle, they moved onto the highway.

"What did they find back there?" Mike asked the sheriff. He was leaning forward in the back seat of the car, his hands cuffed tightly behind him. The sheriff didn't respond, but looked straight ahead up the wet highway.

"Look, Sheriff, I didn't kill Jim. I was handcuffed the whole time he was talking to you on the radio. He wouldn't have left me un-cuffed, not after what happened last time. You can see where he smacked me on the back of the head. I didn't have a chance to do anything but get knocked senseless."

The sheriff looked straight ahead, but he was listening. That's the reason he had made sure the prisoner was put in his vehicle and held there until he arrived. He wanted to hear what Mike had to say.

"The guy you found with Jim is my friend, Sam Jenkins. He killed Jim. He kind of went crazy because of what happened to his face. He came out here to kill me. He somehow blames me for what happened to him. He came up behind Jim after your deputy clubbed me, and hit him with a rock. Then he shot him. Jim had just finished talking to you on the radio. Then Sam turned the gun on himself."

The sheriff continued driving without saying a word.

"What do you think happened back there?" Mike asked, taking a gamble. "That wasn't your imagination, you know. She was pulling you down. That was the spirit of Jeanette Stillman. What happened in the pit, that wasn't your imagination, Sheriff."

"I don't know what it was," answered the confused lawman. "I don't know what the hell I saw. What was that light?"

"Lightning, I guess," replied Mike, "Look, I'm just as mystified as you, but what you saw was real. I saw it too."

"How did you get un-cuffed?" inquired the sheriff, changing the subject to something he understood.

"Sam took them off me. He was going to shoot me, but at the last minute turned the gun on himself. He must have realized what he had done and that I had nothing to do with his problems. Poor guy. Sheriff, we've got to act fast or more of my friends are going to die. We've got to destroy Jeanette's body. All those skeletons back there in that pit are her victims. She killed all of them."

"You're talking crazy," said the sheriff. "If you're thinking of pleading insanity, forget it."

"Look, you've got to believe me. I know you know the truth about the murders back in sixty-six. How Jeanette Stillman killed her daughter and then murdered her seven grandchildren one night, and how she killed herself as the police were closing in. I know about the cover-up and that they left the bodies of the kids and their mother buried in the basement of the old house. They found them just a few days ago. I lived near that house. I swear there was something sinister about that place. The spirits of those dead children were haunting it, sure as I'm sitting here now. You can't bury that much bad karma and expect to get away with it. She must have been killing them like that all along, long before they found her out. It must have been going on for decades. She was having them and killing them to perform her black magic. She practiced witchcraft, Sheriff. She's still practicing it. That was the Stillman family cemetery we were tussling in. That's where she buried them. That's where she was buried. We've got to destroy that body and give those children a decent burial."

Only an hour before, the sheriff would have driven this raving maniac straight to the prison for the criminally insane. After his harrowing experience in the pit, however, and the unmistakable sensation of being pulled under the earth by a pair of bony hands, anything seemed possible.

"Where's Jessica?" he asked, looking hard at the suspect in the rearview mirror.

"Well, that's the problem," answered Mike. "Gee, this is so weird. I don't know how to say it. I know you won't believe me."

"Try me," said the sheriff.

"Jessica's possessed by the spirit of Jeanette Stillman."

Mike let that fact hang in the air. It didn't sound believable to him either, but its belief was critical to their survival. There was no telling what would happen once Jeanette gained full control over Jessica and carried out her intended deeds.

"Where is she?" asked the sheriff again.

"I would guess she's either at Hanna's old house or back at her own place."

Mike gave the sheriff directions to Hanna's house. To his relief they took off in that direction.

Sheriff McGuire drove fast with no lights flashing. They reached the house on Meadowlark Lane in less than ten minutes and pulled into the driveway. Getting out, the sheriff pulled out his baton-size flashlight and his service revolver.

"Take me with you, Sheriff," said Mike. "I know the house."

"You just stay put and shut up," replied the sheriff.

"Don't shoot her by mistake," Mike yelled. "It could get pretty freaky in there."

Sheriff McGuire said nothing as he followed the wide beam of the flashlight up to the tree-covered front porch. He soon gained entry and disappeared inside.

Mike sat back in the seat. His arms ached from being pulled behind him and cuffed so tight. He was worried about what might happen if Jessica was in the house. Either way, he felt vulnerable and helpless, bound with his hands behind him, but all he could do was wait. He could see the faint glint of light in the east, the coming of dawn, but the sky was still dark and starless. The air was damp with the scent of recent rain. After what seemed like an interminable time, the sheriff emerged from the dark building and walked to the car.

"No one in there," he informed him, getting into the vehicle. "I found a chair by the window like you said. But the place has been empty for months."

They drove out of the bumpy driveway back onto the highway.

"Try her house," suggested Mike from the back seat. "She must have gone there."

"She could be anywhere, Russo," replied the sheriff. "I'm starting to wonder if you're just stalling, waiting for a chance to kill me like you did Jim Boone."

"Honest, Sheriff," insisted Mike. "I could have let her pull you under. I could have been long gone. But I didn't. I saved you at great cost to myself. Now all I'm asking is that you give me the benefit of the doubt and check out Jessica's place."

Sheriff McGuire didn't respond as he drove down the highway toward Jessica Wilson's house. Things had gotten too weird.

The suspect's knowledge and explanation of the Stillman case made sense, and actually filled in a few gaps in the story. He had long wondered about it, ever since he had inherited the files from his predecessor. Yes, it all seemed to make sense and explained a lot, like what they had found back there at the Stillman family plot and what was even now occupying an army of state police forensic experts. Everything seemed to fit, that is all except the ghost stories and the witchcraft and the spells and the magic. But then how did you explain what happened back there in the woods? The main thing was to determine the whereabouts and well being of Jessica Wilson. There had been too many deaths tonight already.

They turned off the highway onto the road to Jessica's cottage and were soon pulling into the driveway. The sheriff stopped the car and got out.

"I hope for your sake she's in there and all right," he said, grabbing his flashlight.

"Take me with you, Sheriff," pleaded Mike for the second time that night. "You have no idea what you're up against."

"You just sit there and shut up," ordered Sheriff McGuire in response. "I've had about all I'm going to take from you tonight."

"Sheriff! Sheriff!" Mike yelled as the lawman disappeared into the house, ignoring his entreaties.

As he sat there in the gathering light, a great sense of foreboding overcame him. Mike could sense more than ever the black tentacles of evil reaching for him from beyond the grave.

Jeanette, in Jessica's body, sat in the attic conjuring and chanting her curse. She knew they were coming. She had been projecting her mind, wrestling in the mud with the two struggling men, trying to pull them into the pit with her, when she experienced a momentary disruption of thought, a brief hiccup in her concentration. Distracted for a moment, she found one of them was proving too strong to overcome. Then the intrusion and she was back in the attic again.

Let them come. She watched. There was the big one with his flashlight and gun. She saw him in her mind's eye as he entered the house and searched each room in turn, calling the other one's name, the weak, little white witch she now wore like a sheepskin.

Up the stairs he comes. A lot of good that gun will do him.

You're getting warm. Nope, you're getting cold again. I'm not in the bedroom, fool, nor the bath. Look up and you will spot me. You're under me now. No, fool, you are going to miss me. "Here!"

The sheriff looked up as door flew down with a crash, striking him square on the top of the head. He went down with a thud, out like a bad bulb. The thing that was no longer Jessica walked slowly down the stairs and out of the house. She was completely nude.

Judy lay back in the steaming water, letting it submerge her. She had lost her nerve for a moment and had become afraid of the finality of her act, but now she had her resolve back. She knew what she had to do. The razorblade was tight between her index finger and thumb, poised over her left wrist. Still she hesitated.

Despair welled up in her heart as if to suffocate her, and with it the attending tears began to flow. Life was so unfair, so horribly unfair. She felt her wrist to make sure the stroke would be fatal. Readying herself for the stinging pain, she longed for peace.

"Sorry, Sam," she said to herself out loud, as she made ready to slice the vein. Someone whispered out of the darkness of her blindness.

"Hold on, Judy. Hold on. It will be all right. Hold on."

She stopped and listened, her heart beating wildly.

"Who is it?" she called out. "Who's there? Is that you, Sam? Is anybody there?"

The voice sounded familiar, but it was just a disembodied whisper right above her head. It could have been Mike Russo. It had that type of Boston accent.

Whoever it was, whatever it was, it stayed her hand, at least for the moment. Judy didn't get out of the tub, however, nor let the razor go.

While Judy sat in her house in Jamaica Plain, halfway across the state in the countryside just outside Springfield, another drama was unfolding in the woods only a few hundred yards from old Route 2. Two things were taking place at the same time. Richard, momentarily distracted, had forgotten what he was doing and why, and Sara suddenly remembered who she was and what was happening.

"Richard!" she yelled as she recognized him standing over her with a rather large knife in his hand. The shout jarred Richard's memory even looser. He shook his head to clear it, grabbing it with both hands.

"Richard, what are you doing?" she screamed.

Chapter 28

Mike tried to clear his mind and focus his thoughts. Visualizing white light over him and his friends, he tried to talk to them in his head, sending out words and thoughts of comfort and strength. All this as he sat helpless and handcuffed in the back of the sheriff's car.

He'd had a bad feeling ever since the sheriff disappeared into Jessica's house. That had been fifteen minutes ago and he hadn't heard or seen a thing since. Anything could happen if Jessica or Jeanette or whoever it was, were in there.

Suddenly, Mike saw someone come out the front door. It wasn't the sheriff, but a slim naked woman with long white hair. As she walked toward the car, the first rays of daylight rose from the east and fell on her. She walked with stiff arms and a slight limp. Mike didn't like the dull gleam in her eyes.

"Jessica," he stammered, as she opened the door and yanked him out, throwing him to the ground. He yelled as she brought the butt of Sheriff McGuire's pistol down on his head.

As he lay on the ground in a state of semi-consciousness, she bent over him and unlocked the handcuffs. Dimly, in the back of his half-conscious mind, Mike tried to come to grips with what was happening.

Fortunately for him, she hadn't counted on his hard head. He hadn't been knocked out, only stunned. She started dragging him toward the house. He was surprised how strong she was. Mike had excelled in hand-to-hand combat during basic training. He hoped it would come in handy now, witch or no witch. As they approached the house, Mike swept his foot in front of hers, fast and hard, knocking Jessica's feet out from under her. She fell hard to the ground, the gun tumbling from her hand.

Still dazed, Mike grabbed Jessica and pulled her hands behind her sharply before she could recover. Then he cuffed her and yanked her to her feet, grabbing the gun. Dragging her unceremoniously back to the sheriff's car, he threw her into the back seat, tossing his light jacket over her as an afterthought.

"Big mistake messing with me, sister," he said, as he moved around the front of the car unsteadily. The throbbing pain in his head was making it hard to see and harder to think.

Sliding into the driver's seat, he found the keys still in the ignition. He sat there for a moment and closed his eyes, holding his hands to his face as he tried to clear his head. The pain was excruciating.

He was shaken out of his stupor by the sound of Jessica chanting in the seat behind him. She was saying something under her breath, something in an ugly, foreign, guttural tongue that was better left unsaid. It sent chills down his spine. He looked back and what he saw stopped his heart in terror.

Jessica sat there, her shoulders hunched, her chin down. She looked up at him with black eyes that seemed to be burned into her head. She somehow didn't look quite human, as if she was contorted and about to uncoil.

Snapping out of his daze with a shake of his head, he started the car and pulled out of the driveway, heading back up the road toward the Stillman House. He had the pedal to the floor. He could hear Jessica chanting behind him. The clouds held the newborn sun at bay.

Mike didn't know if Sheriff McGuire was dead or alive, but he couldn't take the time to find out. He'd have to take his chances and finish this once and for all. There was no time to lose.

He drove back up the highway to his old apartment building, fighting the nausea that threatened to overwhelm him. The streetlamps and lights of the other vehicles danced in his vision like laser-beams, all but blinding him. All he could hear was Jessica's awful incantation as it grew louder in his ears. It sounded like she was sitting right behind his shoulder. Suddenly, something loud and heavy hit the top of the vehicle, almost making him jerk it off the road. Thump, it hit again, like some heavy, soft body.

Mike realized he was now in a dream world. Imagining white light over his head, he began invoking a protective spell, a prayer to the Eternal Mother to free him from evil. It was then he noticed his spider scarab on the seat beside him, the one Hanna had given him. The sheriff must have collected it along with Jessica's other charms on his previous visit.

He grabbed the pendent and held it firmly in his hand. It focused his words and gave them power. Soon his prayer was drowning out the sounds coming from the thing that was no longer Jessica. She fell silent and sat rigid in the back seat, as if caught up in an inner battle that was taking all of her concentration. Whatever was hitting them stopped.

Mike pulled the car recklessly into the apartment drive, leaving it slanting partly on the grass, and ran around to the other door, pulling

Jessica out. Going to his pickup, which was still parked in the lot, he grabbed a can of gasoline from the back. He had just filled it up and had meant to leave it with Jessica's lawn mower over the weekend. Now he had another need for it. Guiding Jessica firmly by the elbow, he led her to the woods behind the apartment building. The day was dark and dreary. He started down the path to the scene of his struggle the night before, the Stillman family plot. As he ran through the woods with Jessica in tow, he could only pray that the bones of Jeanette Stillman were still

Only the whites of Jessica's eyes were showing now as he pulled her along the trail. She was gnashing her teeth and foaming at the mouth, but Mike held her tight and concentrated on his protective spell. Then something heavy hit him from behind, sending him sprawling to the ground.

A pair of claws dug into his back. Turning over quickly to face his assailant, he saw a large bird of prey flapping its wings right above him. The giant owl attacked, diving at his face. Mike put up his arms to protect himself and felt sharp talons dig into his flesh. He screamed and hit out at the raptor, which flew away only to attack again then again. Its huge wings battered him. It clawed at his face. In desperation, Mike reached out for the gas can, which lay nearby. Swinging it up hard, he hit the bird square. There was a dull thud and a flurry of feathers, then the thing was gone.

Jumping up, his cheeks bleeding, he grabbed Jessica, and continued up the path. He had the distinct impression she had been urging his attacker on.

He came upon the clearing suddenly. Men in white suits stood in groups examining small piles of bones. Several plastic sheets lay strewn across the ground near the large sinkhole, a pit at least nine feet deep, where the small family cemetery had stood. Broken tombstones lay smashed and cracked in the muddy water at the bottom of the pit. A few of the men looked up as Mike burst on the scene with his handcuffed, mostly naked captive in tow.

He leveled the sheriff's gun, which he had taken from Jessica, in the general direction of the men, and told them to leave. Luckily, it was a group of forensic experts. A few wore guns, but Mike had the drop on them and sent them scurrying unarmed back toward the road. He didn't want anyone to interfere with what he was about to do.

Dragging Jessica along with him, he went to the white sheets and pulled them aside one by one. The skeleton of Jeanette, with her long white hair and wide gaping grin, lay under the second one. Mike jumped back involuntarily on uncovering it, expecting her skeleton to rise at any moment. It remained still. Taking the gas can, he poured most of the contents on the remains.

Suddenly, Jessica ran at him violently, trying to bite him. She bowled him over, clipping his legs out from under him. Somehow she had gotten out of the handcuffs, contorting her arms and shoulders, and began kicking him as he lay on the ground. He put up his hands to protect himself and tried to kick her back, keeping her at bay. She hissed and spat at him, and stomped on his ribs, but again he took her off her feet.

She was strong, but he was able to grab her flailing arms and pull them behind her, holding her down. Then he quickly lit a match and threw it on the pile of Jeanette's bones. They burst into flames like dry twigs. Just then, Jessica heaved him off with a tremendous burst of strength. At that same moment Jeanette's burning body rose from the ground as if on a string, her hair ablaze. Mike screamed, and threw the half-empty gas can at the burning form. It burst into flames like a dry fur tree and was soon just a pile of smoldering ashes. Then all was silent. Jessica had disappeared in the commotion.

As Mike sat and stared at the flames in shock, a dozen armed men with guns drawn and cocked, surrounded the clearing and ordered him down on his stomach. He did as he was told and was cuffed for the third time that day. The angry deputies punched and kicked him as they questioned him. Others ran to put out the fire, which had spread to the surrounding underbrush.

"What have you done with the sheriff?" they asked. "What's going on here?"

Jessica was confused and dazed. She found herself running in the woods naked. What was she doing here? What was going on? Where were her clothes?

She tried to remember. Her mind was a complete blank. What had happened? Had she blacked out? The last thing she remembered was going into that house with Michael, then nothing.

Several miles to the west, Sara had a sudden flash of self-recognition and stopped running. Even without the revelation, she was too out of breath to keep going.

She had turned and fled from the knife wielding man on instinct, her natural sense of self-preservation kicking in. Then she just kept running blindly, like an animal in fear.

Now she remembered everything as she stood bent over gasping for air.

Richard heard her panting long before he spotted her through the branches of the trees. He crept up behind her silently. He remembered nothing. He was filthy and half-starved. He was in the woods and Sara, his wife, was standing in front of him in her pajamas, soaking wet, crying and shivering in the chill morning air. How had they gotten here?

"Sara," he stammered. "Sara, what are you doing? Are you all right?"

She jumped at the sound of his voice, ready to take off again at any moment.

"Don't come near me," she answered. "Stay away from me."

"Sara, what's wrong?" He was confused, uncertain of what was happening. "What's going on?"

"You've been chasing me through the woods with a knife, is what's going on," she replied between breaths.

Richard looked down at the knife in his hand and dropped it like a hot iron.

"Oh, my God! I don't remember a thing," he confessed, suddenly disoriented and unsure of himself. He felt as if he was going to pass out. "I don't know what I'm doing here."

"Just stay away from me," she insisted, as he tried to approach her. She moved back a step, ready to flee.

He did as she asked and tried to win her trust with soothing words and gestures. He promised to turn himself in if she followed him out of the woods. He made her take his threadbare, torn jacket and put it over her shoulders to protect her from the dampness. He showed considerable concern for her well-being and safety, a far cry from what he had been trying to do to her only minutes before.

Though it was all a bit much for Sara to believe, she followed him out of the woods and back to her parent's house, where the police duly took him into custody.

Judy had been shaken by that voice in the night, the one that told her to hold on. It had prevented her from slicing her wrists, but she stayed in the tub for some time oscillating between thoughts of suicide and thoughts of survival. All of a sudden, she realized what she was doing. Getting out of the bath, she threw the razorblade down as if it were a black widow.

She almost stood up too fast and had to hold the towel-rack for balance. Still wobbly, she dried off and walked out of the bathroom, wrapping the towel around her. She was so shocked that she had almost killed herself that it took a full two minutes before she realized that she could see again. She was walking down a sunlit hallway and could see the walls, and the sky beyond the windows, and her legs. She could see her own legs. She yelled out in joy.

"I can see! I can see! Sam, I can see."

No one answered. Running from room to room, she shouted his name, telling him the news. She called Richard and Sara but no one was home. She called Mike, but his phone had been disconnected. She wondered where her friends could be. She had been so consumed by her own personal tragedy that she had no idea what had been going on around her. For some reason, she was afraid for them.

Sheriff McGuire opened his eyes slowly. The dull lump on the top of his head throbbed with pain. He looked up at a ladder descending from a rectangular hole in the ceiling and remembered it coming down on his head. He had heard a voice. He groaned and tried to rise. Grabbing his flashlight, he noticed his pistol was missing. He swore and got the rest of the way to his feet.

Gingerly climbing the short wooden steps, he peered into the dark opening of the attic, flashing his light around the room. After assuring himself the area was empty, he went downstairs and out to his car, which he noticed with alarm was also missing. He went back inside and called the station.

While he waited, the sheriff had plenty of time to think about what Michael had said. Even the part about the spirit of Jeanette Stillman possessing Jessica Wilson was starting to sound believable, especially when they told him they had found her wandering naked in the woods. She didn't remember a thing.

Before long a squad car came to pick him up and take him to the hospital where they bandaged his head. They wanted to keep him overnight for observation, but he refused. Instead, he had his deputy drive him back to the station where they were notified the suspect had been captured.

Reports from the gravesite said that he had destroyed a set of bones, those of an adult female. The sheriff guessed they were the bones of Jeanette Stillman and knew why Michael would have done such a thing. He was glad he had.

Forensics was working around the clock to identify the bodies found in the small cemetery. The more they learned, the more the facts began to fit the fugitive's bizarre story. Sheriff McGuire helped shed some light on the missing pieces and made sure the experts came to the correct conclusions. Lucky for Michael, he now had an ally.

Chapter 29

Mike was due in court at nine in the morning. His lawyer told him not to worry, it was only a formality, but that was easier said than done with three counts of first-degree murder facing him. The fact that he was out on his own recognizance, however, meant something. Sheriff McGuire was mostly responsible for that small favor.

The first few days after his arrest had been touchy. He was saved from a severe beating down at the department only by the timely arrival of the sheriff, who had just come from the hospital with a large bandage on his head. He was able to confirm the latter part of Mike's story, and even more importantly for Mike, was able to keep him from being manhandled by his guards. Unfortunately, Mike still faced three counts of murder.

Jessica had been taken to a local hospital. She didn't remember a thing. Except for a few cuts and bruises and a little malnutrition, she appeared to be fine, and was kept overnight for observation. Other than the fact her hair had turned snow white, Jessica appeared to be back to normal. Mike spent the night in jail.

Over the next few days, the truth slowly began to emerge, at least as much of it as could be believed. Jessica began to tardily get her memory back, at least enough to verify that she had been with Mike the night Linda Reynolds was murdered. However, she still remembered nothing of the deputy's murder.

Mike's alibi coupled with the fact that none of his fingerprints had been found on the murder weapon or in Linda's apartment, eliminated the DA's case for that homicide. They planned to drop it, despite the knife being found in Mike's truck. They reasoned that it had been planted there by the real murderer, who was still at large. State forensic experts verified that Sam Kelly's fingerprints were found on the gun that killed Jim Boone along with the defendant's. Due to the sheriff's influence, it was being considered a murder-suicide, just as Mike had described. So he was being absolved of these murders as well. All he had to do was appear in court to hear the district attorney's proposal. Still, he had been too nervous to get much sleep the night before.

He stood in front of the bathroom mirror trying to tie his only tie. It had been so long since he'd worn one he had forgotten how. Jessica came in and smiled at him.

"Don't know how to tie it, heh?" she said laughing.

"My mom used to do it for me," he admitted shyly. "I forgot how. Can you give me a hand?"

"Sure," she replied. "This is how it goes."

She stood in front of him and wrapped one end around the other with a flourish. "Through and about, turn in and out, and there, it's done."

"How'd you do that?" he asked, grabbing her by the shoulders and kissing her.

"I've had plenty of practice on my brothers," she explained, smiling up at him. She liked the way his shoulders looked in a suit. "You look very handsome today."

"Thanks. I hope the judge thinks so," he replied.

"Don't be nervous. Your lawyer said the DA has already agreed to drop the charges."

"Thank God for you on that. I was afraid you had lost your memory for good and they were going to fry me. Thanks."

"It was the least I could do," she said, hugging him. "I don't usually forget when I sleep with someone for the first time."

"Good thing for me," he said, hugging her back.

"Tell me what happened again," she asked for the umpteenth time. "I don't remember anything after going into the cellar of that house. I seem to recall some strange things. Was that real?" She still wasn't able to trust the memory of what she had seen just before her blackout.

"Yes," he replied. "I guess so, but I don't really know. It was all kind of weird. What did you see?"

She looked at him searchingly for a moment but didn't answer. Mike let it drop.

"What happened after that?" she inquired.

Mike told her the story again.

"Do you think it was Hanna?" she asked when hearing of the bright flash in the pit.

"It could have been. Her image passed through my mind at the exact same time, but it could have just been weird lightning. I don't know."

They left her house and headed into Concord where his trial was taking place in a half hour. He told her how his father had talked to him on the phone.

"He said 'find the Meadowlark,' or something like that. That's how I found you in Hanna's old house."

"That's amazing," she replied. "I've heard of things like that. It makes sense to me, that the dead can turn electrical impulses into audible sound waves like that."

She was shocked that she had been possessed by Jeanette, surprised that a spirit could take over her mind so completely without her being able to put up a fight.

"Oh, you put up a fight, alright," Mike assured her, "even if you don't remember it. Otherwise she wouldn't have been so distracted. You gave me the opening I needed."

Mike told her how he had destroyed Jeanette's molding corpse to end the curse, and returned the bones of her victims to hallowed ground so they could rest. The world now knew of Jeanette's terrible deeds.

They arrived at the courthouse and sat in the car in silence. Neither could fully believe the events of the past few weeks in spite of the fact they had both lived through them. Now Mike had to face an all too real court proceeding. He straightened his tie and got out of the car.

Walking up to the entrance, he saw Sara, Richard, and Judy waiting for him. They smiled bravely and hugged him as he approached. There was sadness in the air, despite their joy at their respective recoveries, miraculous to say the least. Sam had been cremated and put in the ground. Mike and Richard organized the small memorial ceremony, which filled Sam and Judy's local synagogue in Jamaica Plain to capacity. Mike spoke a moving eulogy and they all lovingly remembered Sam.

Both Richard and Sara were beginning to put their lives back together. Richard had moved speedily through his own court hearings and trial. Put under observation for a period, he was soon free, but ordered to stay 200 yards from his wife. The restraining order would remain in effect for ninety days, at which time there would be a wellness hearing. Sara had recovered her memory. She understood as well as anyone the nature of his affliction, but the memory of the savage beatings and betrayal were still strong. She knew he had not been himself, but she still did not totally trust him. She had a lot to deal with. She longed to have her life back to the way it was. Until the terrible curse of Jeanette had haunted them, they had been very happy together. She still wanted to start a family. She still loved him. He was actually a nicer person now than he ever was. They all supported Mike, who they regarded as their savior.

Judy looked at Michael with admiration. In spite of her pain at losing Sam, she could only smile when she saw Michael. He had made her see again. He had saved their lives. He would have saved Sam's too if he could have, and Linda's. But he had been lucky just to protect himself against the evil they had so unwittingly unleashed.

Judy more than any of them realized what Michael had done, what power he possessed in such an unassuming manner, what a miracle he had brought about. He had saved not only her, but all of them, and who knows how many countless others. If Jeanette or her spirit or whatever it was had had its way, who knows how many more would have died. She said a silent prayer for him as she took her seat in the courtroom. Jessica sat next to him in the front row.

Mike looked around the room. As he did he had to smile. Most of his friends were there. Neil Bates, the ex-Jesuit, and his girlfriend Nelly sat near the front. Neil smiled and gave him a thumbs-up. Mike's old work crew was there as well. They must have taken the day off from their respective jobs, the slackers. Mike smiled and nodded discreetly in their direction. Several of his customers and business associates were present, showing support by their looks and smiles. Several waved to him. As a matter of fact, it looked like the whole town had shown up to show that they were behind him.

Mike heard his name called and moved to the front of the court. The clerk read the charge and the judge asked the DA a few questions, which the attorney answered in the affirmative. Then the judge and the two lawyers held a lengthy, mostly inaudible discussion at the side of the judge's bench. When they were done, the judged thanked everybody for coming and asked for the next case. Mike's lawyer had to tell him it was over.

"Is that it?" asked Mike, as he followed his attorney out of the courtroom into a large foyer.

"Yep, just like I told you, just a formality. All charges have been dropped. You're a free man with no criminal record. Congratulations."

Mike shook his lawyer's hand. Soon he was surrounded by well-wishers, and shook their hands as well.

"Good job, Mike,"

"Way to go, Mikey."

"Well done, Michael."

They slapped him on the back and shook his hand, all eager to express their gratitude for what he had done for the town in uncovering the terrible secret and laying those poor children to rest.

After the rather lengthy investigation of the remains by the state police and the FBI, it was determined that events had transpired roughly as Sheriff McGuire and Mike Russo had theorized. Forensic evidence confirmed that from the years 1931 through 1966 when she had been caught, Jeanette Stillman murdered twenty-four individuals, twenty children, all males, and four adult females. All of Jeanette's children and grandchildren showed signs of violent death. The bodies were interred in the local church cemetery where Hanna had been buried, at the express wish and expense of Hanna's family, along with several other knowledgeable members of the community, including Mike and Jessica.

They walked arm in arm out into the clear fall day. The trees were on fire with brilliant orange and dazzling yellows, which splashed across a cloudless sky. It was good to be alive. Despite the elation and joy at being free from the curse that had plagued them, Mike couldn't help feeling sad for the loss of Sam and Linda. He missed Sam's wit and spirit, and Linda's beauty and grace. What cruel twist of fate that his friends should die while he lived. Who determines one person's life and another's death? Why does one survive and another standing right beside them, no better and no worse, no more or less deserving, why does that one perish? None of it made any sense to Mike and often left him pondering his existence alone at night, but he always embraced the next day.

He hugged his friends at the courthouse steps and left them smiling and waving as he drove away with Jessica by his side. They decided not to go home, but to drive up to the site of the old house and toast their friends who hadn't made it. They didn't mention it to the others. They wanted to be alone with their thoughts and each other. They had to bring closure to the whole affair. Jessica had her talismans and crystals, her herbs and objects. Mike had his faith in the Universal Principal that guides creation. Mother Universe, Almighty Father, whatever force and intelligence it is that drives forth its purpose with such searing perfection that nothing can stand in its way.

He pulled his pickup into the drive and set the brake. They got out and walked around to the rear of the vehicle, stopping to hold hands and look at the remains of the old house. Where once had stood a historical landmark, an architectural oddity, a peculiar curiosity, was now a gaping hole with wood and stone jutting out of it like ruins and tombstones. It smoldered as if on fire, although no normal flame had ever burned there. The chimneys stood like red brick towers, slanting in the sun. An empty, glassless window in a half-wall glared at the day. Mike sighed and started toward the ruins.

They performed no magic rituals, made no circles, sprinkled no salt. They burned no candles or incense. Instead, they spread a blanket on the front yard and had a picnic. Putting out cake and tea, honey and cream, cinnamon, oranges, and eggs, they laughed and talked as if a crowd of friends had gathered.

Mike smiled and invited all the spirits of the dear departed to join them, Hanna and his father included, before returning to their long journey into night. He freed them to go their way in peace, in so doing consecrating and freeing the ground and the old pile of stone and wood from any taint that might linger there. The small meal would be a closure, a cleansing, consuming of all negative influences once and for all.

Jessica held a goblet of wine, which she swished around three times in a counter-clockwise motion. They then cut the cakes into tiny pieces and distributed them on the many plates around them in a circle. They sat there together, enjoying the dying day, Jessica's hand in his.

Cars went by hardly noticing them as they sat on the lawn and shared their meal. Mike almost fell asleep with the soft buzz of insects in his ears. The last rays of the sun peeked pink and purple over the trees to the west. The golden light of the day's end made everything soft and empyreal.

Mike stood up and started picking up the remains of the picnic, while Jessica put everything in a plain paper bag. They were happy and at peace, but at the same time sad at the memory of lost friends. Then they heard it, someone whispering in the air right between them.

"Why don't you…"

THE END

To Richy and his love of the paranormal. May he rest in peace.